brenda novak

A Home of Her Own

Meena—
I hope you enjoy
your re[...]
Dun[...]
Best Wishes
Brenda Novak

HARLEQUIN®

TORONTO • NEW YORK • LONDON
AMSTERDAM • PARIS • SYDNEY • HAMBURG
STOCKHOLM • ATHENS • TOKYO • MILAN • MADRID
PRAGUE • WARSAW • BUDAPEST • AUCKLAND

ISBN 0-373-71242-1

A HOME OF HER OWN

Copyright © 2004 by Brenda Novak.

This edition published by arrangement with Harlequin Books S.A.

® and TM are trademarks of the publisher. Trademarks indicated with ® are registered in the United States Patent and Trademark Office, the Canadian Trade Marks Office and in other countries.

www.eHarlequin.com

Printed in U.S.A.

Dear Reader,

Welcome back to the small town of Dundee, Idaho. If you've read the first three books in my series, you already know that Dundee is one of those places where family stands for something. It might not always be what we want it to stand for, but Dundee's definitely a place where a person grows roots. Love the place or hate it, the mountains, the land, the town are in the blood of everyone who lives there. So far, Booker has turned his life around. Rebecca has married her childhood nemesis. And Delaney has given Conner the tether he needed so badly.

So what about Mike Hill? Those of you familiar with Mike know what a good guy he is—and what a great catch. You also know he's nearly forty and unmarried. It's going to take a very special woman to bring this man to his knees. He finds her just about the time he gives up looking—and in a very unlikely place.

I had a great time writing this story, especially because the inspiration for certain plot elements came from my own family background. I'll leave you to guess which ones, but as you read, reserve a smile for those of us who truly understand the cliché "Truth is stranger than fiction."

I love to hear from readers. Please drop me a line at P.O. Box 3781, Citrus Heights, CA 95611, or visit my Web site at www.brendanovak.com, where you can e-mail me or check out excerpts of my books, research articles and win fabulous prizes.

Until we visit Dundee again…

Brenda Novak

To Tonya, my oldest sister. She let her friend offer me my first
(and only) cigarette when I was eight years old and she was
eighteen, then cried laughing when I nearly hacked to death.
She locked me and my other siblings out when she baby-sat
so she could bake cookies and eat them without us. She
refused to let us cross the holy threshold of her room,
where she entranced us (standing outside looking in)
with such mysterious antics as burning incense and
making bottle candles out of crayons.

She also rocked me for hours when I was a baby,
bathed me until I was old enough to bath myself,
married young and let me stay with her almost every
weekend, took the heat from my parents when I stupidly
caused the loss of something important to the family,
taught me how to cook and clean and decorate.
You've been a friend, a sister, a mother to me, Tonya.
For everything, I love you.

Books by Brenda Novak

CHAPTER ONE

THE VACANT HOUSE LOOKED haunted. Large and imposing, with a full moon hanging directly behind, the old Victorian cast a grotesque shadow across the snow, and the windows shone like so many eyes.

Ignoring the gooseflesh that prickled her arms, Lucky Caldwell stood on the ornate porch, braced against a chill wind as she pushed the heavy front door a little wider. She didn't really want to venture inside now that it had grown so late. The house had sat empty long enough that rats, possums, raccoons or other crawling things could easily have taken over. Or maybe she'd find some mass murderer hiding in one of the rooms....

If she was anywhere else, she'd head into town and get a motel for the night. But as soon as even one person in Dundee spotted the distinctive strawberry-blond hair she'd inherited from her mother, word would spread all over town that she was back. And she didn't want to alert anyone to her return just yet. She needed to get her bearings. Coming here was a risk, a *huge* risk, and she'd never been as lucky as her name.

The floor creaked as she stepped across the threshold. Instinctively she reached for the light switch, but then paused. Somehow, waltzing inside and lighting up the place seemed too brazen. She didn't belong here; she'd *never* belonged here.

But she didn't belong anywhere else, either.

Marshalling her nerve, she flipped the light switch anyway.

Nothing happened. The pace of life in Dundee was maddeningly slow but, evidently, not so slow that Mike Hill, executor of the Caldwell Family Trust, hadn't gotten around to having the utility company shut off the electricity. Which, after six years, didn't come as any big surprise. She'd inherited this rambling Victorian when Morris died and hadn't been back since. During that time, she'd received a couple of calls from Fred Winston, the town's only real estate agent and a man she remembered as wearing a cheap brown toupee. He'd told her the paint was peeling and the porch was sagging and asked if she wanted to sell. But she knew who wanted to buy and the answer had been and still was—no. At least not yet. She had unfinished business here in Idaho.

She set her backpack on the dusty floor and searched for her flashlight. Unfortunately, it was already on when she found it and, judging by the weak beam, had been on for several hours.

Lucky considered returning to her car for the extra set of batteries. She'd had to park out front because the roof on the garage had collapsed. But she was afraid she'd lose her nerve if she turned back now. Better to forge ahead....

She hefted her backpack to her shoulder, trained the dim light in front of her and left the door open in case she encountered something or someone she'd rather not meet.

Entering the formal living room, she quickly swept the light around the perimeter. Nothing moved—but the familiarity of the place evoked bittersweet memories. As bad as her childhood had been, she'd been truly happy for a few short months while living in this house. Especially that first Christmas after her mother had married Morris.

In the dark, cobwebby corner to her left, she could easily imagine the splendid tree that had once stood there, proudly bearing a thousand twinkling lights and an abundance of shiny gold balls. That was the first time her family had possessed enough money to buy a tree any taller than a token three or four feet. And to have it flocked with fake snow and decorated so elegantly was really an extravagance. Every year since she'd become an adult, Lucky bought as big a tree as her current abode would allow and always flocked it, on principle. But she'd been living off the money she'd inherited from Morris, which was barely enough to get by on, since she gave most of it away. In order to keep traveling, she'd had to cut down on expenses. The places she'd been renting, for a few months here and six weeks there, had low ceilings and generally weren't the nicest. Which meant she'd never been able to duplicate the opulence of that damn tree.

She wrinkled her nose at the musty smell and glanced back at the open door before moving deeper into the house. The moonlight filtered through the bare, thick-paned windows, painting silver squares on the hardwood floor and, together with the faint beam of her flashlight, made it possible for her to see.

The Georgian-style staircase rose up in front of her. A large office with double doors jutted off to the right, along with what used to be an impressive library. Lucky waved a cobweb out of her way and poked her head into the library, then the office, relieved to find them both vacant of scurrying animals and—thank God—anything larger.

She continued her search, pausing to listen carefully here and there, until she reached the kitchen and family room. Situated at the back of the house, they were more like one big room with floor-to-ceiling windows that curved into a semi-circle and looked out over the pond at the bottom of the hill.

Unfortunately, most of the windows at the back were broken now. Bending to retrieve a small rock lying among the glittering shards of glass on the old stone floor, Lucky tossed it up and caught it again. So much had changed. Morris was dead. Her mother, too. Her brothers, Sean and Kyle, who were both older than she was, had sold the land they'd inherited and moved elsewhere. But the feeling of being unwelcome here, the resentment of this small community, seemed to linger.

Lucky threw the rock away and watched it skitter across the floor. So much for the hope that coming back would be easier than she'd anticipated. Owning a house didn't make it a home.

Considering the state of the Victorian, she wondered whether she should sleep in her car. A metallic blue '64 Mustang, it was fully restored and beautiful. But sitting out in her car would be as cramped as it was cold. She'd be better off inside. Despite the creepy feel of the place, she hadn't seen anything more threatening than a few spiderwebs. Discarded trash here and there indicated that others had been inside the house since it had been closed up, but nothing showed recent activity.

Her tension easing, Lucky delved into her backpack and retrieved her supplies. Ten tall fragrant candles. Three fire-starter logs. Matches. A jug of water. Trail mix. And barbecue-flavored sunflower seeds. Her suitcase, cleaning supplies and bedding were still out in the car.

With its stone floor and broken windows, the kitchen was colder than the front of the house. But the family room portion had a wood-burning stove and provided the most natural light. Come morning, Lucky planned to make the place livable. For now—she blew on her hands to warm them—she just needed to get through the next six or seven hours.

She lit the candles, then arranged them on the marble countertop. They created a dim, ethereal glow and gave off a comforting scent that helped dispel the dank odor of neglect. Building a fire didn't take long, either, thanks to the starter logs. When Lucky was a senior in high school and Morris had divorced her mother and moved back in with his first wife, across town, where he'd lived the final few months of his life, Red had stripped the place bare. She took everything of value down to the drapes, the stained-glass window on the second-floor landing, even the expensive knobs on the cupboards. But, thankfully, she hadn't bothered carting off the wood by the stove. Lucky used the last of the split logs to build up her fire, welcoming the infusion of heat and hoping it would last for a few hours. Then she moved gingerly back, her feet crunching over the broken glass from the windows, which was thickest by the stove, to watch the smoldering orange flames catch and grow.

The fire seemed symbolic somehow—her first step, a beginning. But the settling noises of the old house reminded her that she still needed to explore the upstairs, just to be sure she was as alone as she thought she was.

After tapping her failing flashlight, to no avail, she went outside to collect the sack she'd placed in the backseat of her car. She replaced the batteries, left the front door standing open again for reassurance, and climbed the stairs to the five bedrooms and three bathrooms she knew she'd find there.

A dark spot on the landing showed water damage. Clearly, the wind and rain had pushed through a tear in the plastic her mother had used to cover the hole when she took the stained-glass window. Lucky frowned at the stain, disappointed that she hadn't stood up to Red that day. Red hadn't had any real use for the window. She'd stuck it in a closet of the mobile home she'd moved into when she remarried.

But Lucky wasn't sure, even now, that it would've done any good to fight her mother. Red had been determined to take absolutely everything she could loosely interpret as "furniture"—because that was all she'd been awarded in the divorce, and she wasn't happy that ten years of marriage to one of Dundee's wealthiest old ranchers hadn't netted her more.

The door downstairs slammed shut, and Lucky bit back a startled scream.

"Hello?" she called, pressing a hand to her chest.

All she heard was the keening of the wind through the eaves outside.

She gripped the flashlight more tightly, her heart pounding as she listened for footsteps. She heard nothing but couldn't help imagining ghosts. She certainly wouldn't blame Morris if he'd decided to stick around and haunt this old place. After everything he'd done for her mother, for the whole family, he'd been treated pretty shabbily in the end. It had been his first wife who'd come through and nursed him once his health turned.

But Morris had been a good man. Certainly he had better things to do in the afterlife, Lucky thought wryly. Chances were far greater that Red would be the one rattling chains and roaming the grounds....

"There's not much left here, Mother," she muttered as chills rolled down her spine. "You took everything except the Sheetrock and the two-by-fours."

Silence settled on the house like a fresh layer of dust as Lucky leaned over the banister and shone her flashlight into the corners below. She saw bird droppings, an old rug that looked as if it had been chewed on one end, a broken chair. Lucky's brothers, who'd stayed in Dundee a little longer than she had, once told her that Morris had never returned to the place or fixed it up after Red moved out—and they were obviously right.

Finding nothing of particular concern, Lucky walked

slowly on, still apprehensive as the plastic flapped noisily behind her.

She discovered bed rails in two of the bedrooms, an old mattress with no bed rails in a third. The master had a large sitting area, which had been lovely. But the mirrored doors on the closets and the mirror over the vanity were now cracked. Graffiti covered the walls. *Bitch! Whore! Killer! May you rot in hell!*

A searing pain in Lucky's stomach—her ulcer acting up—made her feel as though she'd swallowed acid. She forced herself to turn away from those nasty words and concentrate on practical matters. That was the trick, wasn't it? To grow a thick skin like her brothers and not let her mother's legacy of shame and embarrassment bother her?

There was so much else to think about, so much work to be done.

She glared over her shoulder at the graffiti. Maybe she'd start by painting. After a few months, when she had the place fixed up, she'd finally sell out and put Dundee behind her forever.

Just as soon as she found what she was looking for.

MIKE HILL BROUGHT his Cadillac Escalade to an abrupt stop in the center of the road and squinted at the property next to his ranch. He couldn't tell for sure, but a light seemed to be burning in the big Victorian. From the dim glow, he guessed it might be candles. Kids in these parts loved to visit his grandfather's old mansion. Occasionally, they broke in to make out or to vandalize it. On Halloween, he'd caught a group of teenagers trying to spook themselves by holding a séance, although they were too drunk to take anything seriously. He knew this because he'd done his best to scare the hell out of them so they'd think twice about coming back, and they'd simply laughed and fallen over each other as they piled out.

He grinned at the memory. Mike didn't mind a bit of fun and games; he'd never been a saint himself. But he was afraid some poor kid would accidentally burn the place down, possibly injuring someone in the process. And he couldn't bear the thought of losing the house. Mike had grown up spending his weekends there, with Grandpa Caldwell. He loved the old Victorian, had always been told he'd inherit it one day.

That hadn't happened. Instead, his grandfather had left all his grandchildren equal shares in a large ranch located in eastern Utah, which they'd since sold. But whether the house belonged to him or not, Mike couldn't stand by and allow it to be destroyed.

Shoving the transmission into Reverse, he made a quick, three-point turn and started bouncing down the long, rutted drive to the house. A set of car tracks cut through the crusty, week-old snow, confirming that at least one other vehicle had recently passed this way.

The tracks led to a vintage Mustang parked behind the silly fountain Red had bought and placed in the front yard. Mike didn't recognize the car as belonging to any of the young people he knew—and in a town of only 1,400 people, most folks knew each other. But it could easily belong to someone from a neighboring town.

Grabbing the cowboy hat sitting on the passenger seat and jamming it on his head, he parked behind the Mustang and stomped the snow off his boots as he approached the door. He listened but didn't hear any noise coming from inside—no music or voices—so he doubted anyone was tearing up the place. More likely it was a pair of young lovers borrowing the old mattress he'd seen in one of the upstairs bedrooms.

He scratched under his jaw. He really didn't want to walk in on something like that. But there was the issue of the candles. And he felt fairly confident that if a couple had to drive

all the way out here for privacy, there was a mother somewhere who'd thank him for rousting them out.

"Damn kids." He tried the door and found it unlocked.
Probably the boy had climbed through a window around back
and let his girlfriend in the front door. That was how they usually did it.

Rusty hinges protested as he poked his head inside, but a
rich vanilla scent greeted him immediately. The light came
from the kitchen. Heat seemed to emanate from that part of
the house, as well. Evidently *someone* was trying to make
things cozy....

"Hello?" Mike banged on the door as he entered. "If you're
undressed, cover up. I'm comin' in."

He heard rustling at the back of the house. Then a flashlight snapped on and the beam hit him right in the face, blind-
ing him before he could take another step.

"Stop right there!"

He put up a hand to block the light. "Or?"

"Or...I'll shoot."

He could tell by the voice that it was a woman. He had no
idea where her boyfriend might be, but she seemed to be alone
for the moment. "You have a *gun?*" he said incredulously.

"What do you think?"

Mike couldn't remember anyone ever being shot in Dundee—unless it was in some kind of hunting accident. But he
supposed anything was possible. "What kind of gun?"

"Does it matter?"

"Just curious." He was still trying to protect his eyes.

"One that'll put a hole in you," she said. "Happy?"

"Not particularly." The quaver in her voice told him she
was probably lying about the gun, which he'd suspected from
the beginning. He could understand why she'd feel a bit intimidated with a six-foot-two, two-hundred-and-ten-pound

stranger barging in on her. What bothered him was the light—that and the question of why she was there. "Who are you?"

"I could ask the same of you," she said warily.

"Mike Hill. I own the ranch next door."

Mike had grown up in these parts. Most everyone knew his family. But if she recognized his name, she didn't say so.

"What are you doing here, Mr. Hill?"

"Do you mind?" He scowled at the light as she stepped closer. "You're the one who walked in uninvited."

She had to be alone, or he would've heard someone else by now. "I came to tell you that you'd better put out those candles and hightail it out of here before I call the police. You're trespassing on private property."

"Is it *your* property?" she asked.

"It should be."

"But it's not, is it?"

He didn't like her tone. The fact that he'd lost the house, of which he had so many fond childhood memories, to a gold digger and her children still bothered him. The fact that he'd been robbed of the time he could've spent with his grandfather in the last ten years of Morris Caldwell's life rankled even more.

"What happens here is none of your business," she went on briskly. "Please go."

Mike had no intention of leaving. No one was going to chase him out of his grandfather's house—especially with nothing more threatening than a flashlight. "Get that damn light out of my eyes."

"Or?" she said, coming back at him with his own line.

Mike welcomed the challenge. "Or I'll take it away from you."

"Then I'll—"

"Shoot? You don't even have a gun. If you did, you wouldn't need to blind me."

She hesitated, but Mike didn't give her a chance to decide, just in case he was wrong about the gun. With two quick steps, he caught her around the waist and pressed her up against the closest wall.

The flashlight fell and rolled away as he pinned her hands to the side. But he'd moved her close enough to the light in the kitchen that he could just make out a straining chest covered by an overlarge sweatshirt, a pale oval face and a thick halo of long curly hair that appeared to be blond. She was young, all right, but older than he'd thought. Certainly not a teenager. She looked small, perfect, porcelain—like an angel. But the glint in her luminous eyes had nothing to do with innocence and everything to do with red-hot fury.

She began to raise her knee, but he managed to maintain his hold on her and protect his groin at the same time. "Let go of me you, son of—!"

"Whoa, calm down, little lady!" He used his body weight to press her more firmly against the wall so she wouldn't try to knee him again.

"Little lady?" She was breathing so hard he could feel every intake of breath. "I suppose you think that kind of condescending bullshit passes for manners out here, huh, *cowboy?*"

Mike cocked an eyebrow at her. "My manners are a hell of a lot better than anything I've seen from you," he snapped.

"I'm not the one who came barging into your house!"

That took him aback. *"What?"*

"You heard me. Whether you think this place should belong to you or not, I own it, so let me go."

Mike didn't budge. The last time he'd seen Lucky Caldwell she'd been a pudgy eighteen-year-old with more than her share of acne. She'd worn her reddish hair in a tight ponytail and waited for the school bus out front every morning, hugging her books to her chest and glaring daggers at him whenever he drove by. "I don't believe you," he said.

"Rumor had it that my mother tried to poison him. Actually, she gave him too much insulin, which she claimed was an accident, but he divorced her and cut her out of his will. Would I know *that* if I was just some squatter?"

"Pretty much everybody knows that," he pointed out, trying to see her more clearly. "At least around here."

"Okay, you bought the land next door from Morris when I was ten and you were about twenty-five. Josh was a couple of years younger. You and he started a stud service with a black stallion that had a white star on his forehead and white socks."

At his surprised silence she added grudgingly, "That horse was beautiful. I used to bring him sugar cubes and apples."

Slowly, Mike let go of her and eased away, wondering why his stallion hadn't keeled over if she'd been feeding it from her evil mother's pantry. Now that he could see her a little better, he couldn't help noticing that she wasn't wearing anything, other than maybe a pair of panties, beneath that baggy sweatshirt. The hem hit her almost at midthigh; bare, shapely legs extended from there.

"It's cold. Where're your pants?" he asked.

"In case you haven't noticed, it's late. I happened to be in my sleeping bag when you so kindly broke into my house and ruined my night. Forgive me for not dressing more modestly."

With that biting edge to her voice, he could tell she still had plenty of spunk. But she'd certainly changed in other ways. Mostly, she'd grown up. Although she had large breasts, especially for such a small woman, the fat had melted away, and her hair was long and curly and tumbled almost to her waist. With the light from the kitchen acting like a halo behind her, he could now see that it was more red than blond.

Mike restrained a whistle and couldn't help wondering whether she would've looked that good six years ago if she hadn't pulled her hair back every day. If so, she might have commanded a little more positive attention from the boys in town. As it was, she hadn't been especially attractive. Nor, with her unpleasant personality, did she have anything else to recommend her.

"Why didn't you tell me it was you?" he asked.

Her hands curled into fists. "Maybe I appreciate my privacy."

More likely she enjoyed being caustic. He remembered Lucky clinging to Morris's arm the day Morris had invited Mike over to meet his new wife and children. Because of his grandparents' divorce and the quick second wedding, it had been a difficult year for Mike's whole family, but particularly for Mike, since he'd always been closest to his grandpa. Everyone else had refused to acknowledge Morris's invitation to come to the house, but Mike had shown up, hoping that everything he'd been hearing was a lie, or at least not as bad as it seemed. He'd thought he knew his grandpa. He'd thought his grandpa would never change. But Morris had been swept away by the excitement of his new relationship and was never the same after falling in love with Red.

Mike had known there was indeed trouble in Eden when Morris hugged Lucky close and introduced her as "his new girl." "This one's a little doll," he'd said, but the moment he turned his back, Lucky stuck out her tongue at Mike and ran away.

Mike blinked, wondering what had brought Lucky back to Dundee. After Red died, his mother had finally stopped talking about how "that woman" and "those children" had stolen Morris's love, as well as his money, then abandoned him when he was old and sick. Those who'd really loved him had taken care of him that last year. She'd also quit telling Mike, every chance she got, that it was Red who'd caused his grandmother to die shortly after Morris did. *The doctors say it was heart failure. Of course it was. Her heart broke when she found out about Daddy's affair. Mother was never the same after she left him and moved to town.* Eventually, the scandal had slipped into the background and Mike hated to see it resurrected. "Are you here to stay?" he asked.

When Lucky threw back her shoulders and brought up her chin, he knew he hadn't done a very good job of concealing his hope for a negative answer. But then, he couldn't imagine her expecting *anyone* to be happy about her return, his family least of all.

"I might stay for a while," she said. "You don't have any problem with that, do you?"

He had a problem with it, all right, but he'd already done all he could about Lucky. As soon as he'd learned that his grandfather had never legally adopted her and her brothers, as they'd all believed, he'd sued her for the house. And lost. Then he'd tried to buy it from her, several times. But she'd refused to sell. Bottom line, Lucky legally owned the place his grandfather had always promised to him; she could stay as long as she liked.

"What you do is your decision, of course," he said, his tone as curt and formal as hers.

"My thoughts exactly." She clasped her hands in front of her. "Now, if you don't mind, it's late, I'm nearly naked, and it's cold."

He leaned sideways to gaze through the short hallway to the kitchen. Aside from the candles and the crackle of a fire, she didn't seem to have many comforts in there. Surely, staying in such a barren, filthy place had to be miserable, especially for a young woman. But he didn't want her to be too comfortable, did he? Then she might prolong her visit.

"Is there anything else?" she asked when he hesitated.

Letting his breath seep slowly between his lips, he stooped to retrieve his hat, which had fallen off when he'd "disarmed" her. "No."

She stalked to the front door and yanked it open.

If she'd been anyone else, he would've said something neighborly, something like, "If you need anything, I'm right next door." Because she was a woman, and young and alone, he had a tough time *not* saying it. But she wasn't just any woman. She was the daughter of the most selfish, grasping woman he'd ever met.

"Good night," he said coldly and walked out, carrying his hat. If Lucky had turned out as much like Red as he suspected, she could certainly take care of herself.

CHAPTER TWO

LUCKY COULDN'T SLEEP. Her presence had been discovered by Morris's first family. Already. Before she could even settle in and begin her research. She didn't peg Mike Hill as much of a gossip, but he was loyal to his family. Now that he'd seen her, he was sure to mention it to his mother, who would mention it to her sister and brothers, and so on until half the town rose up against her. After all, practically everyone in Dundee was a friend or relative of the original Caldwells.

Not that Mike or any of the people in his circle could do anything about her return—except make it unpleasant. Morris had seen to that. Considering what he believed her mother had tried to do to him, Lucky couldn't understand why he'd still loved *her* and why he'd provided for her, especially so well. He'd left her brothers each a sizeable chunk of land, but he'd given her a little more than anyone else when he bequeathed her the house *and* a living allowance. Besides being grateful, she still missed him terribly. He was the best man she'd ever known, one of the few who had room in his heart for a fat, ugly little girl.

Ironically, Mike, one of her greatest rivals, reminded her of the man she'd loved so dearly. There was something about the way he carried himself, the way he smiled. Not that he'd ever smiled at her. When she was a teenager, she used to daydream that the rugged cowboy next door would strike up a

conversation, but she couldn't remember his even acknowledging her. Which was probably why she'd become so determined to get a reaction out of him. She'd even flashed him
one day while he was riding past on a horse and she was swimming in the pond. She'd doubted he could ignore *that*—and
had felt mildly exultant when an expression of displeasure had
flickered across his face.

Pulling her knees to her chest, she tried to shut out the terrible craving she'd always felt for any crumb of approval or
acceptance—especially when it came to Morris's first family—and concentrated on staying warm.

She was tempted to leave this house, leave Dundee. But the
list of names she'd found in her mother's journal was reason
enough to stay.

AFTER A MISERABLE night's sleep, Mike stared at the phone,
wondering whether or not he should call his mother. It was
possible that Lucky didn't plan on staying for any length of
time. She moved around a lot. He knew because he was in
charge of mailing off the monthly check she received from
Morris's trust, and she was forever sending him a new address.
If she saw this as a stopover, if she was only going to move
on in a few days, mentioning her sudden return would upset
his mother, his entire family, for nothing.

But if Lucky was going to stick around, it'd be better to
give everyone some warning.

He'd called his brother, Josh, already, but Josh was in Hawaii with Rebecca and Mike hadn't been able to reach him.

"Mike?"

Mike glanced toward the door. Plump, fifty-year-old Rose
Hilman, who handled the accounting, had just poked her head
into his office.

"Yes?"

"Gabe Holbrook is here to see you."

Forgetting about his mother, his brother *and* Lucky Cald-well, Mike sat taller in surprise. He'd grown up with Gabe. They'd been best friends since they were kids, but ever since the accident, Gabe rarely came around.

"Send him in," he said.

As Mike waited, he felt a surge of guilt and remorse. Over the past few months he hadn't made enough of an effort to see Gabe. The man had had a tough two years, the worst imaginable, but he'd become so remote and moody, it was dif-ficult to connect with him anymore. There didn't seem to be anything safe to talk about. The subjects they used to enjoy—football, rodeo, women—had all become painful reminders of Gabe's loss.

Mike stood as Gabe wheeled himself into the room, slightly heartened that his friend looked so healthy. A long-sleeved T-shirt covered the corded muscles in his broad shoul-ders and arms, which bunched as he forced his chair over the thick pile of the carpet. Obviously he'd been lifting weights. His face was leaner and harsher in some respects, but he pos-sessed the same thick-lashed blue eyes and wavy black hair that had always made him a favorite with women. At least he'd been a favorite before the accident....

"Gabe, good to see you, man." Mike rounded his desk to shake hands.

Gabe's grip was firm. "It's been a while."

Too long, and Mike knew it. If only the sight of Gabe in that damn wheelchair didn't make him feel so...heartsick. He shoved his hands in his pockets, because he suddenly didn't know what else to do with them, and sat on the edge of the desk. "You look good, buddy. You must be drinking more of that wheatgrass juice you made me taste last time I came up to the cabin."

It had probably been two months since that visit, but if Gabe resented the neglect, he didn't let on. "There're more vitamins and minerals in a tablespoon of wheatgrass juice than—"

"I know—a whole grocery sack of fresh vegetables," Mike broke in, chuckling. "And I still couldn't force it down."

Gabe's eyes swept over him. "From what I can see, you're doing okay without it. For an old guy."

Two years younger, Gabe had skipped a couple of grades in school and always teased him about his age.

"Forty's right around the corner," Mike said, "and you're not the only one who won't let me forget it. Josh has been giving me hell for months. So what brings you out to the ranch on such an ugly day?"

Gabe's eyes cut to the window, where snow was falling so thickly Mike could barely make out the barn.

"The roads aren't impassable yet. But your driveway could use some shoveling. How do you expect a cripple like me to get around?"

The way he tried to make light of his situation made Mike more uncomfortable. Gabe's body had been his whole life. Now he was a broken man, could never be fixed, and was living out in the hills like some kind of hermit.

"You seem to get anywhere you want," he said, which was true. If Gabe didn't go out much, it wasn't because he couldn't.

He shrugged. "I manage. Especially when I have a good reason."

"Sounds like something's up."

"I wanted to tell you that my dad's running for Congress in the next election."

"Really?" Mike nearly stood at this news, but remained sitting on the corner of his desk to lessen the height difference between them. He hated towering above Gabe when Gabe was really taller by a couple of inches. "That's great. He's got the background for it. He's been a state senator for…what? Nine years now?"

"Ten, but it'll still be a tough race. Butch Boyle's been in office forever."

"An incumbent is always difficult to beat. But your father's well respected in this state. I think he has a good chance."

"We need some new blood in there. Butch's been in Washington so long I don't think he remembers he's from Idaho."

Mike had to agree. He'd never been impressed with Congressman Boyle. But Mike would've supported Gabe even if Gabe had just announced that his father was running for President of the United States. This was the first sense of purpose he'd felt in his friend since the car accident.

"Fund-raising's critical," Gabe continued. "That's the other reason I'm here. I was hoping you'd help me."

"If you're asking me to contribute, you know I will." Mike leaned over and shuffled through some papers on his desk, looking for his checkbook, but Gabe's voice stopped him.

"I was hoping you'd be willing to do a little more than give me a donation."

Mike raised his eyebrows. "What, for instance?"

"I'd like you to put together a committee. I want to meet with Conner Armstrong and the rest of the investors in the Running Y Resort, and Josh and your uncles and a few other folks in town."

"You don't need me for that."

"Actually, I do. I'm not sure they'll take an ex-football player seriously enough."

Mike suspected Gabe meant they might not take a *crippled* ex-football player seriously enough. No one thought Gabe any less of a man now than he was before, but Mike didn't bother trying to convince Gabe of that. He knew from experience that Gabe wouldn't listen. "Boise is where the money's at, not here."

"Boise is split between the two congressional districts. We've got the more conservative part, which we'll probably lose to Boyle," Gabe said. "As far as grassroots efforts go, we're going to have to do what we can here and up in the panhandle."

Mike rubbed his chin. He'd shaved when he got up this morning, but he could already feel the whiskers that would create a shadow across his jaw by dinnertime. "What kind of money are we talking?"

"Half a million, at least. I'm sure Boyle can easily raise that much, what with Political Action Committees and donations from the timber industry."

"We can't raise half a million from private individuals, no matter how successful our grassroots efforts are," Mike said. "We live in a state that's nearly half-rural."

"I realize that. But there are other avenues."

"Like…"

"The American Federation of Teachers, the American Federation of State, County, and Municipal Employees, the International Brotherhood of Electrical Workers, the Teamsters Union…"

"You've been doing your homework."

Gabe gave him a rare smile. "Damn right."

Mike considered the request. Maybe getting involved in Garth Holbrook's campaign would give him and Gabe something in common again, help them both adjust to who and what Gabe was now.

"Sure," he said. "Josh is out of town with Rebecca for a few days, an early Christmas present. But I'll set up an appointment with him, Conner and the other Running Y investors as soon as he gets back."

LUCKY LEANED against the wall of her old bedroom and rubbed an itch on her forehead with the back of her hand. She'd been knocking down cobwebs and sweeping out the house all morning and didn't want to touch her face with her fingers. The physical exertion of cleaning helped her stay warm, so she'd kept at it while waiting for the snow to let up. But it was already noon and the weather didn't seem likely to change any time soon. If she wasn't careful she could get stranded out here another night.

She was determined not to let that happen, but she didn't have too many options. There wasn't any cell phone service because of the surrounding mountains. She was fifteen miles from town and didn't have anything remotely resembling a shovel with which to dig her car out of the snow. And Mike Hill was her only neighbor.

Mike Hill... God, she couldn't ask him for help! He'd always resented her, and she'd—

She'd nothing. Most of the time, she didn't even exist for him. It was better to pretend he'd never existed for her, either.

Deciding there wasn't anything she could do until it stopped snowing, she headed downstairs for her suitcase so she could hang up a few of her nicer clothes. She'd packed carefully, filling her bags to maximum capacity just in case she stayed awhile, but her belongings were no longer neat and tidy. After Mike had left last night, she had trouble getting warm again and she'd rummaged through them, searching for layers.

Shoving her clothes back inside her biggest suitcase, she sat on the lid to close it, then pulled it over to the stairs and started hoisting it up one step at a time.

"Come on," she grumbled as she strained to keep moving. She made the first curve of the stairs and rounded the second, but the corner of her suitcase hit a spindle, nearly jerking it from her grasp, and the latch gave way. With a curse, Lucky watched in frustration as everything spilled down the stairs.

"That's it, I give up," she said, and dropped the suitcase, too. It banged its way along, hitting the wall and the railing several times before finally crashing to the floor.

Sinking onto a step near the top, she glowered at the wreckage. What was another mess? She was already alone in a house with no utilities, stranded by a terrible storm....

I should leave Dundee as soon as the storm lifts. That thought had been drifting in and out of her mind all morning. She'd already put this place behind her once, along with its ghosts and memories. Why had she bothered to come back?

The black journal that had fallen out of her suitcase, along with everything else, served as a quick reminder. Studying what she could see of the fanning yellowed pages, she wondered once again whether reading it had been a mistake.

Would finding her father really make any difference?

She had no idea. Her brothers hadn't grown up with their father, but they knew his name. According to Red, he'd been a handsome young man named Carter Jones, who'd spent two years in Dundee before breaking her heart and following the rodeo circuit. Except for the money he'd occasionally sent when he was working, they'd never heard from him again.

Her brothers didn't seem to have a problem with that, but she was different. She'd grown up without knowing so much as a name. Until now. Suddenly, she had three possible candidates. She'd come here with the goal of narrowing it down to one. And why not? What better things did she have to do? She'd been traveling from place to place, volunteering at hospitals and food banks and shelters for six years—ever since she'd graduated from high school. There really wasn't anywhere left to go, at least anywhere she'd find the peace she'd been seeking in her volunteer work. This small town hated her for being who she was, but it held all the secrets she needed to gain some perspective on her life.

With a sigh, she retrieved the journal. Maybe returning to Dundee *wasn't* a mistake, but she should've waited for spring. She might have waited, except that she'd wanted to be here for Christmas. The memory of that one holiday, her first in this house, had tempted her back.

She chuckled sadly. God, she was still trying to relive it. How pathetic...

Stepping past the shoes and underwear on the stairs, she went back to her mother's bedroom to confront the vulgar graffiti on the wall. This room, those words, brought back so much of what she'd experienced when she lived here. Her friends' parents' disapproving glances and hushed words: *Julie's brought home that Caldwell girl again. We need to have a talk with her.... Lucky'll turn out to be just like her mother, you wait and see.... We're law-abiding, churchgoing folk. We can't have that kind of influence in* this *house.* The suggestive whispers of the boys in school: *Is your hair that red everywhere? Let's go behind the bleachers and take a look.... With a mother like yours, you ought to know all the tricks.*

All the tricks? Growing up, Lucky had known more about sex than she should have, but certainly not from her own experience.

Sliding down the wall to the bare floorboards, she opened the weathered book she'd found when she finally went through the boxes her brothers had sent her after Red's funeral. The list of male names scrawled in her mother's hand brought back fragments of memory Lucky had tried for years to suppress. Men, coming in and out of their ramshackle trailer while Lucky was small, ruffling her hair or handing her a shiny quarter. Men moaning behind the closed door of her mother's bedroom.

Despite the terrible cold, sweat gathered on Lucky's top lip. She wanted to burn the journal, obliterate the proof. But she couldn't. Dave Small, Eugene Thompson and Garth Holbrook were all listed as having "visited" her mother twenty-five years ago, right around the time a man would've had to visit Red for Lucky to be born. Unless Red was seeing someone she *didn't* write down, which seemed unlikely given her scrupulous records, one of these men was probably her father....

Lucky recognized Dave Small's name, and Garth Holbrook's, too. Both had been prominent citizens of Dundee, giving her some hope that she could identify with or admire her father at least a little more than she did her mother. They might have visited a prostitute several times, but Lucky knew from watching Red that being faithful wasn't easy for a lot of people. It was even possible that they hadn't been married when they'd associated with her mother.

She thumbed forward to the blank pages that represented the year Morris had come into their lives. He'd put a stop to the male parade going through Red's trailer. For a while, anyway. Until Red forgot what it was like to scratch for a living and grew bored with being an old man's wife. Then, while Morris was away on his many business trips, everything had started up again. Only now her mother didn't keep a list, the men didn't leave any money, and Lucky was old enough to have a clearer understanding of what was really going on when her mother said she needed to speak to Mr. So-and-So alone for a few minutes.

Briefly, Lucky closed her eyes, shaking her head at all the times she'd begged Red not to risk their newfound security. As Lucky grew older, Red had quit pretending that Lucky didn't know the truth and started threatening her instead. *You say anything, Lucky Star Caldwell, and I'll kick your ass right out of this house.*

Her mother's voice came to her so clearly, so distinctly, that Lucky glanced up, toward the entrance of the room. But she saw nothing—nothing except herself as a young, insecure girl, peeking into the room in response to her mother's shrill call, "Bring me some damn aspirin."

When things at home became unbearable, Lucky would sneak over to the Hill brothers' barn to be with their beautiful horses. There, for an hour or two at a time, she managed to forget the sick feeling that, by her silence, she was betraying Morris as badly as her mother was. Or the knowledge that, even if she'd had her mother's permission to tell what she knew, which she most certainly did not, she wouldn't have breathed a word of it because she couldn't bear the thought of Morris disappearing from her own life.

Snapping the book closed, Lucky climbed to her feet. She'd tried so hard to distance herself from all that. Once she'd graduated from high school, she'd left Dundee and never looked back. Even when Morris had died and her brothers sent word of her inheritance. Even when, two years later, her mother had a stroke and passed away. Even when Mike Hill contested the will, forcing her to hire an attorney. She'd let the attorney go to court for her and when it was all over, she'd simply petitioned Mike, as executor of Morris's estate, for the check he was supposed to send her each month and left the house to rot.

Until now. Now she realized she could never run far enough from the past and she'd come back do something about the house. But first she had to ask Mike for a favor before she froze to death. She doubted he was going to be very happy about it.

CHAPTER THREE

LUCKY SHIFTED from one foot to the other as she stood at Mike's door. He might be chief among her rivals, but he was also one of the handsomest men she'd ever known and, without running water in the house, she hadn't even been able to shower. She was soaked and shivering from wading through snow, and her nose and cheeks felt so raw she was sure they were bright pink.

Pink had never been a good color on her; pink wasn't good for most redheads. But at this point, Mike Hill was her only option. No one else lived nearby.

A middle-aged woman came to the door. Her brown hair, full of gray streaks, was pulled into a bun with a pencil jammed through it. "You don't have to stand out in the cold, honey. This part of the house is only offices. You can come in."

"Th-thanks." Lucky was so cold she could barely speak.

"You're going to catch pneumonia if you don't get out of those wet clothes and put on something dry as soon as possible," the woman said, her gaze traveling over Lucky's soaked jeans.

Lucky blinked the last vestiges of snow from her eyelashes and managed a smile. "I'm f-fine. Is Mr. Hill around?"

"Which one?"

"Mike."

"He's in his office. Can I tell him who's looking for him?"

Lucky hesitated to state her name. She didn't want to send shock waves through the community just yet. But Mike already knew she was back, which pretty much ruined her low-profile return. "Lucky Caldwell."

The woman's eyebrows shot up to her hairline. "Did you say *Lucky?*"

Lucky clenched her jaw and nodded. Her hands, feet and nose burned as they thawed, but the prickling sensation was the least of her worries. How was Mike going to react to having her appear at his office?

"You've grown up," the woman said. "I didn't recognize you."

Lucky didn't recognize her, either, and it must've shown because the other woman frowned. "I'm Polly Simpson—Mrs. Simpson to you, at least in the old days. I used to work in the attendance office at Dundee High, remember?"

"Oh, of course," Lucky said. But she still couldn't recall Polly Simpson's face. Probably because she'd never missed a day of school in her life. School had been her refuge. She'd rarely visited the attendance office and had probably only passed Mrs. Simpson in the halls.

"I'll tell Mike you're here."

"Wait." Lucky caught her arm. "Is there a Mrs. Hill I could talk to?"

"If you mean Josh's wife, she's out of town. Mike's not married."

"Still?"

Mrs. Simpson chuckled. "Still. Do you want me to get him?"

Evidently, she had no better choice. "Yeah."

With a final curious glance, Polly headed the other way, her panty hose rubbing as she walked. A moment later, she poked her head out of a room at the end of the hall and waved. "Mike says you can come on back."

Lucky quickly removed her boots because the caked-on snow was beginning to melt and create puddles on the plastic protecting the entryway carpet. But when she saw her feet, she wished she hadn't been so polite. There was a hole in her sock, which made her look like the white trash everyone here already thought she was.

"Miss Caldwell?"

Lucky straightened. "I'm coming." Ignoring the hole, along with the wetness of her jeans and her generally haggard appearance, she refused to acknowledge the curious stares of the office personnel and walked down the hall as if she and Mike had been friends for years.

Mike had a large office with a mahogany desk, four soft leather chairs, a wet bar in one corner and several horse pictures hanging on the walls. Huge windows revealed the storm, but Lucky knew that on a clear day, they'd show the barn and the beauty of the land sweeping away from the house.

"Lucky." Mike stood. Cool curiosity filled his hazel eyes, but he didn't come to meet her, and he didn't smile. "Is there something I can do for you?"

Lucky resented having to ask him for a favor, even a small one. But unless she wanted to turn into a Popsicle by morning, she had to. "I was hoping you wouldn't mind letting me use your phone."

"Of course not." He paused briefly, studying her, and she stood completely still, forcing herself to bear the weight of his gaze. She had no doubt that he wouldn't like what he saw. She'd lost a lot of weight since she'd lived here, but her hair color was too light to be the rich auburn everyone seemed to admire, and her skin was too pale.

"You're soaked," he said. "Don't tell me you *walked* over here."

She didn't want him to know how desperate she was for the basics in life, so she shrugged carelessly. "It's only half a mile or so."

"It's storming."

"I guess I could've dug my car out of the snow, but the closest thing I have to a shovel is a broom." She chuckled, hoping to elicit a smile from him and ease the tension between them, but it didn't work.

"In that case, I think you made the right choice." He brushed past her as he dragged a chair across the carpet to a small table in the corner, where there was a phone.

As he swept by, Lucky caught the scent she'd noticed last night. Mike had been in his midtwenties when she was growing up, fifteen years her senior, but she'd always respected him—almost idolized him. And now that she could see him more clearly, she decided he'd changed for the better. Where he'd once been tall and lanky, he was well-muscled and perfectly proportioned. Faint laugh lines bracketed his eyes and mouth, and the skin of his face, hands and neck showed how often he worked outdoors. She liked Mike's rugged virility, his light eyes and brown hair, the aura about him that said he'd been around awhile and knew how to handle life. But last night was the first time she'd ever gotten close enough to connect a specific scent to him. He smelled like the outdoors, like a wintry forest....

"Sit down and make yourself comfortable," he said, but she knew his words were only a polite facade.

She shook her head. "I won't sit, I'm too wet."

He frowned at her soaked feet as if he'd missed them in his earlier perusal—and seemed to zero in on the hole in her sock. Her toes curled before he motioned her into the chair again. "I'm not worried about you getting anything wet."

Clearing her throat, she did as he suggested so she could leave as soon as possible. "Um, do you happen to have a phone book I could use?"

He leaned into the hall and asked someone to bring him a

phone book. "Can I get you a cup of coffee?" he asked, turning back.

Lucky longed for hot coffee. Without electricity, she couldn't brew any for herself. But she wasn't going to press her welcome long enough to drink it. She didn't want to take anything more from Mike than absolutely necessary. "No, I'm fine."

He opened his mouth to speak again but Polly Simpson interrupted with the phone book, which he immediately passed to her.

"Thanks," she mumbled and tried to get her burning fingers to work well enough to turn the flimsy pages.

Mike shoved his hands into the pockets of his Wranglers and leaned against the doorjamb, then seemed to think twice about hanging around to watch. "I'm gonna grab a cup of coffee," he muttered and left, and Lucky breathed a sigh of relief to find herself alone.

It took her nearly fifteen minutes to get through to the power company, and an additional five to reach the other utility companies, but when she finally hung up with her third customer service representative of the day, she had promises that the electricity and phone service would be restored at 215 White Rock Road. She just didn't know exactly when. She'd been told it would happen after the storm, but the storm could last another day or two.

"All set?" Mike reappeared almost the second she closed the phone book.

Lucky took the question to mean that he was as anxious for her to leave as she was to go. "Yes. Thank you." She stood and headed for the door, but knew she'd be stupid not to ask Mike if she could borrow a shovel. If she didn't get power and water today, she'd have to dig out and drive to town. She was down to a small bag of sunflower seeds for food, only half a gallon of water and no more firewood.

Cursing herself for not being better prepared for the harsh Idaho winter, she paused on her way out. "I'm sorry to bother you again, but would it be possible to borrow a shovel? I won't need it for more than a couple of days."

He'd already started working on his computer. He glanced up—and hesitated long enough that she regretted asking.

"If you don't have an extra one, I understand," she said.

"No, that's not it. I'm sure I can find something." Getting up, he came around the desk and led her through the offices. When they reached the outside door, he told her he'd be right back.

She put on her cold, wet boots while he disappeared into the private part of the house. By the time he returned, she was dressed and ready to go, and he was carrying a fair-size snow shovel. "Here you are."

"Thanks. I'll get it back to you as soon as I can," she told him and ducked out into the storm. She thought he said, "There's no rush," but the wind had kicked up so much, she could scarcely hear him.

LUCKY SPENT the next several hours shoveling snow in a veritable blizzard. The work warmed her body but did little for her fingers and toes. Soon her jeans were stiff with ice. She had to stop every few minutes to go inside, take off her boots and stick her frozen feet in her heavy sleeping bag in an effort to warm them.

As the temperature dropped and the sky darkened, she considered heading back to Mike's. It was getting harder and harder to wield that darn shovel, but she had too much pride to beg him for any more favors. She'd get by on her own, like always. She just needed to figure out a way to reach town.

The shovel scraped the gravel of the drive as she jammed it through the snow for what felt like the millionth time. Her back and arms ached, protesting the strain as she tossed a scoop off to the side before digging in again. Who would've thought clearing the driveway could take so long?

She slumped against the car and tried to catch her breath. Shading her eyes against the flakes still blowing around her, she squinted toward the road. She had at least twenty feet to go.

"I had to pretend I was coming home for Christmas, had to see the old place in winter," she grumbled, longing for the cup of coffee she'd refused earlier and a hot bath. She imagined slipping into a steaming tub and promised herself she'd do exactly that—as soon as she had some hot water to do it with.

After another fifteen minutes of sheer determination, she finally threw the shovel down and, completely winded, wiped her nose with the back of her gloved hand. She wasn't making enough progress, and it was getting too dark to see.

Tramping into the house, she flipped the first light switch she found, praying that her electricity had been restored. As hungry as she was, she could get by without food for one more night if only she had heat.

Nothing happened.

Dejected, she yanked off the hood of her coat and went to the kitchen to ransack her backpack. She was hoping to find an energy bar or something else she might have missed, but discovered nothing more than a few gum wrappers and crumbs. To make matters worse, her jug of water contained only a few ounces.

What was she going to do? She needed to finish clearing the drive and get out of here. But she couldn't go back to shoveling....

Returning to the living room, she stared through the large front window at what she'd achieved so far. Maybe she could drive out. It was worth a try, wasn't it?

Encouraged by visions of a hot meal and a cozy motel room, she grabbed her purse and hurried outside again. But she had trouble starting the car, and even after she got the darn engine running, she didn't make it more than ten feet before her tires spun out.

"Come on!" She shifted the transmission into Drive. No luck. She gave the Mustang a quick shot of gas and reversed. Nothing. She was stuck—at least until morning.

Letting her shoulders slump, she hammered her forehead on the steering wheel. What had she been thinking, coming back to Dundee at Christmastime? She, of all people, knew there was no Santa Claus.

AS THE WIND TOSSED tree branches and snowflakes against the house, Mike stared at the ceiling of his room. He was exhausted and wanted to sleep, but this was one of the worst storms he'd seen in years and much as he wanted to forget Lucky, he couldn't do it. He kept picturing her, small and cold with her toe poking through that hole in her sock, and he kept feeling guilty that he hadn't sent over one of his men to shovel her drive. If she'd been anyone else, he would've done it in an instant. But she wasn't anybody else. She was Red's daughter, and she wasn't as sweet as she looked.

He remembered her sticking her tongue out at him and decided he'd done the right thing. She'd been living on his grandfather's money since she turned ten. The physical labor had probably done her some good.

Unless she'd never managed to get her car out of that long drive. Maybe she was sitting over at the house right now, freezing to death....

He thought of the broken windows and the snow drifting inside.

If she'd needed anything, she would've come back to the ranch, he told himself. She'd been over once—and he'd been nice enough.

But he wasn't absolutely convinced she'd return. He could tell she'd had a difficult time appearing on his doorstep in the first place.

Punching his pillow, he rolled over. Mike had made sure his horses were safe in their stalls, each covered with a thick blanket, but he was letting a woman stay alone in a house that had no heat?

Not just any woman, he reminded himself. Lucky Caldwell. Lucky didn't count. Besides, if she was cold, she'd build a fire. She'd built one last night, hadn't she? A fire would keep her warm. He wasn't going to lose any more sleep over the little brat who'd replaced him in his own grandfather's eyes. Lucky wasn't his responsibility, and he didn't want anything more to do with her.

Work…he needed to think about work. With Josh gone he'd have plenty to do come morning. He had clients to call, payroll to sign—

The image of Lucky pressed between him and the wall, her eyes wide with alarm, flashed through his mind.

"Son of a bitch," he muttered and kicked off the covers. Evidently, it didn't matter who she was. His conscience wouldn't let him rest until he made sure she was okay.

MIKE HAD a four-wheel-drive, and one of his men had shoveled his driveway as late as five o'clock, but in this storm, the risk of getting stuck was still high. He decided it'd be better to take one of the snowmobiles he kept out back.

Grabbing the heavy-duty flashlight he used to check the horses, he bundled up in a heavy sheepskin coat and lined leather gloves, pulled on his cowboy boots and shoved his hat low on his head. Then he stalked outside and toward the shed. He'd be soaked and miserable by the time he got home….

The high whine of the snowmobile's engine sounded oddly

subdued in the storm's bluster. The headlight barely cut the dark, but Mike knew the lay of the land. He'd been riding snowmobiles out here since he was five years old—back when both his grandparents were still alive and together and he came to stay with them so often.

As he shot over the snow, icy flakes clicked against his windshield, stung his unprotected face and threatened to rid him of his hat. But it wasn't long before he was climbing the hill to his grandfather's house—Lucky's house now— feeling quite confident he'd find her gone. No one would stay around in a storm like this, he thought. Until he saw her car stuck halfway between the house and the road and knew she'd tried to go somewhere. She just hadn't made it.

The tone of the snowmobile's engine lowered by at least an octave as the hill grew steeper. He compensated by giving it more gas. He couldn't see any lights inside the Victorian, which concerned him. He hadn't really expected the utilities to be restored yet, not in a storm like this, but he assumed Lucky would light some candles or start a fire.

Maybe she'd fallen asleep, and the fire and candles had gone out.

Worry seeped through him, along with the cold, as he came to a stop next to an area that had obviously been shoveled fairly recently. He should've helped her. If she was in any kind of trouble, he knew he'd feel responsible.

The snow came above his knees as he climbed off, grabbed his flashlight and made his way toward the porch. Only this time when he reached the door, he found it locked.

"Lucky?" He banged on the thick wood, but received no answer. "Lucky, are you in there?"

Where else could she be? She seemed stubborn, but she wasn't stubborn enough to try walking the fifteen miles to town, was she? God, he hoped not. If she'd done that, he was pretty certain he'd find her lying frozen in the snow.

His flashlight made a bright circle in the swirling flakes as he waded through the side yard. When he got to the back, he found that door locked, too, but easily slipped his hand through one of the broken windows to undo the safety latch.

The kitchen was barely warmer than the outdoors. She'd been wet when he saw her just after noon. Did she know enough to get out of those clothes? Did she have others? He had no idea what she'd brought with her or how well prepared she was for weather like this, but if what he'd seen so far was any indication, she sure as hell didn't have much of a plan.

He trained his flashlight on the room around him. Lucky had cleaned in this part of the house, but he didn't see her sleeping here.

"Lucky?"

No answer.

His heart pounded as he jogged into the living room, library, office. Empty. Damn!

Taking the stairs two at a time, he headed directly to the master bedroom. "Lucky? It's Mike."

Nothing.

His heart started to pound harder. "Lucky?"

"G-go away."

The sound of her shaky voice brought both relief and more concern. He stopped abruptly and swung around, searching for her. She wasn't in the master bedroom, but she was close, definitely upstairs.

"Are you okay?" he called, hoping she'd answer him again.

"I s-said, g-go away!"

She was in the second bedroom. He strode purposefully down the hall and opened the door to find a round lump in the bottom of a sleeping bag on the dirty old mattress he'd noticed on previous visits to the house.

"What do you think you're doing?" he asked, worry putting an edge on his words.

"Wh-what do you mean?"

Her teeth were chattering so badly he could hardly understand her, especially through the sleeping bag. "You don't have any heat in here."

"Not l-late-breaking news."

"You should've come back to the ranch."

"Because I'd b-be so w-welcome?" She finally poked her head out and, unless he imagined it, she looked blue around the mouth. In any case, her eyes seemed too large for the rest of her face, reminding him how young she was. Twenty-four. He'd barely graduated from college at twenty-four.

"Because you could freeze to death over here," he said. "And my place is your only real alternative."

"Too ironic, d-don't you think? M-me asking you to p-put me up?"

"I would've done it," he said.

"Not h-happily. D-don't think your m-mother would approve of that much ch-charity where I'm concerned."

He didn't want to talk about charity right now, not when he'd ignored her needs the way he had. "That's another matter. Come on."

"What are you t-talking about?"

"You're going home with me."

"N-no, I'm not." She ducked back inside the sleeping bag. "It'll b-be morning soon. I'll d-dig my car out and—"

"Like you did today?" he said.

"D-didn't get an early enough st-start," she grumbled. "It's hard w-work."

"Something you're not accustomed to, I'm sure." With all

the money he sent her from Morris's trust, she didn't need a job and he doubted she'd ever had one.

"P-pardon me?"

"You can't keep a job when you move every few weeks."

"Who are you t-to sit in j-judgment of me? You and your family th-think you're so much b-better."

"That's bullshit," he said. "You don't know me or my family. I passed you on the road a few times when you were a kid. That's it."

"Not quite."

"There's more?"

"Only s-something I've been t-trying to forget."

"What could that be?"

She didn't answer, and it was too darn cold to coax her. "Are you coming or not?"

The fact that she'd already curled up again didn't seem hopeful. He considered his options. He could leave her here and send someone to dig her out in the morning. But then he'd go home, feel guilty and have to come back. Or he could take her with him.

Problem was, he didn't know which he'd regret more....

"If you want a hot meal and a warm bed you'll cooperate," he said.

"I d-don't remember asking you—"

"Look, we've never been friends. I know that. But for tonight, let's forget about the past and pretend we just met, okay? Simple enough?"

"That's m-mighty noble of you, M-Mike, but I'm sure I'll l-live without your help."

Mike wasn't so sure. She obviously didn't realize she could be in real danger. "You're freezing, Lucky."

"My problem, n-not yours."

True. He'd tried to tell himself as much, but... "Are you going to make me do this the hard way?" he asked.

"The hard way?" She began to crawl out again, but he knew she'd only continue to argue, so he made a quick decision. Closing off the top of her sleeping bag before she could emerge, he slung her over his shoulder like a burlap sack filled with rocks and marched into the hall.

LUCKY YELPED as she banged into Mike's back. "What are you *doing?* Leave me alone! Put me down! You egotistical, spoiled, self-righteous son of a—"

"All the traveling you've done in the past six years certainly hasn't improved your personality," he broke in dryly.

Adrenaline finally loosened her tongue. "Kiss my ass, Mr. Hill. You and your whole family can go to— Ouch…" he'd started down the stairs, which made her bump against him with every step "…to hell—ow!—because I don't care who you are or what you—ouch!—have, you're no better than I am!"

"Grown up angry, have we?" His breathing became labored as he reached what she thought had to be the front door.

She tried to slug him or kick him, but she couldn't do anything through the thickness of the bag. She couldn't even tell him off properly, which was probably why he was chuckling.

"I can't breathe in here," she said. "Let me out!"

"You were breathing in there just fine before I arrived. As a matter of fact, that bag might be the only reason you're *still* breathing. So relax. You'll be fine."

"I don't want to relax!"

"You'll thank me in the morning."

"For kidnapping me?"

"I doubt feeding you and keeping you warm for one night qualifies as kidnapping."

Keeping her warm for the night? When she was sixteen and visiting his horses, she accidentally saw Mike kissing Lindsey Carpenter in the barn. She'd replayed that scene in her mind a thousand times, but when she imagined it, she got to be the woman moaning softly as Mike held her against him. For a girl with a mother like Red, a girl who'd learned too much too soon, it was quite an epiphany to see something so sweet and gentle going on between a man and a woman. Watching Mike that day had mesmerized her. The memory of it still did. But the fact that being kept warm by him in exactly the same way appealed to her only added to her humiliation. She'd wanted to slip into town and fix up the house while quietly searching for her father. A simple plan. If only she'd known to expect the worst blizzard of the century. Then she wouldn't be going home with Mike Hill—in a bag!

Mike's boots thudded on the porch, telling her they'd moved outside, and the bumping started again as he descended more stairs. He slowed then, which meant he was probably wading through snow.

"This is ridiculous," she cried.

He set her down on something small and narrow, something she couldn't see or identify.

"What is this? Where are we?"

"Hold still."

She continued to struggle until he let her head out of the top of the bag. The snow immediately lashed her cheeks, but now she could see that she was on a snowmobile and Mike was behind her.

"Sit tight, unless you feel like flying off at thirty miles an hour," he said.

"I'm going back in the house," she said, but before she could move, his arms clamped more tightly around her and she heard his voice, low in her ear.

"Lucky, that's enough!"

She paused, shivering and breathing hard as the wind

whipped at her hair. Why he was doing this? What did he care if she froze to death?

"You're going to be fine," he said, more gently.

The thumping of her heart seemed to echo in her ears. He didn't understand. Of course he wouldn't. She'd bet her life he'd never fantasized about her once. "How do I know that?" she said tentatively.

"Because I've got you."

That was the problem.

"And if I refuse to go?"

"Trust me."

More frightening words had never been spoken. Because she instinctively knew he *was* going to take care of her, at least for tonight.

CHAPTER FOUR

"I WANT IT HOT. Hot, hot, hot," Lucky said, hugging herself and shivering as Mike adjusted the knobs on the tub.

Hot? Mike struggled to keep his eyes from straying to her bare legs. He'd told her to go ahead and get undressed while he drew her bath, but she'd been quicker at it than he'd expected. Now she was out of the spare bedroom she'd changed in and standing next to him wearing nothing but a towel—and *he* wasn't too cold to notice.

Clearing his throat, he ran his hand under the faucet again. "You should bring your body temperature up slowly. This water's lukewarm. Once you get used to it, add some more warm water, then more until you feel normal."

"Isn't that for people who have frostbite?" she said, her teeth chattering.

"You're pale and shaky. I'm just being cautious."

"Okay, okay." She was so eager to get in, it looked as if she'd drop her towel before he could leave the room—which reminded him of that day eight years ago when he'd ridden past the lake while she was swimming. She'd called his name, unhooked the front clasp of her bikini top and flashed him. Out of nowhere. They hadn't spoken in years. She was so young at the time, he'd felt only perturbed; more than anything, it had been an act of defiance. But he was pretty sure he wouldn't mind if she flashed him again now that she was an adult. She might not be his favorite person, but he couldn't deny that she'd turned into an incredible beauty. And the fact that she didn't seem to be aware of her own good looks made her all the more alluring....

"I'll have some sweats ready for you to wear when you get out," he said.

"Thanks." She stepped to the side so he could get past her and immediately focused her attention on the bath.

He allowed himself a quick glance over his shoulder at her bare back as she started to lower the towel, then closed the door behind him.

LUCKY COULD SMELL FOOD—wonderful, glorious food! If not for the scent of bacon and—she sniffed again—eggs and onions, she might never have gotten out of her warm bath.

Just as Mike had promised, Lucky found a pair of sweats sitting on a chair in the bedroom she'd used earlier. But donning Mike's clothes seemed rather personal, considering who they both were, and his sweats were way too big for her. She decided to pull on one of the layers of clothes she'd peeled off before getting into the tub. She thought it might help her remember that she needed to keep up her defenses, that Mike was not her friend.

"There you are," he said as she entered a large country kitchen with wood paneling and flooring and a table that could seat at least twelve people.

His eyes flicked over her stocking-clad feet, faded jeans and burgundy sweater; if he noticed that she'd chosen not to wear his sweats, he didn't comment. "Hungry?"

She was famished but also leery of his sudden hospitality. "You didn't have to cook," she said.

"What have you had to eat?"

"Some trail mix, an energy bar and sunflower seeds."

"That's it? Since when?"

"Noon yesterday."

"God, you must be starving." He motioned to the table. "Sit down. It's almost ready."

She looked around as she made her way to the table, feeling as though she'd just infiltrated the enemy camp. She'd often wondered what Mike's place would be like. While hiding in the barn, she'd seen people come and go from here, imagined it'd be rustic and comfortable, and she wasn't disappointed. In a word, his house was *quality,* yet nothing seemed ostentatious or even new. The kitchen, with its big circular rug, white cabinets and stainless steel appliances—indeed the whole house—was simple, masculine, lived-in and clean.

"Where are your brothers these days?" Mike asked as he put a heaping plate of bacon, scrambled eggs and hash browns with onions in front of her.

"Sean is married and living in Seattle."

"Ketchup?"

She nodded and reached for the bottle.

"And Kyle?"

"Kyle's married, too, and living in Spokane," she said, keeping her focus on the ketchup she was squeezing onto her potatoes.

"They both wound up in Washington? What took them there?"

"It wasn't here."

He capped the ketchup for her, then watched her eat, which made her so nervous she could hardly taste her food. At least the potatoes she shoveled down stopped the hunger pangs.

"Why didn't you follow them?" he asked after a few moments.

"To Washington?"

"Yeah."

She'd always been an outsider, in one way or another, and that held true even with her brothers. They were male, closer in age, less sensitive, and had the same father. They'd weathered their childhood by sheltering together while she'd forged on alone. For whatever reason, the quiet closeness and understanding they shared seemed to exclude her. "I don't know," she said. "I visit them once in a while, though."

"You seem to *visit* lots of places. You just never stay for long."

She thought she heard censure in his tone and couldn't help bristling. "Maybe I like to travel," she said flippantly. But it was a lie. She hated the lack of direction in her life, the temporary nature of everything she did. She just didn't fit in anywhere, had nothing to cling to. What else could she do? Mike, on the other hand, had no reason to leave Dundee. He had family here, a thriving business, many friends, respect. He had a *home*.

Silence fell and she looked up to find him watching her closely. "What?"

"I wasn't criticizing you."

She swallowed a mouthful of eggs. "What were you doing?"

"I guess I was asking why you haven't settled down."

"I'm…still young." She searched for a more credible reason, but she had difficulty coming up with one. Bottom line, Morris's money was both a blessing and a curse. Because she didn't have to earn a living, she didn't need to keep a job or go to school, two major activities that kept other people from rambling around the way she did. "And…I like to travel."

He leaned back and crossed his booted feet. "You mentioned that."

"Right. Well…" She shrugged.

"No men in your life?"

"Aren't you going to eat?"

"Is that an attempt to dodge my question?"

"What do you think?"

"I think moving so often must be hell on your love life."

"Then I guess it's a good thing I'm not seeing anyone right now." She'd never really had a serious relationship. She ended up comparing all the men she met to a cowboy she'd once seen kissing a woman in a barn—the same cowboy who was feeding her right now.

"That surprises me."

She played with her toast. "Why?"

He didn't answer right away. When she glanced up, she could tell that the tenor of the conversation had changed.

"Isn't it obvious?" he said.

Unless she was mistaken, she read appreciation in his eyes—the same kind of appreciation she saw when she crossed a crowded nightclub and a man at the bar turned to watch her. Maybe Mike didn't *like* her, but he found her attractive. The chubby, ugly girl who'd mooned over him all those years had finally caught his eye....

Lucky's heart started to pound at the realization, and she put down her fork. Their eyes met, and he gave her a sexy grin that went to her head quicker than a whole bottle of champagne.

Oh, God! He was flirting with her. On one level, she knew she shouldn't be surprised. A lot of men tried to pick her up. The fact that she was so aloof, that she protected herself too well to let anyone close, seemed to draw them. They liked the challenge—but the idea of responding to any of them left her cold.

That wasn't the case tonight.

But this was Mike Hill. His entire family would hate him just for being *seen* with her. And a man with Mike's good looks, sharp mind and impressive accomplishments wasn't single at forty without being hard to catch. Especially in Dundee, where life was all about getting married and having babies. Obviously, he had commitment issues. She had problems, too: deep down she was still the same little girl who secretly worshipped him.

She had to be careful, play it safe. Otherwise an already difficult visit to her hometown might become intolerable. "It's late," she said, looking away. "We'd better go to bed."

He stood and gathered up her dishes. "Right. You can have the spare room you changed in before your bath."

"Thank you. I appreciate everything you've done." She knew she sounded stilted, but formality seemed the most natural way to distance herself from Mike. She was warm and full. Now she'd crawl into the guest bed and forget that she was even in Mike's house.

All she had to do was fall asleep.

But when she did lie down, sleep wouldn't come.

AS SOON AS LUCKY HEADED down the hall, Mike finished cleaning the kitchen, then flipped on the television. He'd been so tired earlier, when he'd had to drag himself out of bed to check on her. But, strangely enough, now that she was here he didn't feel tired anymore. He suspected he knew the reason. He hadn't liked the girl who'd left Dundee, but he was sure attracted to the woman who'd returned.

Attracted was the key word, he told himself. What he felt was primitive male instinct. Once the storm blew over and he sent the little prodigal to her own house, his life would get back to normal, and normal meant he had to work tomorrow.

LUCKY HEARD Mike pass her room.

Sleep... Sleep, damn it!

She squeezed her eyes shut and forced them to stay that way, but a few minutes later, she realized it was no use. She kept picturing Mike kissing Lindsey Carpenter in the barn and thinking that tonight it could have been her.

After growing up with Red, she'd decided that it was important to save herself. But for what? For more offers from strange men who didn't appeal to her? Was she a fool not to take advantage of the opportunity to be with Mike? When was she ever going to be in his house again? In the future she doubted he'd so much as wave and say hello. Regardless of what occurred, they'd probably both pretend this night had never happened.

So, why not do what she really wanted *and then* start pretending?

MIKE HEARD his bedroom door open and lifted his head in surprise. He lived alone. The woman who did the cooking and cleaning took weekends off. Which left only one possibility.

Squinting to make out the shadowy figure standing in his doorway, he swallowed hard. Sure enough, it was Lucky. And when she didn't say anything, he had a funny feeling he knew what she wanted.

"Is something wrong?" he asked, hoping he could get her a glass of water or another blanket. He'd tried to make her smile earlier—but this…this was a little more than he'd bargained for.

"No." She sounded uncertain. He might've supposed that she was frightened or insecure, but he reminded himself that Lucky couldn't be either. Not with the way she looked, and not at twenty-four.

He knew he should scare her away, but with every heartbeat it became more difficult. He leaned on his elbows to get a better glimpse of her and felt his pulse go crazy. She wore the sweatshirt he'd set out for her earlier. But, like last night when he'd pressed her against the wall, she didn't have anything on underneath it, except maybe a pair of panties.

The thought of her panties didn't help him hang on to his sanity.

He had to say something that would cause her to withdraw immediately, before his desire took control.

But if he rebuffed her, he'd humiliate her.

If he *didn't* rebuff her…

He let his breath hiss out between his teeth. He could barely think above the racket his heart seemed to be making. If he didn't send her away it was probably no big deal, he told himself. She'd been raised by the town's most notorious hooker. Showing up in a man's bedroom probably wasn't anything new for her. And maybe he wanted her here, but it wasn't as if he'd *invited* her.

"Can't you sleep?" he said, stalling.

"No."

Briefly, he tried to summon the self-control to send her back to her own room. But the overabundance of testosterone suddenly flooding through his body muddied his thoughts, made him reckless. Any resolve he'd managed to muster fled the instant he imagined how embarrassed she'd be if he were to turn her away. Somehow it was easier to give in to what he really wanted if he looked at it as some sort of kindness.

"Are you still cold?" More stalling on his part.

She nodded but didn't ask for a blanket. Neither did she apologize for interrupting him and duck out of the room. There was no mistake. She was making him an offer and, heaven help him, he didn't think he could say no. It was the temerity of her stance that was his undoing. He wanted to take her in his arms, reassure her that she'd read his signals correctly.

"Want me to keep you warm?" he asked and lifted the blankets. Because he'd turned up the heat for her sake, he wasn't wearing anything except his boxer briefs. If this wasn't what he thought it was, she'd certainly turn back now. But she didn't. She came toward him.

When she reached the edge of his bed, she quickly pulled off the sweatshirt and dropped it on the floor. Then for a few seconds she stood in front of him wearing only a pair of lacy white panties.

The sheer beauty of the woman she'd become stole his breath. It had been a long time since he'd made love, too long. Yet, oddly enough, he hadn't realized it had been *much* too long until now.

"You're gorgeous," he whispered.

She shook her head, but he couldn't believe she or anyone else could disagree with him on that, and he wasn't really looking at her face anymore. He let his gaze drift appreciatively over the rest of her while making one last feeble effort to talk himself out of making this mistake. He'd pretty much given up dating. He couldn't seem to fall in love like everyone else. But he missed having an active sex life and, mistake or no, he wasn't about to reject Lucky now that she was standing next to him almost naked....

A MOMENT OF ABSOLUTE PANIC nearly sent Lucky running from the room. But the memory of that kiss she'd witnessed in the barn calmed her fears and prodded her to take what she wanted. This was Mike Hill. As indifferent as he'd been toward her in the past, he was a decent man and treated everyone else well. He'd be gentle, even with her. And maybe he'd make her feel like someone who mattered, someone like Lindsey Carpenter or one of the other women who belonged in Dundee. For a few moments, she might even feel as if she belonged with *him*....

He immediately urged her into bed with him, and she felt his bare skin against her breasts as his hands slid up and down her back. "Jeez, you *are* cold."

His body was as hard and sinewy as it looked, but it was the evidence of his arousal that sent sparks through Lucky's veins. *She'd* done that to him. The little girl he'd never acknowledged. The belligerent teen who'd gotten nothing but a frown when she'd unclasped her bikini top.

"You...you feel good," she said before she could stop herself.

She thought she saw his teeth flash in a grin. "You said you wanted me to make it hot, right?" He nuzzled her neck, kissed the indentation below her earlobe. "Hot, hot, hot?"

The bath... She remembered, even though she could scarcely think for all the sensations bombarding her brain. Warm flesh. Hard muscle. Crisp sheets. The scent of clean male.

"That's what I said," she whispered, breathless with the excitement and daring of what she was doing. She'd never initiated a sexual encounter in her life, and she'd actually had the nerve to approach Mike Hill.

"Then—" he rubbed his lips across her cheek "—let's see what I can do."

She turned her head, wanting him to give her the long, slow kiss he'd given Lindsey in the barn—the long, slow kiss she'd been waiting for all her life. But he didn't seem very interested in her mouth. He relieved her of her panties. Then his tongue and his hands worked such seductive magic, she almost forgot about kissing him, at least in such a soulful way. He soon had her writhing and moaning, bursting with need and the absolute certainty that nothing he was doing to her could hurt, whether it was her first time or not. She wanted Mike too badly; she wanted what his fingers promised.

But when he put on the condom he took from the nightstand near the bed and answered her eagerness with a powerful thrust, that illusion shattered.

She stiffened as she tried to absorb the sudden shock of the pain, and he froze.

"What is it?" he asked.

She tried to catch her breath so she could speak, but the desire she'd felt only a moment earlier was fading fast, and she wanted to cry. This wasn't like the scene in the barn. This meant nothing to Mike except physical release. She was doing exactly what her mother had done so many times. Only she'd sold herself for nothing....

"I'm...I'm fine," she managed to say.

"Lucky?"

She could sense his bewilderment. "Are you, um, finished?" she asked when he didn't move.

"Am I *finished?*" he repeated as though it was the oddest question in the world.

"It's...it's okay if you're not. I...I'll wait. I'm okay with waiting." She figured it was the right thing to do, since it was her fault they'd come this far. Whatever regrets she had she'd deal with later, on her own. She couldn't blame him for her own error in judgment. She'd visited *his* room, not the other way around.

He remained hesitant. "What's wrong?"

"Nothing."

"I hurt you."

"No, I... It...felt great. Really." God, she couldn't wait until morning, when she could go back to her rambling, lonely house and never see him again. The anguish of her mistake stabbed into her heart just as he stabbed into her body.

I'm such a fool. What did I think this would do? What did I think it would change?

Suddenly, he cursed and withdrew.

His displeasure stung like a slap in the face. For all his indifference, she'd never seen him lose his temper before. But she'd made him angry. She'd screwed this up so badly. "I'm sorry. I did it wrong," she said. "I didn't know. I— Is it too late? I don't mind if...if you want try again."

"You're kidding, right?"

Her emotions were so scrambled she wasn't sure if she was kidding or not, but she realized it was too late to smooth over her blunder. Blinking against the tears stinging her eyes, she scrambled to get out of his bed.

He buried his head under a pillow while she struggled to get free of the sheets. "Please tell me this wasn't your first time," he said, his voice muffled.

She couldn't answer. She had to get out. She'd ruined it. It was her fault, not his. She'd understood the rules when she came in here. She'd known from the beginning that she meant nothing to him. She'd just thought—she didn't know what she'd thought. She'd just wanted to live the dream *once*. That was all.

Finally free of the bedding, she leapt to the carpet, but he caught her arm before she could go anywhere. "Why didn't you tell me?"

"I…I didn't think it would matter," she said, then yanked away from him and ran to her own room where she put on several layers of clothes and curled into a tight ball beneath the covers, trying to make herself as small as possible. She was shaking so badly she didn't think she'd ever stop, and she wanted to cry. But the tears that had seemed so close a moment before suddenly wouldn't fall.

CHAPTER FIVE

AFTER LUCKY LEFT his room, Mike groaned. Never in a million years would he have guessed that she was a virgin. She was younger than he was by a good stretch—too young for him, really. But she was certainly old enough to know what she was doing when she came to his room. With Red as her mother, she must've learned more about sex by the age of ten than most girls knew at fifteen. She could cuss like a sailor. She'd rambled around the whole United States. She had a body most men would die for. How did a woman like *that* get to be twenty-four without ever having sex?

And why the hell didn't she tell him?

He would've been gentler with her. From the abandon of her response, from the signals she'd been giving him, he'd thought she was ready. Had he known the reality of the situation, he would've made sure—

Had he known, he probably wouldn't have touched her. He'd welcomed her into his bed only because he assumed she'd take their lovemaking in stride—and maybe, after going to all the trouble of rescuing her, he felt somewhat deserving of a small reward. But this… He cringed. This was different. She'd been miserable, and he'd been miserable, and…and what had he expected? This was Lucky Caldwell. Of *course* getting involved with her would result in regret.

He sulked for several minutes, but then had to admit that

there was more to what he felt than sexual frustration and disappointment. Now he could no longer believe that she was exactly like her mother and had therefore earned his derision. Besides her lack of sexual experience, he'd seen something vulnerable and sweet, even giving, beneath Lucky's tough-girl attitude. He'd hurt her and disappointed her—deeply, he suspected—and yet she'd worried about being a generous partner.

I'm sorry…I did it wrong… Is it too late?

The contrast between the two images he now held of her troubled him—but only because he was dwelling on a situation better forgotten. It was for the best that their lovemaking had turned out the way it had; he and Lucky didn't have any business touching each other.

With another curse, he got out of bed, kicked aside the sweatshirt she'd left behind and threw on his clothes. This night was so screwed up he was going to forget it *was* night and go to work. He wouldn't think about Lucky again….

But his footsteps slowed as he neared her room, and he couldn't help poking his head inside, just to make sure she was all right.

"Lucky?" he said softly.

She didn't respond. He could see her curled up beneath the blankets, but he couldn't hear her crying or anything. She must've gone to sleep. Wishing that made him feel better somehow, he closed her door and went outside to check on the horses.

MIKE WAS COOKING again. Lucky could smell the food, but she didn't want to get out of bed. She didn't want to face him. She felt incredibly stupid for ever believing that one night in his arms could change anything in her world. And she knew he had to be asking himself why he'd shown any interest in her.

Going into his room had been as big a gaffe as flashing him—only more humiliating because this time she'd been hoping for a positive reaction.

She rubbed her temples to ease the pounding in her head as she tried to convince herself that last night's embarrassment didn't matter. He'd never liked her to begin with, so she hadn't lost anything. Except a pair of panties. She felt uncomfortable without her underwear, but she wasn't going back to his bedroom for any reason.

Getting up, she dressed and made the bed as perfectly as she could, wishing she could erase any trace of herself. The urge to leave town obsessed her. She wanted to get in her car and simply drive away. But she'd left Morris's house vacant too long already, and the promise of those names in her mother's journal held her fast. Besides, she might've been naive and foolish to do what she did, but she wouldn't be a coward about it now.

After using her finger and a little toothpaste to brush her teeth, she raked her fingers through her unruly hair, which had reached almost wild dimensions, took a deep breath, and walked down the hall to the kitchen.

Mike didn't turn at the sound of her approach. She thought he hadn't heard her until he spoke. "Morning."

Her nails curled into her palms. "Morning," she said.

"Coffee?"

She hesitated. It felt so odd letting him take care of her. She hated the complexity it added to their relationship, hated the grudging appreciation that was getting mixed up with the resentment and everything else. But she didn't have much choice. She could drink his coffee or she could go without. Providing for herself wasn't an option at the moment. "Please."

He filled a cup and set it on the table, where a pitcher of cream and a bowl of sugar waited. "Breakfast is coming right up."

She was hungry, but she wasn't sure she'd be able to keep the food down. Her ulcer was aching, burning. She shouldn't have stopped taking her medication. "Smells good."

He flipped the pancakes on the griddle, then leaned against the counter. She could feel his attention on her but refused to meet his eyes in case he wanted to initiate a conversation that went deeper than, "One pancake or two?"

Unfortunately, that didn't stop him. "So…" he said with just enough emphasis to warn her that she wouldn't like what he was about to say.

Ignoring his lead-in, she crossed to the window, distraught to see that the storm still raged.

"Are you going to explain what happened last night?" he asked.

She kept her back to him. "I don't want to talk about it."

"You should've told me you never had sex with anyone."

"It doesn't matter."

"It *does* matter. A guy should know when he needs to…to take a little extra care and—"

She didn't want to hear this. "You're going to burn the pancakes if you're not careful."

"How do you know? You've barely even glanced in this direction."

"I can smell them."

"I don't care about the pancakes. I'm trying to tell you that—"

She held up her hand. "I know what you're trying to tell me. I was an idiot last night. I get it. But it's not your problem. And I don't need your advice because I won't ever be in that position again. A girl can only lose her virginity once, remember?"

When he didn't respond she turned to see why, and found

him looking stricken instead of mollified. "It didn't have to be that bad," he finally said.

"It couldn't have been any different," she said flatly. "Anyway, I was wondering if maybe I could get a ride into town."

He frowned. "What's the matter, Lucky? You itchin' to run again?"

"I don't know what you're talking about."

"What is it you keep running from?"

"Go to hell."

"Is it that you're afraid?"

She tried to throw him off with sarcasm. "Do you always analyze your bed partners?"

"Only when something happens that I don't understand."

"Forget about it," she said.

"Why, so you don't have to face the truth?"

"*What* truth? You rolled on top of me last night for a few seconds. That doesn't mean you know anything about me."

"That wasn't exactly what happened. First, you came into my room and asked for what you got. And maybe I know more than you think. At least I know what your actions tell me."

"And what do they tell you?"

"You stay in one place for only a few weeks or months and leave about the time most other people begin to form friendships and put down roots. I'm guessing you do that because you're terrified of growing close to anyone, of maintaining a relationship."

"If you're applying that to this situation, we don't even *have* a relationship."

"With me it's something else."

She cocked a challenging eyebrow at him.

"I think you're afraid that if you stay, we might end up in bed again—and next time you might like it."

He'd hit a little too close to the truth, and she couldn't bear for him to know it, so she shot him a withering "as if" look. "There's no danger of that. I may not have the best judgment in the world, but I generally don't make the same mistake twice."

A muscle twitched in his cheek at the insult. She thought he might come back at her with something equally hurtful and much truer: *Who'd want you anyway?* But he didn't. "We can't take the snowmobiles into town because the roads'll be plowed once we hit Third," he said, "but we can try to get you out of here in the truck."

LUCKY GRABBED Mike's arm as they passed the Victorian. "Wait—aren't you going to stop?"

He gave her an incredulous look, and she let go. "We're in the middle of a blizzard. If I stop, there's a greater chance of getting stuck."

"But I need a pair of my own shoes and money to pay for a motel room."

The wipers struggled against the snow and ice although he'd done his best to scrape the windshield clean. "My boots will keep your feet dry," Mike said. "And I'll front the money for the motel and lend you some cash."

"But the house isn't secure with all those broken windows."

He redirected the heat blasting through the vents so it wouldn't hit him dead on. He was warm enough with his big coat. "You're afraid of getting *robbed?*"

"Maybe."

"Whatever you're afraid of losing, you can afford to replace." He slanted her a brooding glance. "I should know. I send you your check every month, remember?"

After last night, and the conversation that had followed this morning, Mike wanted to punish Lucky. For returning to Dundee. For destroying his peace of mind. If he couldn't achieve some kind of resolution or come to grips with what had happened, he at least wanted to vent his displeasure. But Lucky had become so aloof and withdrawn over the past hour that, predictably, she didn't react, which only frustrated him further.

"What I want can't be replaced," she said stubbornly.

"Why not?"

She didn't answer his question, giving him the impression that she wouldn't even if he pressed her. "And there's no need to risk my ID and credit cards," she added.

He drew a deep, calming breath. He rarely had to struggle to get along with anyone, especially a woman. But Lucky had always been trouble.

"Are you going to let me out?" she asked.

"I'm thinking about it."

"I'll jump if you don't." She opened her door. Because they were only traveling a few miles an hour and the snow looked deceptively soft, he believed she just might try it.

With a grimace, he applied the brakes. "Make it quick. I have to stay in the middle of the road because the snow's too deep on the sides."

She hopped out and hunched against the wind as she made her way to the Victorian. A few minutes later, she appeared with a little bag, probably filled with toiletries, her purse and a black book tucked under her coat.

"That's what you wanted?" he said, eyeing the book curiously as she climbed in.

She slipped it farther under her coat, out of sight, and bent over to brush the snow off her jeans before closing the door. "Thanks for stopping." Her tone let him know that she didn't plan to explain.

With a sigh, he managed to get the truck moving again, but the going was slow and tedious and they drove several minutes without speaking. "Why'd you come back, Lucky?" he asked, finally breaking the silence.

Lucky knew better than to answer that question honestly. She might have grown up in Dundee, but she was sure Dave Small, Eugene Thompson and Garth Holbrook, if they were still around, had more friends here than she did. Some people might not appreciate her digging around in their pasts.

She turned to stare out the window. "There's something I have to do."

"What?"

"Nothing that concerns you."

"Or my family?"

She laughed bitterly. "Or your precious family."

"Will you be staying long?"

"I don't know. A few weeks—" she shrugged "—maybe a few months."

"And then you'll be gone again?"

"And then I'll be gone."

The tension in his jaw seemed to ease with this news, which didn't make her feel any better.

"What about the house?" he asked.

She studied his profile. "What about it?"

"Are you planning to leave it empty?"

"Maybe." She'd promised herself that once she found her father, she'd sell out and put Dundee behind her forever. But she wasn't sure she could let the Victorian go. It had come to represent the only love she'd ever known. Morris was associated with that place, along with all her childhood hopes and dreams, which was why she'd hung on to it for so long.

"You know you don't give a damn about the house or anyone here in Dundee," Mike said.

She said nothing.

"So why are you being so obstinate? Why not sell it to me and forget about it?"

He believed she'd refused his purchase offers just to spite him. In all honesty, Lucky knew her feelings toward Mike had played a part, but there was more to it than that. Morris's Victorian meant a great deal to her because she'd never had a real home. But if Mike's family wouldn't relinquish their emotional claim to the property, she could never feel good about living there. So what was she hanging on to? The memory of a man Mike and his family felt they had first "dibs" on? Childhood dreams of warmth and belonging that would never come true?

She thought of that kiss she'd witnessed in the barn, and juxtaposed it to the reality of last night. Mike had finally broken through her defenses when it came to selling the house, but she had too much pride to let him know she was ready to give it up without a fight. Lifting her chin, she met his gaze squarely. "How much are you willing to pay?"

He scowled. "I've already offered you twice as much as you could get from anyone else. How greedy can you be?"

How much were her dreams worth? "I don't know," she said. "But somehow I always seem to be asking for too much."

MIKE DIDN'T FEEL like driving back to the ranch. The roads had to be nearly impassable by now and were only getting worse, making his decision to stop in at Jerry's café a risky one. But he didn't care. He wasn't the unruffled, conservative guy he'd been just yesterday. He was restless and edgy and—

The bell over the entrance jingled. Brooding, Mike glanced up from his coffee to see Gabe roll in and wasn't sure whether he was excited to see his old friend or not. He decided he wasn't. Gabe had seemed more like himself when he visited the ranch yesterday, but Mike didn't want the added pressure of trying to maintain their strained relationship right now. He was still too annoyed about what had happened with Lucky. But he waved anyway. He could hardly go unnoticed. He was the only one in the diner besides Judy, the waitress, and Harry, the cook.

"What are you doing in town in the middle of such a bad storm?" Gabe asked as he wheeled closer.

Too grumpy to bother smiling, Mike propped an arm on the back of the booth and watched his friend. "I was wondering the same about you."

"I had a meeting with the mayor yesterday and stayed too long. Haven't been able to make it home since." Gabe remained in his chair instead of hauling himself out and sliding around the booth as Mike had seen him do before, when the restaurant was busy.

"Too much snow?"

Gabe nodded.

"Considering that you bought the most remote piece of land you could find, I'm not surprised." He took a sip of his coffee. "Did you stay at your folks' place last night?"

"I did. My father and I sat up talking politics." He smiled faintly as though he'd enjoyed it, and Mike was glad that Gabe had at least remained close to his father.

"Where's he now?"

Gabe grimaced. "My sister Reenie and her family stopped by. She drives me nuts, so I thought I'd get out of there for a while."

Reenie spoke her mind. She'd probably said something Gabe didn't want to hear, something that should've been said a long time ago, and Gabe had walked—or rolled—out.

Given his mood, Mike had half a mind to be more honest with Gabe himself. "You still making furniture?"

"If I make much more, I'm going to have to build another cabin just to house it."

Yesterday Mike might have nodded and pretended it was perfectly normal to make piece after piece of furniture and do absolutely nothing with them, but he couldn't keep up with that social farce today. He missed the honesty that had always existed between him and Gabe. "Why are you warehousing it?" he asked.

Gabe blinked in surprise. "What do you suggest I do?"

"What anyone else would do—sell it." Lord knew Gabe's rocking chairs—anything he created, really—were more than mere furniture. They were works of art. But no one else would ever be able to enjoy them because Gabe kept the furniture he made, closeting it away.

"I don't need the money," he said with a shrug.

"This isn't about money."

Gabe scowled and tried to sidestep him again. "Where would I sell it? All the people around here who're really interested have already traipsed up to my cabin to take their pick."

That wasn't true. Since the accident, few folks braved his cabin. Mike was one of those who visited from time to time, and even *he* looked for excuses to avoid interrupting Gabe's sullen solitude. "Who are you trying to kid?" he asked. "Me or you?"

Gabe's expression grew leery. "What's going on with you today?"

"Nothing. Nothing's ever going on with me anymore, because I understand that our relationship has changed." Mike took another sip of his coffee, watching Gabe over the rim.

"Changed?"

"We've been best friends most of our lives, yet ever since the car accident, I'm only allowed to smile and nod and talk about the weather."

Gabe's eyes narrowed into silvery slits. "If you've got something to say to me, Mike, say it."

"Okay." Mike set down his coffee cup and leaned forward.

"It's time for you to be productive again, to stop feeling sorry for yourself."

Gabe rocked back as if Mike had just landed a right hook. "God, it's Reenie, isn't it? She's been shooting off that mouth of hers to you, too."

"No." Mike shook his head. It wasn't Reenie at all—it was Lucky. She was bringing out the worst in him all around. But he was halfway into this conversation and he wasn't backing out now. "What I think has nothing to do with Reenie. If she's saying things you don't like, it's probably because she's as tired as I am of seeing you cut yourself off from everyone who cares about you."

The muscles in Gabe's arms bunched, revealing the anger circulating beneath his carefully controlled exterior. Since the accident, Mike had sensed the explosiveness of that anger—everyone sensed it—which was why most people chose to stay away. But until now, Gabe had kept a tight rein on his emotions. "Unless you know what it's like to be sitting in this damn chair, you have no right to criticize or advise," he growled.

Mike felt terrible about the accident and guilty for having two strong, functioning legs while his best friend would never walk again. But he could finally see that his pity wasn't getting Gabe anywhere. Maybe he was foolish to risk their relationship by pushing too hard, but he couldn't let Gabe slip any further away from the man he used to be.

"You're letting it beat you, my friend," Mike said evenly. "And I can't stand to watch."

Gabe's lips curled into a snarl, but before he could let loose, Judy came up behind him.

"Well, look who we have here." She tucked her bleached hair behind her ear and smiled appreciatively. "I haven't seen you in forever, Gabe."

A mask quickly descended over Gabe's face. Swiveling in his chair, he managed a tight smile. "Hi, Judy. How are you?"

"I'd be better if you'd drop by a little more often. Are you such a health nut these days that you can't eat a greasy burger once in a while?"

Gabe muttered something about stopping in again soon, but Mike could tell he didn't mean it. Gabe didn't like being singled out, even for such a simple greeting. The exchange reminded Mike far too much of the polite nonsense that had overtaken his own relationship with Gabe.

"So what can I get you today?" she asked.

"Nothing." Gabe glanced malevolently at Mike. "Go ahead and take care of Mike—if he'll let you. Suddenly he's an expert on everything."

Judy propped her hands on her hips and frowned as Gabe wheeled himself out. "Wow, what's gotten into him?"

"Nothing new," Mike said with a sigh.

She put her order pad back in her pocket. "I take it you're not having a very good day, either."

He rubbed a hand over his stubbly jaw. That had to be the understatement of the year. In the past twenty-four hours he'd slept with his rival and alienated his best friend.

CHAPTER SIX

LUCKY SAT on the bed in her cheap green-and-brown motel room, ignoring the noisy storm outside as she stared at the three names in her mother's journal. Dave Small, Eugene Thompson, Garth Holbrook. What were they like?

From what she could remember of Dave Small, he had a short, stocky build, a large extended family and a pizzeria near the Honky Tonk. He also served on the city council and had two sons about ten years older than she was. Smalley took after his severely overweight mother and was one of the biggest men she'd ever seen. At nearly half his weight, Jon favored their father. Both boys were married, or at least they had been when Lucky left Dundee. But she couldn't remember much more than that. She'd bumped into Dave here and there, but she'd never spoken to him. The only interaction she'd ever had with the Smalls was when Smalley and Jon rode past the Victorian one day and knocked down the Dave Small for City Council sign her mother had posted in the yard. Before they peeled away, they spotted her watching them from the shade of the porch, and hollered that their daddy didn't need the support of a two-bit whore like her mother.

Lucky had immediately thrown the sign away. She hadn't liked the smirk on their faces any more than she appreciated what they had to say. But she couldn't get too indignant about that incident anymore. On the night of Smalley's high school graduation, he and Jon were both listed in her mother's journal as having visited, along with a note that read *Collected $50 from Theril.* Several other entries indicated that Theril was another member of the Small clan and something of a regular.

Closing her eyes, she shoved the diary aside. Surely she wasn't related to the Smalls. She could only imagine how warmly they'd embrace her. Considering Dave's position in the community, she had a difficult time believing he'd even acknowledge her existence.

For much the same reason, she doubted she'd have any better luck with Garth Holbrook. He'd been elected to the state senate a few years before Lucky left and was still in office. She'd checked the Internet a few weeks ago and studied the publicity photo and biography on his Web site. Of the three men, he seemed to represent everything she'd like her father to be. Tall and stately, he possessed a full head of dark wavy hair with a touch of gray at the temples, classic features and gray eyes. He looked intelligent, self-composed, honorable.

Of course, a politician was supposed to look honorable, so maybe she was falling for a carefully constructed illusion. His Web site also revealed that he'd been married for forty years to the same woman, which meant he'd already had a family by the time he visited Red. It didn't reflect any better on him that his relationship with her mother had lasted longer than a one-time "Oops, I made mistake" kind of visit. According to the journal, he'd stopped by Red's place often over a three-month period. He'd even bought her a car.

Getting off the bed, Lucky went into the bathroom to gaze at herself in the mirror. Did she look like any of these men? She remembered Eugene Thompson as an old cowboy with callused hands and worn jeans. But there wasn't anything on the Internet about him and she hadn't seen him since Red married Morris. He could have moved on, or died.

With a sigh, she leaned closer to her reflection. She couldn't see a resemblance to anyone except Red. She had her mother's oval face, slightly slanted green eyes and high cheekbones. But her hair wasn't quite the same flaming color as her mother's, and she didn't have any freckles. Her figure was significantly different, too. She turned to the side. She wasn't nearly as buxom as Red had been, but buxom wasn't necessarily the ideal anymore. Appearance-wise, she wasn't bad, was she? Certainly she was no longer overweight.

Mike's comment suddenly came to mind. *You're gorgeous.* She'd immediately discounted that compliment as foreplay. When her mother drank, which wasn't often but wasn't pretty when it happened, she began dispensing advice. Her favorite warning was, "A man will tell you anything to get in your pants, Lucky. Don't believe a word of it."

But Mike had seemed sincere. Sure, the huskiness in his voice had left little doubt about what he wanted, but she hadn't been making him work to get her clothes off. She'd already shed her sweatshirt at that point. There wasn't any need for him to tell her anything.

Maybe he was just being kind. Whether she wanted to admit it or not, he'd been kind in several ways last night.

No more of Mike. Purposely turning her thoughts in another direction, she undressed so she could take a long, hot shower.

The telephone interrupted her. Assuming it had to be the front office, she hurried over, wondering if there was a problem with her credit card.

"Hello?"

"Lucky?"

Mike. Chills rolled down her spine, and she felt very exposed even though she was alone in a locked motel room. "Yes?" she said, automatically covering her bare breasts with one arm.

"You don't have a car."

"I know that."

"How are you going to get home when the storm lifts?"

"I—" She hadn't made any plans. This morning her only thought had been to remove herself from his company. "I'll hire someone to drive me or…or thumb a ride."

"Do you hitchhike very often?"

"Sometimes, why?" she said, even though she'd only done it once before, in Kansas City, when she'd gone to a bar with some friends from the food bank and wanted to leave before everyone else was ready.

"It's not safe."

"This is Dundee," she said.

"I don't care if it's Timbuktu. I don't want to be responsible if something happens to you."

"How would you be responsible?"

"I'm the one who dropped you off at the motel."

She couldn't help laughing. "So? If my body was found on the side of the road, the whole town would probably launch a celebration, and you and your family could lead the parade."

"Is that what you think I'd do?"

"I know how you feel about me."

Silence. "Then why did you get into bed with me last night, especially when you've never been with anyone else?"

She didn't completely understand the answer to that question, wasn't ready to examine it. "I was cold," she said because it was the first thing that popped into her mind. Only after the words were out did she realize they were true. She *had* been cold—cold inside—and stupid enough to believe he could warm her.

"That's it?"

"That's it." She glanced in the mirror again, trying to view herself as he might have seen her last night. "Will you answer a question of mine?"

"Maybe."

"Did you mean what you said when…when I took off that sweatshirt?"

There was a slight pause, then his tone changed, became deeper, earthier. "What did I say?"

She could tell he remembered. He was challenging her again. But she wasn't going to let him scare her away that easily. "That I was…" She swallowed. Asking proved awkward for her, which was, presumably, why he demanded she spell it out. "That I was…you know…"

"No, I don't. Why don't you tell me?"

"You said I was gorgeous," she finally blurted, hoping for some small concession she could take away from their painful experience. It wasn't as if she cared about embarrassing herself in front of Mike. She'd already done a fine job of that—on more than one occasion.

"Now I remember," he said, his tone huskier still.

"Okay, so…did you mean it?"

"Honestly?"

Her stomach tensed, drawing a complaint from her ulcer. Of course he hadn't meant it. What had she been thinking? She'd been stupid to open herself up, to let him toy with her. "No, never mind."

Silence. Then he asked, "Will you call me when you're ready to come home?"

"Sure." She had no intention of contacting Mike Hill for anything, but she was so eager to get off the phone she would've agreed to almost anything. "I'll talk to you later."

"Lucky?"

"What?"

"I meant it," he said and hung up.

MIKE DIDN'T KNOW what to do. He found himself creeping slowly along Main Street—the storm kept him from going very fast—bored stiff. He had plenty of work back at the ranch, yet he found himself reluctant to return. He knew Lucky had something to do with his desire to hang around town, and Gabe, too. They'd both left him frustrated, although in different ways, and he hated that. He wasn't used to negative emotions interfering with his daily life, because he always made such an effort to be cautious and courteous, regardless of the circumstances. He didn't create false expectations, especially with women. He didn't make promises he couldn't keep, especially with women. He didn't allow his relationships to drift toward any extreme, especially with women. He'd never fallen in love and didn't relish the idea of a messy break-up. So why, after dating for more than twenty years, did he suddenly feel so unsettled?

If my body was found on the side of the road, the whole town would probably launch a celebration, and you and your family could lead the parade.

The fact that Lucky actually believed she mattered so little *to everyone* bothered him. Maybe he'd resented her over the years, but he'd never expected her to care, or even notice. Because she'd always seemed so damn tough, like her mother, he hadn't given a second thought to how she might feel.

Now he had to consider the possibility that maybe she wasn't so tough. Maybe her prickly behavior was only a front. After last night, he could believe it. She'd certainly put up other fronts, like the one that had led him to assume she looked at sex in a casual manner. Last night might have ended badly, but those few minutes before her abrupt departure had been anything but casual. Lucky seemed to put her whole heart and soul into her lovemaking, which was why he'd temporarily lost control.

His blood warmed as he remembered the way she'd responded to his touch. She'd abandoned all reservations, trusted him completely, although she'd never been with anyone else and had given him no warning that she hadn't…

His parents' street came up on his left, and he slowed to make the turn. His mother was always telling him he needed to stop by more often. He decided today might be a good day. The local high school would probably be closed due to the storm, so his father, who coached the varsity football team, would most likely be there with her. At any rate, Mike needed a distraction.

"Hello? Anyone home?" he called, walking in without knocking.

"Mike? Is that you?"

He heard his mother's voice in the basement and used the banister to jump down the stairs the way he had when he was a kid.

"What's going on?" He ducked his head as he entered her craft room, because the ceiling was so much lower than anywhere else in the house.

She glanced up from her sewing machine where she was nearly buried in shiny purple fabric. "I'm making a bridesmaid dress for Beatrice's daughter."

"Who?"

"Melanie Jamison, the neighbor's daughter."

"Oh, right. That's nice of you."

"I love weddings," she said pointedly.

He slouched into one of the fold-up chairs surrounding the table. "I know, and you don't have any daughters. I've heard this before."

She arched a meaningful eyebrow at him. "Obviously not enough. I could have *two* daughters-in-law if only my oldest son would take pity on his poor mother, settle down and start a family."

"Josh is keeping up that end of things."

"Rebecca has difficulty getting pregnant. You know that. It was a miracle they managed to have little Brian. They may not be able to have another child."

"Isn't one enough?"

"No. And you're almost forty, Mike."

"Don't make me regret stopping by," he grumbled.

"You won't regret it because I'll feed you before you leave."

He crossed his legs at the ankles. "I like your tactics."

She shrugged. "I go with what works."

"Where's Dad?" he asked. "Don't tell me he had to teach today."

"No, they canceled school. We've got a leak upstairs. He's trying to figure out how the water's getting in."

"You think he needs a hand?"

The sewing machine whirred into action as she bent over her work. "You could ask him."

"Ask me what?"

Mike twisted to see his father step into the room. "Did you find the leak?"

"I did. Soon as the storm passes, I'll get up on the roof and patch it."

His father was pretty spry for sixty-three, but Mike saw no reason to risk an accident. "Don't climb onto the roof. I'll take care of it this weekend."

"What brings you by this time of day? And in a storm like this?" his father asked. "Did you lose power out at the ranch?"

The sewing machine fell silent and his mother peered at him over her reading glasses, waiting for his answer.

Mike cleared his throat. "No, I had to give Lucky a ride into town because she was stranded at Grandpa's house without any heat or water."

"Did you say *Lucky?*" His mother blinked as though he'd

just spoken gibberish. The lines on his father's forehead formed an instant V.

"Lucky Caldwell's back," Mike said.

His mother promptly pushed all the fabric out of her lap and onto the table. "You're kidding."

"No."

"But why? Why is she back after so long?"

"Because she owns property here, I guess." He remembered Lucky saying there was something she had to do and wondered about the book she'd gone after, despite the rough weather. But he didn't see any point in mentioning it. He didn't have any idea what she had planned.

"That house should belong to us," his mother said.

His father walked over to massage Barbara's shoulders. "Do you know if she's staying for good?" he asked Mike.

Mike removed his hat and scratched his head. "I don't think so."

"That's hopeful, anyway." His father bent to give his mother an encouraging smile, but the unhappy expression on her face lingered.

"I wish she'd sell us that house and be done with it," Barbara said. "But she won't. She's a mean-spirited, nasty person just like her mother."

Mike had come here hoping to bolster his dislike of Lucky. But his mother's harsh words didn't sit well. "Mean-spirited?" he repeated.

"What else would you call her? She has no use for that house. She doesn't even like Dundee. She thumbed her nose at us and ran off the second she inherited it, and no one's heard from her since. Unless it's to send a forwarding address for her monthly check."

"She left as soon as she *graduated*," he clarified, "not as soon as she inherited it."

"It happened about the same time. She took off, that's the important part, and she abandoned the house to the elements."

What Mike had once viewed as indifference now seemed to have a variety of interpretations. "Maybe she didn't feel accepted here."

His mother shook her head. "She was born here! She just couldn't wait to start traveling across the country, living the high life on my father's money."

Mike was the one who'd told them about Lucky's nomadic lifestyle, but now that he knew she'd never even slept with a man *until him*, he doubted she'd spent all her time partying. What he'd previously imagined as Lucky living the wild single's life suddenly seemed like a pretty solitary existence. "Grandpa's trust doesn't give her *that* much every month," he said.

"She gets enough to support herself," his father pointed out.

"True, but I've offered her more than half a million for the house. If she really wanted to live the good life, don't you think she would've liquidated as soon as possible?"

His mother's cheeks grew mottled as she stood and moved closer to him. "Why are you *defending* her?"

"I'm not." He shrugged as if he wasn't particularly concerned one way or the other. "I'm wondering if there isn't a little more to the story, that's all."

"You lived next door to her while she was growing up. You know what she's like. Josh told me she stripped off her clothes in front of you once."

"It was only her top and—"

"Only her top! She had no business doing that. What a little…tramp," she finished as though the word had been difficult for her to say but was too fitting to avoid.

Mike's irritation spiked in spite of his efforts to retain control. "She's *not* a tramp."

A pained expression claimed his father's face. "Maybe

you're not used to hearing your mother say such things, but you know Lucky's reputation, Mike."

Mike knew of Lucky's reputation, all right. He'd made assumptions based on that reputation and he'd found them to be totally false. But without telling his parents *how* he came to know her reputation had been largely exaggerated, he couldn't convince them that they were wrong, so he decided it'd be smarter to back off.

"Look, she's not my favorite person, either, okay?" he said. "I want Grandpa's house, and I'm still hopeful she'll sell it to me and move. But if she doesn't, let's…" He allowed his words to fade away, because he wasn't sure how to frame his request.

"What?" his mother demanded.

"Let's not make a big deal about her being here. Live and let live, you know?"

"When have *we* ever hurt *her?* I've hardly spoken two words to her."

"I'm just saying that maybe we could cut her a little slack. This whole mess is really her mother's fault."

"Lucky was part of it, too," Barbara argued. "I remember how she used to fawn over my dad. 'Daddy, it's cold out. Don't forget your coat. Daddy, I shined your boots the way you like them.' She hung on your grandpa's every word and smiled up at him as though he was the moon and the stars, all the while hoping to get her hands on his money. It kills me that he fell for it."

"We don't know about her motivation, Mom. She was only a child."

"She wasn't a child when you took her to court."

Mike couldn't help scowling. How was it that he ended up on the opposite side of every argument lately? "Morris gave her the house. What did you want her to do, apologize and hand it back?"

"Yes!" his mother said. "Why not? What makes her think she's entitled to it? She was part of my dad's life for only ten years. Her mother tried to kill him, for heaven's sake!"

"We're not positive about that."

"Of course we are. Maybe we couldn't prove it, but that doesn't mean it didn't happen."

"Even if it's true, Lucky didn't have anything to do with it."

"Who knows?"

Mike stood and stretched his neck. After last night he was sure Lucky hadn't had anything to do with the insulin overdose. She wasn't the kind of person to harm an old man. His mother, who was usually one of the most generous people he knew, simply couldn't divorce her emotions from the situation long enough to see it from any perspective but her own, and trying to force the issue was only creating a bigger problem. "Look, Mom, I'm sorry Lucky's back, okay? But there's no need to get so upset. Everything will be okay."

A tear trickled down his mother's cheek. "The way I feel isn't right," she said, suddenly deflating. "I've never hated anyone in my life, but I hate Red, whether she's dead or not, and I hate Lucky." She turned her face into Larry's chest, and he put his arms around her.

"You're entitled, honey," he soothed. "You've been through a lot because of them."

Mike couldn't believe he'd made his mother cry; she typically cried only at weddings and funerals. First he'd hurt Lucky, then Gabe, and now his mother. Evidently he was making a clean sweep of everyone he came into contact with today.

So much for being Mr. Nice Guy....

CHAPTER SEVEN

MIKE LEFT his parents' house as soon as possible, even though his mother insisted on feeding him. The conversation over lunch was too stilted. Mike could tell his father wasn't happy that he'd taken Lucky's side of the argument. And the word *tramp* kept flashing through his mind like a cue card, making him feel guilty for allowing their misjudgment to continue when he knew for a fact that it wasn't true. Problem was, defending Lucky any more valiantly than he already had could cause his poor mother to have a nervous breakdown. Just imagining a scene where he told his family that he knew Lucky wasn't a tramp *because he'd taken her virginity* was enough to make his blood run cold.

He shook his head and eased his SUV over to the right because his tires kept slipping on the snow-packed road. Considering how much his association with Lucky would upset everyone who cared about him, he was going to choose the lesser of two evils and keep his mouth shut. He needed to go home and get some sleep. Maybe then he could gain some perspective on all of this.

But as he passed the Timberline Motel where Lucky was staying, he couldn't help craning his head to get a glimpse of the door to her unit. Was that a light glimmering through the crack in the drapes? What was she doing? Reading that black book? Had she eaten since breakfast?

Probably not. She couldn't have gone anywhere on foot in this storm. Which meant she had to be hungry.

Not your problem! he quickly reminded himself. But when he found the highway out of town closed because of the storm, it came as no surprise. And although Lucky wasn't his problem, that didn't stop him from buying her a burger and fries and heading straight to the Timberline.

WHEN SHE HEARD a knock at the door, Lucky shoved her mother's journal, which she'd left on the bed, into a drawer and went to check the peephole. "Who in the world—"

Mike again. She couldn't believe her eyes. What was he doing here? He'd already destroyed what little peace of mind she'd possessed when she returned to Dundee. Why couldn't they make things easy on each other and avoid contact now that they had the chance? She was certainly trying to do *her* part.

She wouldn't answer the door, she told herself. She wasn't dressed for company. After her shower, she'd pulled on a T-shirt and sweats without a bra.

But it looked as if he was carrying something that could be food. And he'd already seen a lot more of her than she was showing now.

Opening the door, she braced herself against the wind and snow that rushed in and stared out at him. "Don't tell me you're stuck in town."

"Actually I am."

"Why didn't you go back earlier?"

"I guess I had to cause some problems first."

"What kind of problems?"

"Never mind. Are you hungry?"

"Not really," she said above the wind, but she knew her eyes had betrayed her when they flicked to the sack.

He grinned knowingly. "A double cheeseburger. With bacon."

The smell alone made her salivate. A double cheeseburger with bacon was better than sex—and now she knew what she was talking about when she used that expression. "Well…I wouldn't want it to go to waste," she said, trying to sound indifferent so she wouldn't have to thank him too profusely. "Let me get my purse so I can pay you."

The wind would have slammed the door against the inside wall had she left it standing open. She asked him to hold it and turned to retrieve the promised money, expecting him to wait right where he was. But without her to bar the way, he stepped inside.

Lucky whirled around when she heard the door click shut to see Mike, shaking off the snow and cold. His mere presence seemed to gobble up half the space in the room.

"Here you go." Grabbing the first bill she could find in her wallet, which turned out to be a twenty, she held it out to him. She knew a double cheeseburger couldn't have cost that much, but she wasn't going to squabble over ten or fifteen bucks if it meant getting rid of him. "I appreciate the food."

Ignoring the money in her outstretched hand, he gave her the sack, removed his coat and slipped around her to sit on the end of her bed. "You're watching ESPN?" he said.

"I like sports." She frowned at the coat he'd just discarded on her vinyl chair.

"Did you catch Monday Night Football?"

"Half of it. I couldn't take watching Green Bay lose."

"You're a Packers fan?"

She was a Brett Favre fan, but she didn't think she needed to get specific. Most men didn't pick their favorite team based on the build of the quarterback. "I like the Raiders, too."

"What about basketball?"

"My favorite is definitely the Kings. No team's more exciting to watch, although the Denver Nuggets have a lot of talented young players. They might become a championship team, if they can only keep the crew together."

"You think the Kings will ever win a championship?"

"It's certainly their turn."

"What about baseball?"

"What about it?"

"Do you like that, too?"

"Not as much as basketball and football, but if there's nothing else on…"

"Who do you follow?"

"The Mariners, mostly."

He studied her. "How do you know so much about sports?"

"From watching games, I guess." No matter where she went, there was usually a local sports bar that served a good dinner and provided a casual, friendly atmosphere in which to spend a few hours. Whenever she moved to a strange city, she felt most comfortable sitting in one of these bars, eating buffalo wings and watching basketball on the big screen. It also gave her something to do when the other volunteers where she was temporarily working invited her out and she didn't want to go with them that night.

"You're nothing like I imagined," he said simply.

"Yeah, well, it's hard work being a villain full-time. We need a little rest and relaxation occasionally."

Ignoring her sarcasm, he picked up the remote and turned up the volume.

"Hey, don't you have somewhere to go?" she asked.

He cocked an eyebrow at her. "In this weather?"

"Why not? You have a four-wheel-drive. I'm sure your parents would *love* to see you."

"Sorry, just came from there."

Her heart skipped a beat at the thought of the family conferring on how they might oust her from Morris's coveted mansion. Selling was one thing. Being forced out was another. "Great. Did you tell them I'm in town?"

"Of course."

"What'd they say?"

"My mother started crying."

She tossed the sack onto the bureau despite her hunger. "Gee, thanks for sparing my feelings."

He leaned back, resting his weight on his palms. "I didn't think you'd care."

Lifting her chin, she gave him her best glare. "I don't."

The brim of his hat shaded his eyes, making it difficult to read his expression. He didn't comment further, so she shoved the money he'd ignored a few seconds earlier into her pocket and glanced at the food. She wanted to eat, but there was still the small problem of persuading Mike Hill to leave her room.

"Aren't you on your way out?" she asked.

He doffed his hat and stretched out on the bed she'd been using. "Actually, after what you did to me last night, I'm pretty tired, and—"

"What I did to *you*?"

"—there really isn't anywhere I'm burning to go, at least not until the storm lifts."

"I'm sure they have other vacancies."

She caught a flash of white teeth as he grinned. "What's the matter, Lucky? Do I make you nervous?"

They were sharing a twelve-by-twelve-foot room with two double beds. Of course he made her nervous. But she wasn't about to admit it. "What makes you think you *could* make me nervous?"

"The fact that you keep fidgeting with the hem of that T-shirt, for one."

"It's a habit. I do it all the time whether I'm nervous or not."

"Right." He jerked his head toward the food. "Eat and watch the game. When the storm's over, I'll take you home."

MIKE FELL ASLEEP within minutes, leaving Lucky to sulk about the way he'd taken over her room. He had lots of money. Why was he foisting his presence on her?

Her only escape was the bathroom, but she'd already taken a shower.

After trying unsuccessfully to become absorbed in the game, she decided she needed some sleep, too. With the television on to help drown out the storm, she climbed into the other bed, faced the wall and curled up. But a few seconds later, she couldn't help rolling over to stare at Mike's profile. Making love with him hadn't been everything she'd hoped, but deep down she knew she was probably to blame for that more than he was.

And she had to admit, regardless of his identity, she'd never met a handsomer man.

LUCKY WOKE UP to silence. The wind had died down, the television was off and it was dark—so dark that she couldn't tell whether Mike was still in the room.

Squinting to see in the glimmer of light that crept in from the parking lot, she rose up on one elbow and leaned toward the other bed.

"Is something wrong?" he said.

She jumped at the sound of his voice. He was still there, all right. On the near side. So close she could reach out and touch him.

The idea of touching him made her heart pound, and she immediately slid away. "No."

"I shut off the TV. I hope you don't mind. You were tossing and turning and didn't seem to be sleeping well."

"That's fine," she said. "What time is it?"

"Nearly two."

"Is the storm over?"

"I think so, but it'll be a while before the roads are clear enough to travel."

"We can probably go home in the morning, though, huh?"

"Probably."

There was nothing left to do but sleep some more—except, for some strange reason, Lucky was tingling all over. She knew she couldn't lie still, so she decided to get up.

"Where are you going?" Mike asked when the bed creaked.

"My muscles are a little tense. I think I'll take a hot shower."

He didn't say anything, so she slipped into the bathroom and closed the door.

MIKE LISTENED as Lucky turned on the water. He pictured her taking off her T-shirt and sweats, pictured her dropping them carelessly on the floor and stepping beneath the hot spray. He could see the water sliding over her head and shoulders and rolling down between the breasts he'd kissed last night—

His body reacted so strongly, he cut off his thoughts. Since awakening almost an hour ago, he'd finally understood what had upset him about last night. It wasn't Lucky so much as it was him. He felt he hadn't done her justice. She was a beautiful woman who'd waited a long time to make love with a man. She'd offered to make love with him, and he'd taken her virginity as though it was nothing. He wanted to go back and do it right, wanted to show her what her body could feel beneath the right touch. That was the real reason he hadn't been able to leave town, wasn't it? The real reason he'd gotten himself snowed in and stayed in her motel room when he could have rented his own? He'd been looking for an opportunity to amend the recent past. But she was so intent on keeping her distance, she wouldn't even let her fingers brush against his when he'd handed her that sack of food yesterday.

Still, there had to be some reason she'd trusted him in the first place....

Getting up, he decided there was nothing he could do but take the same risk she'd taken. If she rejected him, she rejected him. If she didn't, they could try to live last night over again. Then maybe he wouldn't feel he owed her anything and he'd be able to put her powerful attraction behind him once and for all.

LUCKY FROZE when she heard the door open. She was sure she'd locked it, but the lock wasn't hard to unfasten, even from the outside. A fingernail or coin could open it easily enough and, evidently, Mike had used *something* because she felt fairly certain he was standing inside the bathroom. All doubt about that disappeared when the door closed and the lights went out.

He was definitely in the bathroom.

"Mike?" she said, wishing her voice didn't sound so thin.

"Yeah, it's me."

She hovered closer to the far corner of the tub, although she knew he couldn't see her. It was so dark, neither of them could see anything. "I—I'll be out in a minute if you'd like the shower."

He didn't answer.

"Are you still there?"

"Yes."

She was relieved to realize he hadn't moved from the door. "What is it you want?"

There was a long pause, but he finally responded. "You."

Her... Lucky's heart jumped into her throat. That was exactly what she'd suspected.

"Tell me now if you want me to leave," he said.

The thick darkness, heavy with steam, made her feel slightly disoriented, slightly out of touch with her normal faculties. She had to be disoriented. She couldn't say anything. She wasn't even breathing.

"Silence means I stay," he told her, as though wanting to be perfectly clear.

Her mind raced and she bit her lip. She had to speak now if she wanted to avoid a repeat of last night, but she could think of only one word. She wasn't sure if that was because he'd just said it or because it was what she really wanted, but "stay" seemed to echo through her head. And then it was too late. She heard him pull the shower curtain aside and felt his hands move slowly around her waist.

He hadn't been presumptuous enough to take off his clothes, she noticed, but his mouth found hers in the dark, and he kissed her gently. Like a young boy might kiss a girl on a first date. His second kiss was even better—like that kiss she'd observed in the barn. It was real. She was living it.

He didn't say anything more after that, but his touch, even his kiss, asked a question: *Will you let me try again, Lucky? Let me try again. Trust me one more time....*

Lucky told herself she was crazy, but he'd melted her resistance by telling her he wanted her, and she could hardly think while he was pulling her bottom lip into his mouth. A warm sensation swept through her as his tongue met hers. Her first taste of him almost made her knees buckle. She felt hot, languid and fluttery all at once.

He didn't seem to care that he was getting soaked. He kissed her more deeply, and she swayed against him, slowly letting go of last night, of everything that had happened before this moment—until he started sliding his hand up and over her rib cage. Then she stopped him.

"I won't hurt you," he whispered above the hiss of the water. "Relax."

"I don't think we should—"

"Shh," he interrupted. "I'll take good care of you this time, Lucky, I promise."

In the dark, enclosed space, she could almost convince herself that this was a dream. Just another of the many dreams she'd had about Mike Hill. Only his hands and lips felt better than she could ever have imagined, much better than before. He used the water sluicing over her body, his hands, his mouth. At some point his clothes came off—she wasn't sure exactly when because her mind seemed to be floating instead of functioning correctly. The crinkle of a wrapper told her he'd come prepared, so she didn't worry when he lifted her up and, much more carefully than last night, eased himself inside her.

"Are you okay?" he whispered.

She could feel the muscles bunching in his arms and shoulders as he bore her weight, understood he was holding back.

"I'm fine," she said, although she'd never been happier in her life, and felt him relax a little.

He began to move, slowly, almost leisurely at first, so she could feel every exquisite sensation. Then everything seemed to swirl together and run hotter, higher, faster. She was spinning and spinning and spinning, until, finally, she shuddered against him.

"That's it," he coaxed, chuckling as she went limp. "That's what I wanted."

She clung to him even after he set her on her feet; she felt so weak she feared she might slip right down the drain. The experience had already surpassed all her expectations, but he wasn't finished yet. After she'd had a few seconds to recover, he said, "Again."

"No, it's your turn."

He ignored her and went back to kissing her—and stroking her. This time it took only seconds until every nerve in her body tensed and seemed to cry out his name in bone-melting pleasure.

"Did you like that?" he murmured, pressing his forehead against hers as they caught their breath.

"It was…good."

"Then let's do it again."

"What about you?"

"Shh." He nibbled at the corner of her lip, and she didn't argue further. Mike held her to him as though she might disappear completely if he let go. She sensed that he was giving her something of himself he hadn't given before. She wasn't sure what it was, but it went far beyond the physical. And it made a huge difference.

"Enough," she said hoarsely when she was so sensitive she couldn't take any more.

Mike let the water pound onto them both for a minute, burying their heads in the spray. Then he traced a bead of water down her neck to the tip of her breast and started moving again. But this time it was his turn, and Lucky knew she'd never again feel as powerful as she did right now. She wrapped her legs around his hips, drawing him even deeper inside her, and he groaned in absolute abandon.

CHAPTER EIGHT

EVEN BEFORE MIKE OPENED his eyes the next morning, he felt a smile across his face. Every muscle complained when he tried to move, but he didn't mind. It was a good kind of complaint. And he knew that, this time, he didn't have anything to feel bad about as far as Lucky was concerned.

Lucky… He pictured her clinging to him in the shower last night and felt a fresh wave of desire stir low in his belly. Then he realized that her soft body wasn't curled against him, as it had been from the moment they'd dried off and fallen into bed.

Forcing his eyelids open, he glanced around the room. The storm was over, and he was hungry. He knew those two things right away. But he didn't know where Lucky was. He couldn't see her inside the bathroom. He couldn't see any of her stuff.

He pushed into a sitting position. She was gone. Where and how, he couldn't say, but he knew she wasn't coming back.

It was better this way, he told himself when he felt a sharp stab of disappointment. He would've liked to make love to her one more time. She was so warm, honest and unbridled in her responses, he found it almost intoxicating. But he would've wanted to buy her breakfast, and being seen around town with Lucky Caldwell would not be a good thing. Better to leave well enough alone. He felt satisfied—or mostly so; he hoped she felt the same. Now he could move on.

But twenty minutes later, as he sat at Jerry's Diner and had breakfast alone, he couldn't quite relegate what had happened at the motel to the past. He felt cheated that she'd disappeared so quickly and kept wondering what she might have ordered at breakfast, what she might have said. Sipping his coffee, he remembered her head on his shoulder and her hand sliding possessively over his chest as they were falling asleep, and couldn't help admitting that she really had left too soon.

LUCKY CLEARED HER THROAT to gain the attention of the dark-haired man sitting in the office of Booker T. and Son's Automotive Repair.

He swiveled in his chair and looked up at her. He was on the phone and had a toddler in his lap, a little boy who'd been drawing on sheet after sheet of paper with a black marker. "Be right with you," he said, patiently batting away the child's attempt to scribble on his face.

She nodded and shifted her belongings. He directed the child's hand to more paper before going back to his conversation.

"I can't. The tow truck's out already, Harvey. I sent Chase over to help Helen Dobbs get her Suburban out of the ditch ten minutes ago… Who knows?" He chuckled. "Drove right into it, I guess… But she's lived next to that ditch for twenty years… You bet. I'll call you when he gets back." He hung up, capped the marker and stuck it in a cup with some pens before letting the little boy, who'd started agitating to get down, wriggle to the floor.

"Can I help you?" he said, unzipping his black leather jacket.

Lucky smiled, feeling awkward for appearing out of nowhere with such an unusual request. But Dundee, Idaho, didn't have any taxis. "Cute kid," she said to ease into the conversation. "Is he yours?"

"Yes. This is Troy. He's helping me at work today because his mommy's home feeling nauseous."

"Looks like he knows his way around."

Troy had already opened one of the desk drawers and was pulling out a big bag of sunflower seeds. "Seeds? Seeds, Daddy? Troy eat seeds?"

"Not right now. Your mother wasn't too pleased when I let you get hold of them last time." A sheepish expression stole over the man's face. "He swallowed quite a few of the shells." Taking the bag of seeds away, he set it up high, on a filing cabinet that already held a number of items that looked as though they'd been strategically placed out of reach of the child's chubby hands.

"It's nice that you own your own business and can help your wife out." She watched Troy toddle through the office, searching for another distraction, and caught her breath when he headed straight for the space heater humming in the corner. Fortunately, his father intercepted him and turned him in the other direction before he could get too close.

"I like having Troy with me," he said.

"I won't take up much of your time," she said. "I was just wondering if you might know someone I could hire to give me a ride out to White Rock Road."

He stood and glanced out the front window, and she knew he was looking for her car. "Are you broken down somewhere or—"

She explained about the storm and getting stuck and how she'd had to catch a ride into town because she didn't have any food, water or heat.

"But White Rock Road... The only thing out there is High Hill Ranch."

Mike's ranch... But Lucky wasn't going to think of Mike. Last night had been too overwhelming to even try to catalogue it emotionally. She'd felt closer to him than anyone else in her whole life and knew she'd always treasure the memory, but last night was over. Now she had to get back to real life. "Actually there's a house next door. I own it."

His eyebrows lifted. "That must make you Red Caldwell's daughter."

Obviously she was so notorious that even this complete stranger had heard of her. "Yes, well, no matter what you've been told about me, I don't cavort with the devil, chant incantations over a bubbling cauldron or fly on a broomstick at night."

His lips twisted into a wry grin. "That's too bad."

"Why?"

"I like a good hell-raiser."

His comment caught her off guard, and she chuckled. "You're not among the self-righteous?"

"There's never been anything righteous about me. Ask anyone." He offered her his hand. "I'm Booker Robinson."

From the way he treated his son and—she guessed—his wife, she doubted Booker was half as bad as he made himself sound. Still, she appreciated his efforts to make her comfortable and liked him instantly.

"Where were you six years ago?" she muttered. "I might've been able to stand this place."

He stopped his son from climbing into the trash. "I think I was just getting out of prison."

Another surprise. "Seriously?"

He shrugged. "I did some dumb things when I was younger. Fortunately, I've learned what's truly important in life."

His eyes followed Troy, and she knew what he held dear. "A real education sometimes takes a while."

He shoved his dark hair out of his eyes. "Exactly."

"What made you settle in Dundee?"

"My grandmother used to live here, and—" he seemed to consider his surroundings "—somehow it's home."

Maybe someday she'd find a home, too—but it wasn't in all the cities she'd traveled to so far, and it most certainly wasn't here.

With a quick movement, he scooped Troy into his arms and grabbed a set of keys off a hook near the door. "Let me tell Delbert I'm leaving. I'll give you a ride myself."

Lucky raised a hand to stop him. "I can't go home just yet. I need to make a few calls and buy some groceries."

"So you're going to Finley's?"

"Yeah."

"That's several blocks from here."

"I don't mind the walk. I only stopped in because your business is one of the few that's open today, and I didn't want to miss you if you decided to close early."

"I see. Well, you said you needed to make some calls. Why don't you use my phone while I talk to Delbert? We'll stop by Finley's on the way to your place." He waved her past him to the desk, then stuck his head into the garage and hollered, "Delbert, can you come here for a second? I'm going to need you to watch the office."

Lucky recognized Delbert Dibbs the moment she saw him through the inside window. She was surprised to find him working here, or anywhere, really. A couple of years older than she was, he had a mental disability that had always come between him and a normal life. He used to ramble aimlessly around town, as shabby and lean as a stray cat.

He looked greasy now, but happy as he hurried to the door, a huge rottweiler at his heels. "Bruiser and I like to watch the front. We can even baby-sit Troy for you, if you want. We'd never let anything happen to Troy, would we, boy?" he said to the dog.

The dog showed his agreement by wagging his tail and letting his tongue loll.

Troy clapped his hands and reached for Delbert. "D'bert! Hi, D'bert, hi!"

Delbert frowned at his blackened hands. "Sorry, Troy. I'm too dirty to hold you right now, but we'll play blocks tonight, okay?"

"I'm taking Troy with me," Booker said as Troy changed his focus to the dog.

"Dog!" he said, his eyes going round as he pointed.

Booker squatted so Troy could pet Bruiser while he continued to speak to Delbert. "Just check the front every once in a while to see if anyone's waiting."

Delbert seemed to notice Lucky, standing behind Booker and holding the phone, for the first time. "Hey, do I know you?"

Lucky smiled, and since she hadn't dialed yet, pressed the disconnect button. "I used to live here a long time ago. It's good to see you again, Delbert. You seem to be doing well."

"I work for Booker," he said proudly. "I change oil and fan belts and...and tires." His grin revealed the same crooked teeth as before, but everything else about his situation seemed greatly improved.

"What a nice job to have."

"Yeah. This is my dog, Bruiser. He's big but don't worry, he'd never hurt you."

The dog laid his ears back and whined a quick hello, as if he knew he'd just been introduced.

"He's a handsome animal."

"He's the best dog in the world," Delbert said, positively beaming.

"I'll bet he is."

"Did Booker tell you about the new baby?"

Lucky looked to Booker, who was busy stuffing toys in his son's diaper bag.

"My wife and I are expecting another child," he explained.

"She's sick 'cause of the baby," Delbert chimed in, "but the baby will be here in twenty-eight weeks and three days. Then she'll be fine again."

"Twenty-eight weeks and three days?" Lucky echoed.

"That's when the baby's due," Booker said. "Whether or not she'll actually arrive on time is anybody's guess."

"She?"

He grinned. "They're pretty sure it's a girl." Taking the diaper bag, he started moving into the garage. "I'm going to go over a few things I want Delbert to do while we're gone. Let me know when you're ready."

"Okay." She waved goodbye to Delbert and his dog before calling the power company. Customer Service came on the line right away, but the first woman she spoke to transferred her to a man who transferred her to another woman, and no one could tell her when she'd have service.

"I'd appreciate it if you could see to it as soon as possible," she told the last woman and hung up with a sigh.

FINLEY'S HADN'T CHANGED much in six years. The small, family-owned grocery now had a tiny health food section, in which Lucky found the almond milk she liked on her cold cereal, and an expanded deli. But everything felt, looked, even *smelled,* the same. A table near the front doors held the usual seasonal display of cheap Christmas dishes that could be purchased with coupons. The same dime-store-quality chocolates and stocking stuffers filled the shelves near the greeting cards. And, unfortunately, Marge Finley still worked the register. Marge had never been too friendly to Lucky. She was one of those who'd chosen between Morris's first family and his second, and had never hesitated to make her loyalties known.

Booker remembered he needed teething gel. He took Troy and strode off toward the baby aisle just as Lucky got in line to pay for her groceries. She could feel Marge's eyes repeatedly dart her way. But every time Lucky tried to challenge the other woman's gaze, Marge focused on her current customer.

When Lucky set her groceries and other supplies on the conveyor belt, Marge instantly threw the switch that stopped it from moving and left the register without a word. Lucky didn't know what was going on until she saw Marge picking up a few boxes of cold cereal that had fallen into the aisle. At that point, she suspected Marge was trying to send the message that she wasn't a priority.

Finally Booker came around the corner. "Where's Marge?"

Lucky jerked her head toward the cashier, who was now rearranging cereal boxes on the shelf.

"Does she know we're ready to go?"

"Probably not," Lucky said because she didn't want to explain that Marge had purposely kept her waiting.

"Hey, Marge! I think we're all set here," he called.

"Right. Coming, Booker." She pushed to her feet—no easy task with the weight she'd gained since Lucky had been away—and squished over, moving from side to side because her legs were so big she could no longer walk straight. "How's Katie?" she asked.

"Better, I think," he said. "I called her before I left the shop. She told me she managed a nap this morning."

"Crackers, that's the only thing that helps with morning sickness," Marge responded.

"I'm going to get her some of that homemade soup she likes from the diner as soon as I give Lucky a ride home."

Marge's lips pursed at the mention of Lucky's name, but she made no comment.

Lucky stood taller and withdrew her debit card. Eavesdropping on Marge's conversation with Booker as they went on to discuss Troy and the new words he'd recently added to his vocabulary, and what they each had planned for Christmas, made Lucky feel terribly out of place. No wonder she preferred strange towns and new cities—being anonymous was better than being shut out.

She paid for her groceries. After Booker paid for his, they put their bags into one cart and were just heading outside when a tall, dark-haired man with graying temples brushed past them on his way in.

"Morning, Booker," he said.

Booker nodded hello and continued walking, but Lucky stopped midstride. It was Garth Holbrook. She recognized him from the picture on his Web site.

"It can be slick right here by the door so watch your—" Halting the cart that was carrying his son as well as their groceries, Booker turned back when he realized she wasn't with him anymore. "Lucky?"

Lucky swallowed hard as a sudden, poignant longing washed over her. She'd tried to prepare herself with realistic expectations, knew even if she found her father, he probably wouldn't accept her. But the sight of Garth Holbrook looking so handsome and carrying himself so confidently made her long for a connection with him. He was everything her mother had not been. He had dignity, commanded respect. And she was willing to bet he was emotionally stable.

Booker's eyebrows gathered as he followed her gaze. "Do you know Senator Holbrook?"

Holbrook rounded a corner toward the bakery section and disappeared, and Lucky forced her rubbery legs to carry her forward again. She didn't want to raise too many questions.

"Not personally, no," she said. "I just recognized him, that's all."

Booker navigated the cart around a large puddle and into the snowy lot. "He's a good guy."

"How do you know him?"

"He brings his Navigator to the shop occasionally. Last week he brought in his wife's Town Car."

Mention of Holbrook's wife didn't help the odd feeling in Lucky's stomach. Even if Holbrook himself wasn't averse to taking a paternity test, she felt fairly certain a normal wife wouldn't give her blessing. "What's Mrs. Holbrook like?"

"Celeste? She's nice, too." He grinned affectionately. "She's always on some kind of mission."

"What does that mean?"

"She's involved in a lot of fund-raisers and the like. Lately she's been raising money for a charity that provides Christmas toys to underprivileged children. She sends quilts to Ukraine. She runs Friends of the Library and is a big advocate for schools. I'm sure there's even more I don't know about."

Celeste sounded like a saint—but would she be saint *enough*?

"Do you know anyone by the name of Eugene Thompson?" she asked, turning her mind to other possibilities.

"Never heard of him."

"What about Dave Small?"

He grimaced. "Everyone knows him."

"You don't like him?"

"Not especially."

Lucky hadn't expected Booker to be quite so frank, but she supposed she shouldn't be surprised. He'd been pretty direct from the first moment she'd met him at the shop. "Why not? What's he like?"

"Arrogant. Pompous."

Not exactly a high recommendation. "Is he still in politics?"

"Yeah." Booker pressed the button on his key ring that unlocked his truck and put Troy in his car seat in the back of the extended cab, where she also unloaded the groceries. "He's been talking about running for Holbrook's seat in the state senate should Holbrook go to Washington," he went on. "He might even try for mayor when Rebecca's dad retires. Fortunately—" he gave her a look of relief as she climbed in across from him "—Rebecca says her father isn't planning to retire anytime soon. I'd hate to see Dave wield any more power in this town than he already does."

"Who's Rebecca?" she asked as he started the engine.

"Don't you remember Rebecca? Tall, wild, unique." He grinned as if saying she was "tall, wild, unique" was about the best compliment he could pay a person, and Lucky remembered his comment about hell-raisers. "She married Josh Hill about three years ago. Now they have a three-month-old baby."

"Where do they live?" Certainly not at the ranch house, or Lucky would've seen some evidence of it.

He twisted to see behind them as he backed out. "They built a home several acres away from Mike, closer to the lake."

"I see."

"What makes you ask about Dave Small? And the other guy—Eugene, was it?"

"I'm just curious."

He eyed her skeptically.

"I met them a long time ago, and I was wondering if they were still around."

While that was a lie, it wasn't a big one, and it allowed her to keep asking questions. "Does Dave still have family in town?"

"Of course." Booker pulled into the recently plowed street. "The Smalls will never leave. They think they own this place."

"Then it must get pretty crowded with the Smalls *and* the Caldwells."

Booker cut her a sharp glance. "You're not going to let bygones be bygones?"

Lucky wasn't surprised that Booker seemed to know the whole story. Her mother had been dead for four years, but the people of Dundee probably hadn't stopped talking about her. "The Caldwells are the ones who're holding a grudge."

"From what I heard, Morris and your mother are both gone and the will's been settled. What's left to fight about?"

Lucky thought of the way Marge had treated her in the store. "Resentment can linger for decades."

He withdrew a toothpick from his ashtray and stuck it in his mouth. "It doesn't have to. The Caldwells are good people. Especially Josh and Mike."

Lucky remembered Mike's closeness in the dark, misty bathroom…. Remembered the shower curtain sliding on its railing…and felt the giddiness she'd experienced as he touched her.

"If you say so," she said, because she didn't want to talk about Mike or his family anymore.

They drove several miles in silence, then Troy grew impatient in his car seat, and Booker asked Lucky to give him a cracker. While she dug through the diaper bag on the seat between them, he said, "Where've you been for the past six years, Lucky?"

"Nowhere in particular. I've traveled a lot."

"What brings you home?"

Locating the crackers, she calmed Troy's impatient squeals by giving him one. "I'm here to fix up the Victorian."

Booker chewed on his toothpick for a few seconds before glancing over at her again. "So how does it feel to be back?"

Propping her elbow on the window ledge, she gazed out as they passed the Arctic Flyer restaurant, and a memory flashed through her mind. She was in high school and had gone to the Friday night football game to escape the house. Morris was out of town; her mother was "entertaining" again.

Reluctant to head home, she'd hung out later than usual and had wound up at the Arctic Flyer. A portion of the football team showed up a few minutes later, with several of their cheerleader girlfriends.

Hey, how 'bout climbin' into the backseat of my car and giving me somethin' to celebrate our win, huh, Lucky? Mitch Hudson had called out. Physically more mature than the other boys his age, Mitch had whiskers—and his words were slurred enough to tell her he was more than a little drunk.

Hell, don't touch her, Mitch. You're likely to get a disease, someone else had said and the pretty little cheerleaders in the group, who'd almost certainly had a lot more sexual experience than Lucky did at the time, laughed as uproariously as everyone else.

She considered Booker's question: *How does it feel to be back?* Not as good as it was going to feel to leave again. But she liked Booker too much to say so. "Fine, I guess. At any rate, I won't be staying long."

CHAPTER NINE

WHEN HE DROVE past the Victorian after breakfast at the diner, Mike couldn't tell whether or not Lucky had returned. Neither could he tell whether she'd had her utilities restored. He doubted it; the place was still dark.

It'll happen soon, he decided and spent the afternoon in his office, mostly making calls for Gabe's father's campaign and trying to convince himself that she could take care of herself even without immediate heat and air.

But she hadn't done a very good job of taking care of herself so far and, as darkness fell, he started imagining the worst. She'd hitched a ride with the wrong kind of guy. She hadn't thought to buy food. She needed something and didn't have telephone service so she could call for help.

Finally, he gave up on the offer he was trying to draft for the purchase of another mare and picked up the phone. He'd promised himself that he wouldn't have anything more to do with Lucky, but he didn't need to contact *her* to put his mind at rest. There were other ways to find out what was going on next door.

Rob Strickland answered his call to the phone company. Mike had grown up with Rob and recognized his voice instantly. They chatted about Rob's wife and four kids, then Mike swung the conversation to the purpose of his call. "Could you tell me if 215 White Rock Road has any telephone service yet?" he asked.

"Isn't that your grandpa's old place?"

"Yeah."

"I'll check." Rob put him on hold for several minutes. "Not yet," he said when he finally came back on the line. "And it doesn't look like it's going to be any time soon. I found the work order, but Eloise Greenwalt just told me that once she realized who'd requested service, she stuck it at the very bottom of the stack, after all the trouble calls and everything."

Mike pictured Lucky sitting in that old Victorian, its broken windows welcoming the biting wind. "Eloise Greenwalt did *what?*"

"She stuck it in the bottom of the stack," Rob told him, chuckling. "Lucky Caldwell might have walked away with your grandpa's house and a chunk of his money to boot, but no one who cares about you or your family is going to make things easy on her now. I bet she won't stay the month."

Mike's grip tightened on the handset. "She's living in that house *alone.*"

"So?"

"It's cold outside. She needs service."

Mike could sense Rob's surprise that he wasn't happier with Eloise's spiteful game. "You want us to hook her up?"

"Hell, yes, I want you to hook her up!"

"Jeez, Mike. What's gotten into you? It's getting pretty late in the day and—"

"I don't give a damn how late it is," Mike said. "Do it now."

"We can't do it now," Rob responded, his tone injured. "Most of the crews have gone home for the night."

"Shit." Mike scrubbed a hand over his face.

"What's wrong? It's not as if she's going to die without phone service."

"Just get her a working line as soon as possible, okay?" he said. "And tell Eloise…" Tell her what? That she had no right to make such a decision? He was willing to bet she didn't even know Lucky. But if he stepped in and tried to shield his new neighbor, it'd only evoke more resentment—like it had with his mother earlier today—and his relatives and their friends would treat her that much worse.

Gritting his teeth, he did his best to reel in his temper. "Tell Eloise she doesn't have to get even with Lucky for us. We've got that handled already."

Mike hung up, thinking about all the people he knew at the power company and the water company. Then he got back on the phone, going from one person to the next until he managed to wrangle promises that Lucky would have both water and power. *Tonight.*

LUCKY COULDN'T BELIEVE IT when her lights came on. At six o'clock she'd decided that the power wouldn't be restored today and resigned herself to spending another cold night. Thanks to Booker, who'd insisted on staying long enough to cover the broken windows with plastic, the house wasn't quite as drafty as before. She wasn't exactly comfortable, but she wasn't panicked either. She had food, water, new candles, a fire she'd built with the wood she'd purchased at Finley's and her sleeping bag.

She'd just made her bed on the floor of the living room and situated a mug in the embers of the fire so she could heat water for cocoa when the lights flickered on.

"Hallelujah!" she cried and ran upstairs to turn on the central heat.

A clang echoed through the house the moment Lucky threw the switch. She held her breath, waiting to see if the HVAC system had weathered the past six years as poorly as some other parts of the house—and breathed a sigh of relief when, after another *chung,* air began pouring through the vents. It took a few more minutes for that air to get warm, and would take even longer to raise the temperature of the whole house, but at least *some* of her utilities had been restored.

She picked up the phone to see if she might have a nice surprise waiting for her there, too, but there was no dial tone. Evidently telephone service would have to wait a while longer.

Heading back to her makeshift bed, she decided to go to sleep. It was still early but too cold to do anything else, and she was exhausted because she'd barely closed her eyes last night. After she and Mike had made love until they were both spent, he'd dropped off almost immediately. But she hadn't wanted to miss one moment of lying next to him. Maybe their lovemaking had meant nothing to him, but she'd given him everything she had, everything she *was*. When she was with him, sleeping seemed a terrible waste of time, so she'd stayed awake to study his profile, feel the warmth of his big body, listen to the gentle rasp of his breathing.

But now that she knew what she was missing, she felt even lonelier than before. And while she was in this house, this town, she couldn't stop thinking about Morris and how unfairly her mother had used him. She regretted missing the opportunity to pay her last respects to him, although she knew she'd been right not to come to Dundee when he died. She hadn't wanted to turn his funeral into a battleground. She'd wanted everything to be peaceful and good, wanted Morris to receive the kind of eulogies he deserved. So she'd spent his funeral in a strange church in Texas, begging God to take care of him for all he'd done for her. Then she'd let him go.

It was certainly a cold winter here in Dundee, she decided. Yet the few hours of happiness she'd experienced in Mike's arms had been well worth the price. She didn't bother arguing with herself over that. For the first time since she could remember, she'd taken exactly what she wanted, and for a few short hours, she'd felt content. She'd been the girl pressed against the side of the barn; she'd had Mike's undivided attention. Now she had to do the same thing she'd finally done with Morris—and let go.

BARBARA HILL TURNED OFF her headlights and crept closer to the old Victorian before pulling to the side of the road. Mike had said Lucky was back, but Barbara didn't want to believe it. After everything she'd been through, it didn't seem fair; Red had had enough impact on her life already.

But a blue Mustang sat in the snow midway down the drive and light shone from the windows of the house. Someone was there; of course it was Lucky. Mike had seen her.

Knowing that Lucky was once again living in the home in which Barbara had been raised brought back all the negative emotions she'd experienced during her father's final years. She could still see Red flouncing into the diner while Barbara was trying to have breakfast with her brokenhearted mother, flaunting the huge diamond Morris had given her. She could still hear Red going on and on about how much Morris loved her and her children, how he was finally happy now that he had them. Red had even told everyone they were thinking of adopting a baby together. A baby! When Morris was nearly eighty years old! It was so absurd Barbara hadn't known how to respond. She'd always admired her father. He'd been an astute businessman, a throwback to the old days when a man's word was his bond. But he seemed to become a different person once he hooked up with Red. He let her dye his hair a tacky shade of auburn, dress him in matching shirts, turn the house into something garish, kiss and rub against him suggestively in public. Couldn't he see how silly he looked?

Then there were the things that had happened later, as the

situation grew worse: the infidelities, the lies, the greed, the attempt to kill him with an overdose of insulin.

Sickened by the memories, Barbara rested her forehead on the steering wheel. She could no longer look at the house. Morris had expected his first family to welcome Red and her children with open arms. For a short while, at the very beginning, Barbara had tried. Even though she felt terrible for her mother, who was lost and miserable without Morris, living in that small duplex just off Fifth Street. Even though Red's reputation already spoke volumes about her and she knew Red was after her father's money. Despite all that, she and her sister Cori had met Morris and Red for dinner in Boise one evening. But that night had been one of the worst of their lives. Red had flaunted her control over Morris, made them all look foolish. And, not too long after that, their brother, Bunk, told them that Red had come on to *him* when he and Morris were working on a land deal together and Red had come over to pick up a check.

Barbara knew Red must've had serious self-esteem issues to need such constant acknowledgement of her sexuality, but it was difficult to be understanding when Red had wreaked such havoc in the lives of the people Barbara most loved—and for so many years. Because Red threw a jealous fit whenever Morris contacted his first family, he'd stopped associating with them. Her father had allowed a woman like Red to tear him away from the people who really loved him. How could he do that? The betrayal bit so deeply, Barbara could only pound the steering wheel with her fists. Damn him! Damn Red and her greedy, self-serving children....

And now Lucky was back—to live in Barbara's childhood home and serve as a constant reminder of it all.

THE PHONE WOKE Mike from a dead sleep. Lifting his head, he saw that it was nearly midnight and he'd nodded off at his desk. Probably because he was so reluctant to return to his own bed. He knew he'd only start remembering what had happened when he'd slept there last: the moment Lucky had slipped into his room, pulled off that sweatshirt and…

Another ring shattered the silence, and he groped for the phone. "Hello?"

"Mike?"

Josh. Mike rubbed his eyes. "Yeah. How's the vacation?"

"We're finding out it's not easy to travel with an infant."

Josh sounded rueful enough to make Mike chuckle. "You should've left Brian with Mom. She's missing him already."

"Rebecca would never have agreed to that. Besides, Brian's still nursing."

"Of course. I forgot."

"Speaking of Mom…"

Mike heard a subtle change in the inflection of his brother's voice. "What about her?"

"She says Lucky Caldwell's back."

Obviously, word was spreading fast—all the way to Hawaii. "She is."

"What does she want?"

"To fix up the house, from what I can gather."

"Why now?"

"How should I know?" Mike dimly realized how irritable he sounded, but he was feeling more and more torn about Lucky and didn't want his family to bring her up every time they talked.

"Mom said you gave her a ride into town. Didn't you speak to her?"

"She didn't have much to say."

"Did she tell you what she has planned for the house once she finishes fixing it up?"

"She might sell."

"To us?"

"Maybe."

"That's a switch. Are you sure?"

"That's what she said. But she didn't make any promises."

"No, I don't suppose she would," Josh said. "Mom says she likes being in the power position, likes knowing she has what we want."

Feeling defensive of Lucky again, in spite of himself, Mike raked a hand through his hair. "That might've been true about Red, but I don't think it's like that with Lucky, Josh."

"Maybe not. But Mom wants us to go over there and see if we can talk Lucky into selling *before* making the improvements. She said she can't spend Christmas knowing that Red's daughter is living in the house."

"Christmas is in less than three weeks."

"I know. To be honest, I'd rather ignore the fact that Lucky's even around. Grandpa gave her the house and there's nothing we can do about it. But Mom can't see it that way."

"Josh…"

"What?"

"I don't want you going over there."

"Why?"

"Just leave her alone, okay?"

"Why?" he said again.

"Because I said so."

Mike's words resulted in a strained pause.

"What's going on?" Josh asked at last.

"Nothing."

"Bullshit. I know you too well to believe that."

Dropping his head in his hands, Mike began kneading his forehead. "Where's Rebecca?"

"She's in the other room, watching TV and feeding the baby. Why?"

"Because I'm going to tell you something that stays between us."

"What's that?" Josh said, sounding hesitant.

"I slept with Lucky last night."

Shocked silence. Finally, "What do you mean, you *slept* with her?"

"What do you think I mean?"

"I don't believe it."

"It's true."

Josh cursed softly under his breath. "What the hell were you thinking?"

Of the regret he felt for bungling the night before. Of allowing himself one night to satisfy them both. Of the water pounding down on Lucky's naked body… "It just…happened, okay?"

"Were you drunk? I hope to hell you were drunk, Mike. At least then you might have an excuse."

"I wasn't drunk."

"Isn't she young? *Really* young? Like…*twenty?* And if I remember right, she's none too pretty."

She was beautiful now, but Mike wasn't about to say so. He knew sharing that information would make him sound more affected than he wanted to appear—than he really was. "Would you quit it?" he snapped. "She's twenty-four. Twenty-four is old enough."

"You're nearly *forty!*"

"Lower your voice before Rebecca hears you. You're not helping the situation."

Josh blew out an audible sigh. "I'm trying. I'm focusing on the age difference and her less-than-pleasing appearance because, the way I see it, those are the least of your worries. Just wait until Lucky starts talking. Word'll spread like wildfire that you jumped into the sack with her, and Mom will feel like the brunt of the biggest joke ever to hit town. She'll be crushed."

"What happened between Lucky and me doesn't have anything to do with Mom," Mike growled.

"But she'll take it as a personal betrayal. You know that, don't you?"

Mike shoved away from his desk so he could stand up and pace. "Lucky's not going to say anything to anyone."

"How do you know?"

He didn't. He knew neither one of them had planned on what had happened. But whether or not she'd use recent events to her advantage, he couldn't say. Considering how people in this town were treating her, like some kind of leper, she might be tempted to strike back.

In any case, it probably wouldn't be long before he found out.

WITH ONLY THREE WEEKS before Christmas, Lucky knew she had to get busy if she wanted to make any progress on the house. First she needed to have the windows fixed. Next she had to meet with a loan officer at the bank to arrange an equity line of credit so she could finance the improvements, which would cost at least thirty thousand dollars. Then she had to rent some basic furniture, solicit estimates on the rehab and hire a contractor.

As soon as she could dig her car out of the snow, which was slowly melting beneath a much warmer sun now that the storm had passed, she drove to the bank. Fortunately, she had no problem borrowing against the value of the house. She got approval on her loan the very next day. It was her first call after receiving telephone service.

She didn't have any difficulty getting the windows fixed or renting some furniture, either, but it wasn't easy to find a contractor. There wasn't much building going on in this part of Idaho during the winter, so there weren't many people engaged in that line of work.

By the end of the week, she'd found a man by the name of Fredrick Sharp, who seemed capable and was willing to start on December seventeenth. But he refused to stay on the job any later than the twentieth because he had family coming from out of town.

"That means you'll be pulling off the job after only four days," Lucky said, unable to conceal her disappointment when she met him at the diner on Saturday morning.

He gave her a copy of the contract they'd just signed and put the other in his shirt pocket. "I can start again after the first."

January first! At this rate she'd never get the house done. After that night with Mike, she felt as if she needed to finish her plans and leave as soon as possible—before she was reduced to sitting at the window, hoping to see him drive by. Or sneaking out to his barn to watch him work, the way she used to as a child.

"What about quitting the twenty-second? Two more days would make a big difference. Christmas Eve isn't until the twenty-fourth."

He finished his coffee and pushed his cup off to the side. "Sorry, my wife would hang me by my toenails," he said with a lopsided grin. "It's *my* family who's coming." Tossing a five-dollar bill onto the table to pay for their coffee, he got up as though no was his last word on the subject, and Lucky realized this barrel-chested, ruddy father of five wouldn't budge on his work schedule.

"Okay." They shook hands to finalize their deal and walked across the street to pick out the paint. But they hadn't been in the hardware store more than five minutes when she heard a familiar voice coming from the next aisle over.

"So now you're thinking about replacing the whole roof?" It was Mike. She knew because her knees went weak and she immediately recalled that same voice whispering to her, coaxing her to relax in the steamy shower.

"That roof's twenty years old," someone else, an older man, replied.

"But it's winter." Mike again. "No one replaces a roof mid-winter unless he's crazy or has no choice."

"I'll have two weeks over the holiday break. It'd be nice to get it done while I'm off work, if the weather will—"

"Listen to Mike, Dad. You don't want to risk it," a third voice interrupted.

That had to be Josh, Lucky decided. Josh, Mike and their father, Coach Hill. Lucky had strictly avoided Mike and Josh's father when she was in high school. Like everyone else, she'd had to take P.E. in order to graduate. But she'd signed up for dance, even though she preferred track—anything to avoid facing Coach Hill day after day.

"Let's just patch the roof, then paint the living room. One major project is enough," Mike said.

"Is something wrong?"

Lucky started when Mr. Sharp touched her elbow. He'd been talking about gloss and semi-gloss paints and asking how often she planned on washing her walls, but she'd lost track of the conversation.

Lowering her voice, she said, "No, nothing."

A curious expression crossed his face. "Why are you suddenly whispering?"

"I'm not whispering," she said, but she was, and she wasn't about to stop until Mike, Josh and their father left the store. She didn't want to attract their attention. She knew Mike probably wouldn't acknowledge her while he was in the company of his family and she wasn't sure she could handle such a snub after what they'd shared.

"So, do you want the semi-gloss?"

Lucky nodded. At this point, she didn't care what she ended up with as long as Mr. Sharp piped down for a few minutes.

Instead of falling silent and staying in place, as she'd hoped, he picked up two gallons of cream-colored paint and headed toward the cashier, obviously expecting her to follow so she could pay for it.

"Don't you need anything else before we check out?" she asked, her voice rising only slightly to cover the distance.

He scowled as he glanced over his shoulder. "I already told you, I have all the other supplies."

"Oh…right."

"And I have to give old man Bedderman an estimate on remodeling his bathroom at ten, so we'd better scoot."

She'd forgotten about his other appointment. "Of course. Well, *you* scoot. I'll—" Before Lucky could finish, Josh and his father turned the corner and nearly barreled into her new contractor. While everyone jostled to avoid a collision, Lucky bent over a can of varnish and began examining the label, just in case there was still a chance Mike's brother and father might pass by without seeing her.

"Lucky?" Sharp said, his voice impatient. "You'll what?"

Lucky's stomach tensed as the full focus of all three men landed on her, but she looked up, anyway. Of course it'd come to this. In Dundee, she'd always had to deal with her demons head-on. "I'll pay for the paint in a minute and take it home with me. Just leave the cans at the register."

"Right. See you next week. Josh, Coach," Mr. Sharp said in passing. Then he was gone, and Lucky was alone in the aisle with Mike's father and brother.

Standing, she threw back her shoulders and took a deep breath. She might be willing to cower in the corner when Coach Hill and his sons didn't know she was around, but she'd never let them *see* her cower.

Coach Hill had frozen in place the moment recognition dawned. "Lucky."

She nodded cautiously as Mike rounded the corner carrying some sort of tool. As soon as he saw her, a frown creased his handsome face, the face she'd studied so earnestly in the motel.

"Maybe it's a good thing we bumped into each other," Coach Hill said.

His words were nice enough. The Caldwells were always careful not to lose control. But the coldness in his eyes sent chills down Lucky's spine.

"Maybe you wouldn't mind coming over to the diner with us," he went on. "We have some business we'd like to discuss."

"No, we don't," Mike said.

His father gave him a dark look. "Yes, we do."

Lucky wasn't sure what to think, but she knew she didn't want to let the three of them corner her in a booth at the diner. "What kind of business?"

"We'd like to buy the Victorian."

"I already know that," she said. "I…I'm considering it."

"We'd like to buy it right away. Today."

She shook her head. "I'm sorry, but I'm not quite ready to sell."

"When will you be?"

"Maybe in a few months."

"You've got to make sure you ruin everyone's Christmas first, is that it?"

"Damn it, Dad, come on." Mike physically pulled his father in the other direction, but Coach Hill jerked out of his grasp.

"Just sell us the house and be done with it," he said to Lucky. "No one wants you here. No one even wants to talk to you."

The pain and anger flowing through her tempted Lucky to tell him that his own son had done a little more than *talk* to her. She was so tired of the arrogance, the derision. She wanted to shock and hurt him as badly as he was hurting her. But when she glanced Mike's way, she knew she'd never do it, even if he felt exactly as his father did. She cared about him too much.

"I don't remember asking for anyone's approval," she said instead, but her voice wasn't nearly as belligerent as she'd intended. Terrified that they'd realize how close to tears she was, she narrowed her eyes and glared at them haughtily.

"She has as much right to live here as we do," Mike said.

"Mike's right, Dad," Josh chimed in. "Let her be, okay? We can get the paint later."

Coach Hill's face turned bright red. For the first time, Lucky was seeing a crack in the family's cool disdain. "I'm tired of you holding that house over our heads. Just leave," he said as his sons dragged him away.

When they were gone, Lucky put a shaky hand on the paint rack to steady herself. She'd heard it all before, she told herself. She had a thick skin. They couldn't hurt her. She'd *expected* this.

But *something* hurt—so badly she could scarcely breathe. Maybe it was the realization that, despite what had happened between them, Mike didn't want her here, either. That night at the motel had been no more real than all the times she'd dreamed of being kissed by him the way he'd kissed Lindsey Carpenter.

MIKE'S HANDS CLENCHED the steering wheel as if someone might try to rip it away from him. He couldn't remember ever being so angry, or so frustrated. What could he have done differently in that damn hardware store? Nothing. He'd tried to shut his father up and get him out of there as soon as possible. But it hadn't worked….

"You're grinding your teeth," Josh said, riding in the passenger seat of Mike's truck as they drove back to the ranch.

Mike didn't answer. He didn't want conversation. Josh might be more forgiving toward Lucky than their folks. But Mike still didn't want to discuss her with him. Too many conflicting emotions roiled inside him—split loyalties, compassion, guilt, a desire to be fair.

"At least now you know she's as bitter as Mom and Dad have said."

"Bitter?" Mike echoed.

"Yeah. Didn't you see the way she looked at us?"

Incredulous, Mike stared at his brother. "Dad *attacked* her," he snapped. "She could've leveled him by telling him about me, but she didn't."

"I'm just saying there's nothing to be upset about," Josh said. "It was unpleasant but nothing big. She doesn't care what we think of her or she probably would've told him."

Mike chuckled humorlessly. Josh was either delusional or trying too hard to make him feel better. And if he was trying to make him feel better, it wasn't working. Mike had wounded Lucky, and he knew it. He'd drawn blood simply by allowing that incident at the hardware store to happen.

She hadn't even tried to defend herself....

"Let it go," he told Josh.

"Mike—"

"What?"

"She's a big girl. She'll be all right."

"I know," he said so Josh would shut up. But he couldn't accept such flimsy solace. Lucky wasn't nearly as big as he was. And she had no one on her side.

CHAPTER TEN

THAT NIGHT MIKE tried to distract himself from thinking about the incident in the hardware store by calling Gabe. Dealing with his best friend and the handicap that had changed Gabe's life suddenly seemed the easiest of several difficult situations, and Mike needed to resolve *something*. He couldn't remember ever being at odds with so many people or feeling so uncomfortable in his own skin.

But Gabe didn't answer. After three rings, his machine came on. "This is Gabe. Leave a message."

"Answer the phone, Gabe." Mike felt fairly certain Gabe was at home. He rarely went out, and it was getting late. "Gabe?"

Nothing.

"We've got business to discuss. I've arranged a few meetings for you."

Still nothing. Maybe he'd already gone to bed. Or he had a saw running and couldn't hear the phone.

Mike hung up and called again.

This is Gabe. Leave a message.

"Call me," Mike said, then slammed down the phone. So much for resolving the ill feelings between him and his childhood friend.

Frustrated and tense, he pushed away from his desk and wandered out of his office. He wanted to go to bed and forget the events of the day. But when he reached his room, he couldn't think of anything except the white lace panties he'd shoved into his underwear drawer so the housekeeper wouldn't find them. Lucky's panties.

Pulling them out, he toyed with the small scrap of silky fabric, remembering the sight of Lucky standing before him wearing nothing else. It was a beautiful image, one that instantly tightened his groin. Only it was quickly followed by the memory of the hurt that had flickered across her face at the hardware store today.

All evening he'd been recounting her sins, fighting the urge to go over to her place and apologize. Lucky had thumbed her nose at them for years. She'd refused to sell him the house he loved and left it standing vacant so long it was falling apart. She'd gloated, at times, over the fact that she'd managed to supplant him in Morris's affections. She hadn't even returned for Morris's funeral after inheriting so much of his money. She'd rambled around the country as if…as if…

As if she were lost, he realized.

Sinking onto the bed, he picked up the cordless phone on his nightstand and called information for new listings. Calling wasn't the visit he would've preferred, but he wasn't sure he could trust himself to show up at Lucky's door, apologize and leave it at that. As conflicted as he was about her, he knew two things. One, she hadn't told a soul about them or she would've told his father today. And two, the satisfaction he'd achieved that night at the motel wasn't nearly as long-lasting as he'd hoped it would be.

He was craving her already.

LUCKY JUMPED when her phone rang. Except for the movers who'd delivered the furniture she'd rented from a place in Boise, the contractors who'd given her bids and the bank that had made her the loan, no one had called her since she'd received telephone service. She had acquaintances all over America, but no one she considered close, except maybe her brothers. She knew she'd hear from them at Christmas, but she hadn't even passed on her new number. It wasn't Christmas yet.

So who was calling her at nearly eleven o'clock?

She used the remote to turn down the TV and leaned over the end of the couch to reach the phone, which sat on the floor because she had nowhere else to put it. She'd rented only essential furniture—a bed and dresser for the smallest of the bedrooms upstairs, a couch, a TV and a few lamps for the living room and a kitchen set. She didn't want a lot to move when she painted or replaced the carpet, and this way she'd have less to return when it came time to leave.

"Hello?" she said hesitantly. After her confrontation with Coach Hill in the hardware store this morning, she feared there might not be a friendly voice at the other end of the line. Her homecoming had obviously stirred up as much anger as she'd anticipated.

"Lucky?"

"Yes?"

"It's Mike."

Lucky pulled the blanket she'd curled up in more tightly around her. "What can I do for you, Mike?" she asked, as if they'd never so much as kissed.

Then she remembered his father's words: *Just leave*....

Wincing, she clung even tighter to her blanket. The Hills didn't have to worry. She *would* leave—as soon as she found her father, finished the house and figured out which food bank or Red Cross branch needed her most.

Mike cleared his throat. "I was checking to see—"

"Whether or not I'd packed my bags like your father suggested?" she said.

He sighed audibly. "No. I'm sorry about this morning, Lucky. My father was way out of line."

Lucky cursed herself for letting the encounter get the best of her. If only she hadn't slept with Mike, if only she wasn't completely infatuated with him, then she could've fought back instead of standing there withering beneath their scorn. "There's no reason to be sorry," she said. "I know I'm not wanted here. What your father said came as no surprise."

"I wouldn't let what happened today—"

"Thanks for calling," she said and hung up. She couldn't talk to Mike anymore. Caring about him only forced her to acknowledge that she wasn't as indifferent to the people here as she wanted to believe. And she had to be completely indifferent or they'd succeed in chasing her away before she was ready to go.

A WEEK LATER, Mike watched Josh hand Brian to Rebecca, wondering why he'd been feeling so tense lately. Sure, he'd spent a restless night last night. Since Lucky had moved in next door, he'd spent a lot of restless nights. But work was going well. They already had more mares lined up for breeding season than ever before. And he generally enjoyed Sunday dinner at his folks' place.

"Can I get you another soda?" his mother asked as his father dozed on the end of the couch.

Mike shook his head.

Josh sat across from him and lightly kicked the bottom of his boot. "You've barely said a word since you arrived."

"I'm tired," he said, but he was actually preoccupied with trying to figure out where Lucky had been earlier. When he'd passed her place, he'd looked for her car, but couldn't see it. He hadn't spotted it when he drove through town, either.

"Mike?"

He blinked and glanced up at his mother. "What?"

"What do you think of my tree?"

He studied the Christmas tree, which she'd decorated with big red bows and little tin soldiers. "It's nice."

"You put up a tree at the office, didn't you?"

He had, but only because she'd called to remind him. He liked buying presents, but decorating seemed a waste of time and energy, especially when he had no children and only a handful of employees during this part of the year. He'd said as much to his mother, but she'd acted as if he'd just denounced Christianity and insisted that an office tree was important to some people. He figured she meant those in the office, because he hadn't met a cowboy yet who cared one way or the other. "I did," he said.

"Did you decorate it with the blue-and-silver balls I sent over last year?"

He couldn't remember what his housekeeper had put on the tree. He'd left the task up to her and hadn't really looked at it since. "I think so."

Rebecca, who was gently rocking baby Brian to sleep, laughed at his response. "You should know better than to ask Josh or Mike about something like that, Mom," she said. "Nori Stein could've put up a cactus for all the attention they pay to that sort of thing."

"So, is it pretty?" Barbara asked.

Rebecca shrugged. "Nori's not much of a decorator, but it's not bad for an office tree."

"It's a great tree." Josh spoke around a bite of homemade bread buried in jelly. "I cut it down myself."

"Only because I insisted," Rebecca said. "*You* wanted to buy a fake one."

He managed to swallow. "I would've settled for buying a real one from the lot."

"Those are old before you even get them home," Rebecca complained. "Their needles are ready to fall off."

"What are you giving the employees for Christmas?" Barbara asked Josh.

"A turkey, I guess." He looked to Mike for confirmation.

"That seemed to work last year," Mike responded.

His mother adjusted her apron. "Would you like me to make each of them a tin of fudge?"

Barbara loved feeling important to him and Josh by taking care of details they typically neglected. Mike was usually grateful. But tins of fudge suddenly seemed pretty inconsequential. Maybe it was because he was having trouble concentrating on the rituals of daily living. "That'd be great," he said, mustering what enthusiasm he could.

"I'll do it tomorrow." Seemingly satisfied, she got up to take Josh's empty plate before he had a chance to do anything with it himself.

"One more thing." She turned back at the kitchen doorway. "Your father and I are planning a service project. The Bagleys at church are going through tough times, what with Bart being ill. Last I heard they don't even have a tree. So your father and I were thinking we'd leave some gifts on their front porch Christmas Eve. I thought you boys and Rebecca might like to help."

Nervous energy caused Mike to bounce his leg. He felt terrible about the Bagleys' misfortune, but he couldn't remember the last time he'd been so uninterested in what was going on around him. "Sure," he said. "I'll donate five hundred dollars."

Josh and Rebecca said they'd donate, too, and Rebecca volunteered to help with the shopping.

Considering his familial obligations met, Mike stood. "I'm

gonna head back out to the ranch. I've got some work piling up on my desk."

Shifting Brian to her other shoulder, Rebecca raised her eyebrows in surprise. "We haven't even had dessert yet. What's so pressing?"

"Just paperwork. Lots of…paperwork." His voice fell to a mutter, because he really didn't have anything all *that* pressing, but he didn't care. He wanted to go.

"What's gotten into you lately?" his mother asked, catching him before he could reach the door.

Mike paused. "What do you mean?"

"You're acting strange."

"What's new about that?" Josh said. "Mike's always been strange."

Mike knew Josh was doing what he could to cover for him, but their mother ignored the comment. "You've been aloof, preoccupied."

"You're imagining things," Mike said with a scowl. "I'm fine. I'll see ya'll later." He slipped out into the cool evening air, and took a deep breath. But his sense of freedom didn't last long. Josh came out of the house and flagged him down as he was backing into the street.

Letting the engine idle, Mike lowered his window while he waited for his brother to come close enough to speak.

"What's wrong, man?" Josh asked, leaning against the door.

Mike slung one arm over the steering wheel in a deliberately careless motion. "Nothing."

The easygoing grin Josh had worn in the house was gone. "This doesn't have anything to do with Lucky, does it?"

"Of course not."

"I can understand you being attracted to her, Mike. I have to admit she's changed…*a lot*. But you're not still seeing her, right? You know how crazy that would be."

"I'm not still seeing her. I'm not even attracted to her," Mike said.

Josh studied him a moment longer, then nodded. "Okay, I'll take your word for it." With a farewell thump on the truck, he walked away.

Mike cursed under his breath as he drove off. He didn't lie to his brother often, but he'd lied to him today. He was *extremely* attracted to Lucky—and the more he tried to ignore it, the worse it got.

LUCKY SHIFTED in the car to better see across the street. Part of her felt like a Peeping Tom, hanging out near Dave Small's house, hoping for a glimpse of him. The other part believed she could tell a lot about the kind of man he was simply by observing him in his own element.

The front door of the Smalls' new stucco rambler opened and closed, and a chubby little blond girl wearing a snowsuit hopped into the yard, with a puppy bouncing after her. Dave had to be in his early sixties, so Lucky guessed this was another grandchild. Earlier there'd been several children in the yard.

A woman passed in front of the kitchen window. Lucky squinted, trying to make out whether or not it was the same person who'd arrived with the five kids in a minivan about forty minutes earlier, or if this could be the councilman's wife. Lucky was almost as curious about Liz Small as she was about Dave. She knew his liaison with her mother was a secret, or there would've been some kind of public outcry, so the impression she received of his wife would figure heavily into whether or not she decided to approach him. She wasn't out to destroy the Smalls' marriage or break anyone's heart. She only wanted to answer the biggest question of her life.

The woman at the window was too far away to see clearly. Tempted to pull closer, Lucky put her hand on the ignition, then hesitated when a dark sedan passed her and turned into the drive.

Dave had finally joined the family gathering, she realized when a man stepped out. His hair was now sprinkled with gray, but she recognized his compact body immediately from having seen him around town when she was a child.

He dug around in his back seat, came up with a briefcase and an overcoat and greeted the blond girl who ran over to hug his leg. He looked as though he'd just returned from a long day at the office, but Lucky couldn't imagine that he'd been working on a Sunday afternoon. Maybe he had some type of social function or he sang in the church choir or something.

She watched him carefully as he piled everything he'd been carrying into one arm so he could lift the girl with the other. As he carried her into the house, she pointed to the puppy, and he waited for the furry little creature to catch up to them before closing the door.

Maybe Booker was wrong about Dave. Dave seemed like a family man. He seemed to care about his grandchildren.

Taking a deep breath, she started her car. It was getting dark; she wasn't going to see anything else tonight. But she didn't want to go back to her empty house. At least here in town she could admire the Christmas lights and the plastic Santas and wire reindeer that adorned so many snow-covered lawns.

Maybe she'd drive past Garth Holbrook's house again. She'd found his address in the phone book, along with Dave Small's. But when she'd gone by the senator's place earlier, it had been dark and empty. She hadn't been able to find a listing for Eugene Thompson. She was just wondering how she might track him down when a knock sounded on her window.

Jumping at the unexpected sound, she turned to see Jon Small standing on the curb next to her car, looking far older than he probably was. Puffy bags beneath his eyes and a belly that was beginning to roll over his belt suggested he drank too much; his hair was thinning and his complexion seemed paler than she remembered.

"Who are you and what are you doing here?" he asked, his dark-blond eyebrows knotted into a foreboding slash, his breath misting on the cold air.

Lucky lowered her window and attempted a disarming smile. "I'm out looking at the Christmas lights."

"Megan said you've been sitting here a while."

"Megan?"

"My sister-in-law."

"I was watching the children play earlier." She widened her eyes. "Am I bothering you?"

His expression cleared. "No, not really. Megan was just worried that you might be a child snatcher." He rolled his eyes. "Like we've ever had one of those in Dundee. She watches too much TV."

"I'm no child abductor," Lucky said, chuckling. "Actually, I used to live here."

She could tell he didn't recognize her.

"I'm Lucky Caldwell."

Based on their earlier encounter years ago, she braced herself for a negative reaction and was surprised when he merely sized her up. "You've gotten real pretty, Lucky."

"Thank you."

"You married?"

"No, but if memory serves, you are, right?"

"Not anymore. Leah ran off with the neighbor."

"I'm sorry to hear that. You have kids, don't you?"

"Four of 'em. Custody battle hasn't been easy." He shoved his hands in his pockets and hunched against the cold. The temperature was dropping rapidly now that the sun had gone down. "Listen, I know I'm a few years older than you are, but if you're free sometime, maybe we could take in a movie."

Jon could be her half brother—and she had no interest in him, anyway. "Actually, I can't," she said. "I'm not married, but I am in a committed relationship." Committed to *avoid* a close relationship.

He shook his head and spit on the sidewalk. "The good ones are always taken."

"I'm sure someone will come along." She shifted into Drive. "I guess I'll get home. It's pretty chilly."

"Give me a call if you change your mind."

She nodded and waved before she drove away. But she knew she'd never call him, and she didn't go home. She drove past Garth's house. It still looked empty, so she sat at the diner for almost an hour, nursing a cup of hot cocoa and reading the paper. Christmas was less than a week away, and she hadn't done any shopping for her nieces and nephews yet. She needed to do it soon; she couldn't seem to get into the spirit of the season. She generally spent Christmas serving dinner to the homeless, but there weren't any soup kitchens in Dundee. She'd been crazy to come here, especially now. What had she been thinking?

She'd been thinking of that Christmas long ago when she'd moved into what felt like a castle, and there'd been so many presents under the tree she thought she'd become a princess.

Finally, Lucky paid her bill, gathered up her purse and her keys and went home. It wasn't quite eight o'clock, but she figured she could watch television for a couple of hours before bed. Mr. Sharp was supposed to arrive at six in the morning to finish painting the downstairs, so she planned to turn in early.

But the minute she stepped inside her dark house, she knew something was different. The air smelled strongly of fresh pine, a scent that definitely hadn't been there before. What was going on?

A large, amorphous shape to her right made her jump. "Hello?" she said, struggling to keep her voice steady.

No one answered. She flipped on the light, then felt her jaw drop. In the middle of her previously empty living room stood a giant Christmas tree, freshly cut from the smell of it. Next to its base sat a cardboard box, which held several brand-new strands of lights and the most unusual assortment of ornaments she'd ever seen. It looked as if someone had gone to Finley's and bought everything at random—red, green, blue and white balls; dancers, drummers and Santa ornaments; plastic candy cane garland, gold garland, a silver star for the top and a lighted angel, even two colors of tinsel.

But who had bought all this stuff? And how did they get it into her house?

CHAPTER ELEVEN

LUCKY SAT on the floor as she piled all the decorations back in the box. It had to be Mr. Sharp, she decided. He'd mentioned her lack of a tree, and he was the only one who had a key to her house. She'd given it to him so he'd have access whether she was home or not. She wanted him to get as much work done as possible before he pulled off on December twentieth.

But when she called him a few minutes later, he sounded genuinely surprised.

"Thanks for *what* Christmas tree?"

"The one standing in my living room."

"I didn't know you had one in your living room. You told me you weren't going to bother this year."

"I didn't. Someone else did."

"Who?"

"That's what I'm trying to find out," she said. "I thought it was you. You're the only one with a key to my house."

"I put the key over the door."

"You *what?*"

A note of defensiveness crept into his voice. "I didn't want to lose it."

"Why didn't you tell me?"

"I didn't think of it. I hide a key on every job."

Over the door was a mite obvious for "hiding." But this was Dundee. "That means anyone could've gotten in."

"Were you robbed?" He sounded a bit sheepish.

"No. At least, not that I'm aware of. I haven't checked up-stairs, but I doubt a thief would take the time to put up a Christmas tree or buy me a bunch of decorations."

"You needed a little holiday cheer," he said. "Must've been Santa Claus."

Santa Claus, indeed, Lucky thought as she pressed the End button on her cordless phone. If there *was* a Santa Claus, he was more than a little late getting around to her.

She stared up at her tree. It was tall and full, perfectly shaped. A tree like that at the lot in town would cost seventy or eighty bucks. And the decorations weren't cheap. Whoever had delivered this gift seemed indifferent to price. The hodge-podge of ornaments and garlands further suggested that he or she didn't have a clue about decorating.

It was a man, Lucky figured. A man who wasn't worried about money. Someone close enough to know she didn't have a tree. Someone who wouldn't think twice about entering her house.

She rubbed her lip thoughtfully. Mike. He was the only one besides Mr. Sharp who'd even been over, and judging by the way he'd barged in that first night, he had no problem mak-ing himself at home.

Picking up the phone she'd put on the floor beside her, she dialed information for his number and soon had him on the line.

"Someone put up a Christmas tree in my house," she stated without preamble.

Evidently, he recognized her voice because he didn't ask her to identify herself. "No kidding. Who do you suppose might've done that?"

"I'm not sure, but I'm thinking it was someone close by, someone like…" She glanced at the decorations. "You, for instance."

"Why would it have to be me?"

"No one else lives out this way."

"Josh and Rebecca do. I've got office staff who come and go each day, a housekeeper who only goes home on the weekends, at least during the cold months, Fernando, my ranch manager, and a few cowboys to help us get through the winter until breeding season starts and things really get busy."

"You expect me to believe Josh or Rebecca, or even someone who works for you, did this?"

"I don't expect you to believe anything. I'm just saying it *could* have been them."

"And it *could* have been you."

"I thought you said I'd lead a parade through town if something ever happened to you."

Was he teasing her? He didn't sound serious. "You would, because then you'd finally get the house."

"So why would I bother to buy you a Christmas tree?"

That was the one question Lucky couldn't answer. She hesitated, wondering if she could've guessed wrong, after all. "I suppose you wouldn't," she said, backing off. "Sorry to bother you."

"Lucky?" he said before she could hang up.

"Yes?"

"Christmas is only a week away. When were you going to get a tree?"

"I wasn't."

"Why not?"

Closing her eyes, she rubbed her temples. Decorating for Christmas smacked too much of belonging. She'd chosen to leave the Victorian as empty as possible to remind herself that she wouldn't be staying long.

Don't get attached. You can't forget you're not wanted here....

"Maybe I didn't want to scare you and your family," she said flippantly.

"Scare us?"

"Into thinking I might be getting comfortable."

"No one would begrudge you a good Christmas, Lucky."

She could've reminded him that his parents begrudged her *everything*. But she didn't want to talk about what had happened in the hardware store. She was too busy realizing how much she liked it when Mike said her name. It told her that he was finally dealing with her as an adult instead of ignoring her as he had when she was younger. That in itself was a victory of sorts, although she wasn't sure why. Especially when her name on his lips brought back memories she was better off forgetting. He'd said her name a lot that night at the motel. He'd also said other things he couldn't possibly have meant.

Jerking her thoughts back to the conversation, she lightened her tone. "I have too much to do to worry about Christmas this year."

"Will you be spending the holidays here in town, then?"

He didn't add "alone," but the implication was there, and the humiliation of having no one, not one friend or family member to share the holiday with, wounded Lucky's pride. Especially when he was so admired and well-liked that she couldn't imagine him ever facing the same situation. "No, of course not. Why would I stay here? My brothers have invited me to Washington," she said, even though she hadn't even called to let them know she was in Dundee. "I'm going to fly up there at the end of the week."

"That's a good idea."

She heard relief in his response; no doubt he was already planning to pass the good news on to his mother. "It should be fun." She paused briefly. "You'll be busy with all your family's festivities, huh?"

"My mother insists on cooking a big dinner every Christmas Eve."

"Is your extended family invited?"

"Yeah. That's when we exchange gifts."

Lucky pictured his big, happy family all gathered together to eat and laugh and talk. She could imagine the camaraderie....

"But Christmas itself should be pretty quiet," he went on, as if he might be aware of her feelings. "We reserve that day for individual families. I usually work, believe it or not."

He'd be home on Christmas Day. She'd have to keep that in mind if she didn't go to Washington.

"Have you already done your shopping?" she asked.

"Most of it."

She liked the image of Mike rambling through a department store, trying to find things other people might like. "Where did you buy your gifts? Boise?"

"So far I got everything online."

"That would be easiest."

"When you live where we do."

"Right. Well, have a good holiday," she said, and started to hang up.

"Lucky?"

She paused again. "What?"

"That night at the motel was—"

Disappointment stabbed through her as she anticipated his next words. "Don't finish. I already know what you're going to say."

"What's that?"

"It was a mistake and now you regret it. I regret it, too, of course, but what's done is done."

Silence. Lucky held her breath, waiting. Finally, he said, "That isn't what I was going to say at all."

She nervously smoothed her left eyebrow with two fingers. "What, then?" Her tone challenged him to let her have it, promised that nothing he said could hurt her. That was what she wanted him to believe.

"I'm sorry you regret it," he said, "because as far as I'm concerned, it was unforgettable."

His response left Lucky speechless for perhaps the first time in her life, but he didn't wait for her to recover. He hung up, leaving her so dumbfounded she couldn't move.

"WHO WAS THAT?"

Mike glanced up as his brother strode into his office. Mike normally didn't expect Josh to knock or give him any other kind of notice when he was around. They used to live together, still worked together and owned the ranch as equal partners. But Josh had been working at home more and more since he'd married Rebecca and only now did Mike realize how accustomed he'd become to being alone after hours and on weekends.

Mike didn't want to tell Josh he'd just been talking to Lucky, so he deflected his brother's question by asking one himself. "What are you doing here?"

"Checking in."

"How'd it go at Mom's after I left?"

"Good."

"Where's Rebecca?"

Josh crossed to the window and stared out toward the barn. "She took Brian home. He was getting cranky."

"Why didn't you go with her?"

"I had to pick up some paperwork. Old man Hackett is driving me nuts. First he wants to buy Hezacharger, then he doesn't. I'm not sure we'll ever come to terms, which makes me a little hesitant to go out on a limb and buy Mira's Love. We're going to need plenty of operating capital over the next few months."

"The breeding season is shaping up nicely. We're booked solid," Mike said.

"Still, if we have to keep Hezacharger, maybe we should hold off on new acquisitions."

Mike shrugged. Normally he felt pretty strongly on this subject. He thought Mira's Love was one of the best stallions he'd ever seen and didn't think they should pass up the opportunity to buy him, regardless of whether or not they could sell Hezacharger, but his mind wasn't on business today.

"Where were you earlier?" Josh asked, leaning a shoulder against the wall.

"What do you mean?"

"Where'd you go after you left Mom and Dad's?"

Mike scowled. "Does it matter?"

Josh didn't answer right away. Finally, he said, "Gabriel Holbrook's been trying to reach you."

"You talked to Gabe?"

"When no one answered out here, he called Mom and Dad's."

"I must've been outside." Hating how quickly this new lie rolled off his tongue, Mike focused on straightening his desk. He and Josh had always been honest with each other. But he knew his brother wouldn't understand why he'd spent his afternoon doing what he'd done. *He* didn't even understand it.

"Gabe's pretty excited about his dad running for Congress, isn't he?"

Mike looked up now that the conversation had returned to a neutral topic.

"He told me he just got a commitment for fifty thousand dollars. From one guy," Josh went on to say.

"That's great."

"Poor Gabe. I'm glad he's focusing on something. If it wasn't for that damn car accident, he'd have a Super Bowl ring by now."

"At least he's alive," Mike snapped.

Josh blinked in surprise.

"How can we expect him to get past what happened to him if we can't? Just because he can't run anymore doesn't mean his life is over."

"Gee, aren't we sensitive today."

"Being sensitive is one thing. Making him feel useless because he isn't fulfilling our dreams is another."

"You don't think they were *his* dreams, too, Mike?"

Mike knew they were, but he also knew that the expectations of others had made the situation worse. "He can set new goals."

"Am I right in guessing that you've already expressed your 'suck it up' opinion to him?"

"Why do you say that?"

"He was pretty remote today, and that would certainly explain it."

"In case you haven't noticed, he's been remote, in more ways than one, ever since the accident."

"Are you sure you have to be so hard on him?"

Mike glared at his younger brother. "I want my best friend back."

Josh shook his head. "I'm not sure what's going on with you."

Mike didn't respond. He couldn't explain it. His life had been moving smoothly along for nearly forty years. And then Lucky had returned, and suddenly he was easily irritated, completely preoccupied and dissatisfied with everything that had once fulfilled him.

"We have a meeting here, Tuesday at ten," Josh was saying.

"I thought it was at one."

"Gabe said his father couldn't make it after lunch, so we changed the time. One of us should let Conner Armstrong know."

"I'll do that."

"Fine." His brother slid his hands into his pockets and started for the door, then hesitated at the entrance as though he had something else on his mind.

"See you tomorrow," Mike said, hoping to encourage his departure.

Josh turned and hooked his fingers over the door frame. "I ran into Jon Small when I was gassing up."

"And?"

"He had a few questions for me."

"About what?"

"Lucky."

Mike narrowed his eyes. "What kind of questions?"

"When did she get back? Have we seen her? Hasn't she turned into a beauty? You know."

Mike and Josh often thought alike, but Mike couldn't figure out where his brother was going with this. "What's your point?"

"He said something that struck me as odd."

"Which was?"

"He told me she'd spent the afternoon sitting in her car across the street from his father's house."

Mike sat up taller. "What?"

"She was there so long—"

"Doing what?"

"Just watching the house, apparently. Anyway, she was there so long they were afraid she might be some kind of stalker, bent on stealing one of the kids. So Jon crept up from behind and confronted her."

"Did she say why she was there?"

"She told him she was looking at Christmas lights."

As far as Mike knew, Lucky had no connection to the Smalls. He couldn't help wondering why she'd been there, but he didn't want to add fuel to the suspicion in Josh's face. "So?" he said, pretending to shrug off the information. "Maybe she likes Christmas lights."

"It's freezing outside," Josh replied. "Why would anyone,

let alone a young woman, sit in her car all afternoon and watch one house? That's not a lot of lights, Mike."

"I don't know. Why don't you ask her?" Mike said, trying to act as disconnected from the subject matter as possible.

Josh didn't fall for it. Cocking one eyebrow, he said, "Fernando told me he helped you carry a Christmas tree into her place a couple of hours ago. Considering that, I thought you might see her before I do."

CHAPTER TWELVE

MIKE LEANED against the porch rail, waiting for Lucky to come to the door. He could have called her. He probably *should* have called her instead of traipsing over to her house. But she wasn't the most receptive person in the world, and he wanted to see her face when he asked her about the Smalls.

"Can I come in?" he said when she opened the door.

Dressed in a pair of low-riding jeans and a black, form-fitting sweater, she hesitated but finally swung the door wide and stepped back.

The scent of her perfume as he moved past her evoked images of her silky skin beneath his lips. His muscles contracted as he tried to resist his body's instinctive reaction.

"Would you like to sit down?" she asked.

The house was spotless. It smelled of furniture polish and Lysol, but except for a new area rug and the Christmas tree he'd brought, which still didn't have a light or a bulb on it, the front room was bare.

"Where?"

She frowned as if she hadn't expected him to accept the courtesy but waved him back into the kitchen area.

"Why haven't you decorated your tree?" he asked. "According to my mother, women really like that sort of thing."

"Is that why you brought it over?" she replied, obviously baiting him.

Mike walked to the windows, which looked out over the land he loved. "Tell me what I want to know, and maybe I'll return the favor."

Their eyes met, and Mike couldn't help thinking how difficult it was to erect barriers they'd already broken down. He didn't quite trust her, hated that she seemed to pull him away from all the people he knew and loved, and yet...

"What do you want to know?" she asked.

"I'm curious about why you were at the Smalls today."

"How'd you know I was there?"

"Jon mentioned it to Josh."

She grimaced. "Word spreads fast."

"This is Dundee, remember?"

"How could I forget? Can I get you a glass of wine?"

He knew better than to agree. Drinking and relaxing would lead exactly where he *wanted* it to lead. But what they'd done so far had complicated his life enough already. Maybe, to a certain extent, he could excuse himself for that night at his place and then at the motel. Lucky had dropped into his life out of nowhere, and the attraction he felt toward her had taken him by surprise. But now that he'd had a chance to realize what he was doing, he had no excuse for making the situation worse. "No, thanks."

She sat on the couch behind him and hugged her legs to her chest. "So, what about the tree?"

He turned to face her, his gaze immediately falling to her lips. Maybe he couldn't touch her again, but looking didn't hurt. "You haven't told me what I want to know."

"Can't a woman drive through a neighborhood to admire the Christmas lights?"

"Jon said you were out there all afternoon."

"It was only an hour or two."

"Why?"

"I wanted to see someone."

The jealousy that trickled through Mike surprised him. He wasn't the jealous type. "Not Jon."

She laughed. "No."

"Who, then?"

"Did *you* buy the tree?"

He moved closer, to sit on the arm of the couch. "What if I did?"

"I'd want to know why."

"Because you didn't have one, I guess."

"So?"

"I didn't like it that you didn't have one."

Their eyes met and locked, and a provocative smile slowly curved her lips. "If I wasn't Red's daughter, would you want to spend time with me, Mike?"

"Yes."

Her lips parted and her eyes widened when he answered so quickly; he'd shocked her a little.

"And it would help if you were about ten years older, too," he added.

"My age bothers you?"

"I'm too old to...spend time with you," he finished, borrowing her words.

"Who says? We're both adults."

He was glad, at this point, that he'd refused the wine. "Who did you want to see at the Smalls?"

"Dave."

"Why?"

She shrugged. "I haven't seen him since I left."

"What's that supposed to mean?"

"I was just wondering how he's doing, what kind of person he is." She propped her chin on her knees. "Do you like Dave?"

Mike generally kept his feelings about other people to himself. "I don't have much to do with him."

"You're avoiding the question."

"Okay, I don't particularly like him. Do you?"

"I don't know." She bit her lip, then took the conversation in a whole new direction. "Have you ever been in love, Mike?"

He coughed in surprise. "What does that have to do with Dave?"

"Nothing."

She didn't apologize for the question or retract it, and Mike found himself considering the women he'd dated and sometimes slept with. Had he been in love, or had he simply cared for them? "I don't think so."

"Not even with Lindsey Carpenter?"

"Maybe with Lindsey Carpenter, but it didn't last, and I don't remember feeling too bad when she broke things off."

"I always thought you loved her."

"Why?"

"I thought you'd have to love her to kiss her that way."

"You saw me kiss Lindsey?"

"When I was sixteen."

"Are you saying you used to spy on me?"

She chuckled. "Not exclusively. I just loved going over to your place, being with the horses, hearing the cowboys talk back and forth." She hesitated, then said more softly, "Knowing you were close by."

Her admission evoked a protectiveness he knew he was better off not feeling. "Why did you want to see Dave?" he asked, heading back to safer ground.

She let go of her legs and grabbed a throw pillow instead. "Can I trust you not to tell anyone?"

A funny feeling washed over Mike, something that warned him not to commit himself. He was already far too sympathetic to her, didn't need anything else to soften his heart. But he didn't feel any particular loyalty to the Smalls, so he figured he wasn't taking much of a risk. Besides, she'd kept the secret of their rendezvous at the motel. He could certainly keep a secret for her. "Sure."

She gave up on the throw pillow and reached up to twist her long hair into a knot. "He slept with my mother twenty-five years ago."

He tried not to notice how her breasts lifted as she moved, and concentrated instead on the relief going through him. This news didn't really surprise him. A lot of people had slept with Red. Maybe Dave tried to present himself as a paragon of virtue, but Mike knew he generally did whatever he could get away with. "Why is his contact with your mother of more interest than anyone else's?"

"Because he could be my father."

That took a moment to sink in. Her *father?* Mike had always just accepted that Lucky had no father. He'd never dreamed that it could be someone well-known, someone who was married at the time she was conceived. But it made sense now that he thought about it. Red had slept with a good number of men, and they weren't all single. Take his grandfather, for example.

Finally, he gave a low whistle. "Have you told him?"

"No."

"Are you going to?"

She got up and poured herself a glass of wine. "I don't know. Maybe. I haven't decided. I only found out a few months ago."

"That's why you came back here," he said as understanding dawned.

"See? I tried to tell you I didn't come back just to torture you and your family."

"Is that why you're telling me about Dave, to put me at ease?"

"Were you nervous?"

He wasn't nervous. He just hated being in the middle. And, in some ways, her real motivation made him even more uncomfortable. Digging up the secrets of the past was never a very safe occupation. And yet he had a tough time begrudging her that information, when it was only natural she'd want to know. "Not exactly. How'd you learn about Dave?"

"My mother kept a journal."

Mike remembered the black book Lucky had tucked under her coat when he'd taken her into town during the storm and suddenly understood what it was and why she'd considered it important enough to retrieve. But what she'd said had him seriously concerned, for Lucky and for Dave. "You need to be careful, Lucky. I wouldn't tell anyone. Dave's too ambitious."

"I can take care of myself."

"He has a lot of family here."

"So do you. And I've managed to get by in spite of all of them."

"Dealing with my family doesn't qualify you to take on the world."

"Tell me something," she said.

"What's that?"

"If you could have anything you want for Christmas, what would it be? A new stallion?"

He couldn't answer that without revealing too much. The only thing he seemed to want this Christmas was another night with her. "I don't know. What about you?"

"I'm happy with my tree."

He grinned—and loved the smile she gave him in return.

"Will you help me decorate it?"

Mike told himself he'd be a fool to stay any longer. He

probably shouldn't have come here in the first place. But helping her with the tree seemed so innocuous. What was another hour or two?

LUCKY DIDN'T HAVE a stereo, so Mike went home to get a boom box. He said the people in the office had been listening to Christmas music for weeks and proved it by bringing over several holiday CDs, which he put on while they worked. He cursed when a strand of lights he'd weaved through the topmost branches wouldn't turn on, which meant he'd have to take them all off, but when Lucky laughed at him, he started laughing, too.

"And this's supposed to be fun?" he grumbled.

Lucky was having fun. Mike had acted pretty cautious and self-contained at first, but as the minutes passed and they talked about everything from the ranch and his horses to the annual rodeo, he seemed to relax.

"You want the silver balls to go on the tree, too?" he asked.

She didn't have the heart to tell him they didn't match. "Sure," she said and they loaded the tree with everything in the box. The angel that went on top had a beautiful porcelain face and slowly moved, waving two little lights in her tiny hands.

When they sat on the floor together an hour later, admiring their efforts, she glanced over at him. "Are you hungry?"

He checked his watch. She sensed that he was growing wary again and expected him to say something about going home, but he surprised her. "What do you have to eat?"

"I could make a quick pasta."

"Sure," he said, "why not?" He followed her to the kitchen, where he stood near the island, talking to her while she cooked.

When it was ready, she lit a couple of candles for the table and sat across from him. He refused a glass of wine, for the second time, but ate two platefuls of pasta. While they ate,

Lucky told him about some of the places she'd visited and some of the people she'd met. The conversation remained fairly light until she stood up to carry their dishes to the sink.

"Why didn't you tell my father about us that day in the hardware store, Lucky?" he asked.

She piled the plates on the counter. "Why would I?"

"Because it'd prove that you're not what folks think."

"What do folks think?"

"That you're exactly like your mother."

"How will telling them I've slept with you change that?" she asked.

"*I* know you were a virgin."

"So? You could always deny it."

"I wouldn't."

Silence stretched between them, and the scenes from the motel—the memories she'd been trying to ignore all evening—grew more vivid in Lucky's mind. Earlier, he'd called that night "unforgettable." She wondered if he was remembering it now. "People around here have known you, looked up to you, all your life," she said. "They'd be shocked and… and disappointed to learn about the motel."

"Maybe. But I wouldn't lie about it. You know that, don't you?"

"I won't use you to build my own credibility." She started running hot water in the sink. "You're crazy to even suggest it. What if I were to take you up on the idea?"

"You won't," he said.

"How do you know?"

"Because you'd have done it by now."

Their eyes met, and Lucky felt a tremor of excitement and desire pass through her. She'd never purposely do anything that might compromise him, regardless of his family, the past, her own situation. But she didn't say so. She felt far too vulnerable and exposed already—and feared he was beginning to suspect how deeply she cared. "Thanks for your help with the tree," she said to cover her weakness for him.

Taking her cue, he stood up and collected his hat.

Lucky wanted him to stay. She suspected he wanted the same thing. But she also knew because of how careful he'd been this evening that he'd already chosen his family. She'd never expected him to choose differently. She even admired his loyalty.

"Dinner was excellent," he said.

She dried her hands so she could show him out. "You earned it."

When they reached the front door, she turned on the porch light so he could see, but he flipped it off again. Then he pulled her to him and kissed her lightly on the lips before he left.

Apparently he'd decided to allow himself one more concession.

DURING THE NEXT TWO DAYS, Lucky did her Christmas shopping in Boise and overnighted the Lego sets she'd bought for her three nephews, the softball glove and slider she'd bought for her oldest niece and the Barbies she'd bought for Trisha, Sean's five-year-old daughter. Mr. Sharp made noticeable progress on the house, too. Lucky told herself everything was going well. But that wasn't completely true. She hadn't heard from Mike since they'd decorated her tree. And she was finding it difficult to get close to any of the men who might be her father, so difficult that she'd started toying with the idea of calling Garth Holbrook at his office. From what she could tell, he seemed like a decent man. If they could have a private conversation, she'd ask him if he'd be willing to take a paternity test.

Lucky went through every approach she could imagine before actually picking up the phone.

The worst he can say is no, she reminded herself. "No" wouldn't make a big impact on her life. She'd never had a father before; "no" simply meant nothing would change. If he refused, or his DNA sample didn't match, she'd approach Dave Small. If Dave refused or his sample didn't match, she'd put more effort into tracking down Eugene Thompson. It was a straightforward process of elimination, right?

Still, her heart seemed to rattle around in her chest while she dialed and waited for Holbrook's secretary to pick up.

Finally she heard a melodic voice say, "Senator Holbrook's office."

Lucky could barely squeeze enough air into her lungs to speak. "Is the senator in?"

"He is, but he's on another call. Can I take a message?"

Squeezing the phone in a death grip, Lucky hesitated. "Could I hold, please?"

"Certainly. Your name?"

"Lucky Caldwell."

"May I tell Senator Holbrook what your call is regarding?"

"It's…a private matter."

The other woman's pause indicated that she wasn't pleased with her response. "Does the senator know you?" she asked cautiously.

No. She and Garth Holbrook had never exchanged the most basic of greetings, which would only make this woman that much more reluctant to pass on her message. And if Garth recognized her name and connected her to her mother, he might not accept the call even if he got the message. "Just tell him it's important."

"One moment."

Lucky paced in agitation as two minutes turned into three and three into four. When she'd been holding for nearly ten minutes, she began to think she'd been forgotten, but his secretary came back on the line right before she gave up.

"I'm sorry, Ms. Caldwell, Senator Holbrook told me to tell you he's late for a luncheon appointment and will have to call you later."

She was getting the brush-off; she was sure of it. Disappointment brought Lucky's agitated movements to a halt, and she sank onto the couch. "Fine, no problem," she said. But when she hung up she doubted she'd ever hear from Senator Garth Holbrook.

PARKED IN THE UNDERGROUND LOT beneath the building where his office was located, Garth Holbrook sat in his black Lincoln Navigator and stared down at the message he'd crumpled in his palm. After twenty-five *years*—just when he'd begun to believe he could forget—Red's daughter had contacted him. Why? What could she possibly want?

"Private," he muttered, reading his secretary's rolling script.

Lucky knew about him and her mother. She had to know. What other private matter did they have to discuss? Why else would she call him out of the blue when they'd never so much as spoken? From what he'd heard about her, she was a gold digger of the first order, like her mother had turned out to be. She was probably going to make him pay dearly for her silence in order to save his career. But he wasn't worried about his career. Not as much as he was worried about his family.

Crumpling the message in his fist once again, Garth thought of Gabe and cringed. Since the accident, Garth was the only person Gabe would open up to. If Lucky told anyone what she most likely knew, it would destroy his relationship with his son. Gabe would retreat even further into himself. And what about Reenie? Hardheaded, outspoken

Reenie would conclude that she didn't know her own father. She'd *hate* him.

And for good reason. His torrid affair with Red had lasted nearly two months. He'd betrayed them all, again and again— just for a little of the raunchy, sweaty sex his wife abhorred.

Panic clutched at Garth's chest, and he scrambled to loosen the blasted tie that seemed to be choking him. So what if those two months were his only indiscretion. So what if he'd tried to compensate his wife and children for his foolish blunder, tried in a million different ways. They wouldn't realize that. And he couldn't, *wouldn't,* disgrace Celeste or himself by telling his children how dissatisfied he'd always been with her on a sexual level.

So what, then? What did he do?

Dropping his head in his hand, he sighed heavily. He had to call Lucky before she tried to contact him again, or started spreading what she knew. For Gabe and Reenie's sake, he had to move quickly.

CHAPTER THIRTEEN

LUCKY HAD HER HEAD and part of her upper body in the cupboard beside the stove when the phone rang. Since Mr. Sharp had stopped work for the holidays, she'd been cleaning the nooks and crannies of the house and doing some of the painting.

"Hello?" she said, grabbing the phone on its fifth ring.

"Ms. Caldwell?"

Her breath caught in her throat. It was a voice she didn't recognize, an older, gravelly voice she felt sure belonged to Senator Holbrook.

"Yes?" she said hesitantly.

"This is Garth Holbrook."

God, she was right; she had him on the phone. This man could be her father. Of the three possibilities, she had her hopes pinned on him.

But what now? What did she say?

"Ms. Caldwell? Are you still there?"

"Yes, I'm here, sorry."

"I got your message."

And now she had the audience she desired. She could hardly believe it. "Senator Holbrook, do you know who I am?"

"Yes."

She couldn't read the emotion behind that one word, but she sensed something far from passive. "Well, first off, I want to assure you that I'm not trying to make trouble for you or anyone else."

"Of course not," he said.

The sarcasm in those words made Lucky rush to explain. "I found your name listed in my mother's journal from twenty-five years ago, and was just—"

"She kept a journal?"

"Yes."

He swore softly under his breath, and Lucky winced even though she'd expected him to be upset. How many men wanted the fact that they'd broken their marriage vows recorded? And he was a politician, which made him especially vulnerable.

"How much do you want for it?" he asked.

"Excuse me?"

"How much are you asking for the journal?"

"I'm not asking anything for it. It's not for sale."

"Then why did you call?"

Lucky gathered her nerve. "I was hoping that maybe you'd be willing to…to take a paternity test." Curling her nails into the palm of her hand, she squeezed her eyes shut as she waited for his response.

"You're kidding. You think there's a chance… No. That isn't possible."

"Actually, you were with my mother right around the time I was conceived and—"

"Listen, I'm not your father. I might have been a fool, but I wasn't irresponsible enough to get her pregnant."

"She told you she was on the pill, right?"

Fear dug deep into Holbrook's soul—Lucky could feel it through the phone, could almost hear him asking himself if Red had lied about birth control. But what she'd intimated only made him angry.

"What's the real story here? Morris's money isn't enough for you? Now you've got to come after *me*?"

"I'm—"

"Just tell me what it's going to take to make you leave me alone. A hundred thousand? Two hundred thousand?"

She couldn't respond right away. Despite all the self-talk of the past few months, she must've hoped for a better response because she felt crushed by the anger and contempt in his reaction. "I don't want your money," she said softly and hung up.

THE MUSIC FROM the Honky Tonk spilled into the street every time someone opened the door. Lucky was drawn by the beat of Toby Keith's "I Love This Bar," and the happy voices that both sang and competed with his recording. Yet she hung back in the shadows of the tavern's porch, wondering if she was doing the right thing by coming here. The Honky Tonk was a popular local hangout where she could chance upon just about anybody, which was why she'd avoided it until now. But she knew it wasn't wise to stay at home alone. Especially after her disappointing telephone conversation with Garth Holbrook this afternoon. She'd secluded herself for too long as it was. She needed to be around people, even if those people were from Dundee and didn't care much for her. Even if she was just an onlooker. Besides, she didn't have to worry about anyone being unwelcoming. At this hour, most of the Honky Tonk's patrons would be too drunk to bother with her. She'd waited until nearly eleven o'clock just to insure it.

"You comin' in, little lady?"

A tall man in a taupe cowboy hat had spotted her and held the door expectantly.

Little lady. Mike had called her that her first night back in town.

A grudging smile claimed Lucky's lips as she finally emerged from the deeper recesses of the porch. Dundee was so different from the cities she'd visited, particularly back East—Boston, New York, Philadelphia. No one ever said "little lady" in those places.

"Thanks." She drew a deep breath before stepping into the dark, noisy tavern.

Someone from a table to the right immediately hailed the man who'd held the door for her. He tipped his hat at her before striding off to join them, and she hurried to the bar, where she planned to get lost in the crowd and enjoy the heat and energy of the place. But no sooner had she taken a seat than Jon Small tapped her on the shoulder.

"Hey, I've been hoping to run into you again. How's it goin'?"

Lucky glanced longingly at the college football game playing on the television to her left. "Fine, and you?"

"My ex is suing me for more child support, but other than that…"

"I'm sorry your divorce has been so difficult."

His face darkened. "I never would've expected it from Leah. She was always so…mousy. Couldn't even decide where to go for dinner." He shook his head. "I guess people change, huh? I just never saw it coming."

Lucky had no comment. She didn't know Leah, and the bartender was moving in her direction.

"Can I get you something to drink?"

She ordered a glass of wine, but as soon as the bartender turned away, Jon invited her to dance.

Lucky didn't want to get out in front of people. She craved some of that anonymity she'd enjoyed at half the sports bars across America. But he was already tugging on her hand.

"Come on. You're the prettiest girl in town, and I could use a little distraction."

His slurred words told Lucky he'd had quite a bit to drink. She was afraid it might cause more of a scene to tell him no than to simply dance with him and get it over with.

Allowing him to lead her to the edge of the floor, she looped her arms loosely around his neck. Faith Hill was singing now and the tempo had slowed.

"How do you like being back?" he asked.

"It's great," she lied.

"There's no place like Dundee."

A quick glance at his face told her he meant it. "I guess."

"There's room to breathe out here, to spread out, to be yourself."

"Maybe if your father's name is Dave Small," she muttered.

He grinned. "I guess it doesn't hurt that my father's something of a local celebrity."

"Do you admire him a great deal?" she asked, suddenly hoping Garth Holbrook wasn't her father, after all. Maybe it was Dave Small or even Eugene Thompson….

"I guess. He was strict growing up, but he's mellowed a lot."

"I've never met him."

Jon jerked his head toward some tables by the jukebox. "He's here tonight. I can introduce you if you like."

Lucky thought she should give herself time to file away Senator Holbrook's rejection first, but she didn't have the opportunity to speak to Dave every day. And it wasn't as if she'd mention her mother or the journal. After this morning, she had no further plans to take the direct approach. She'd just say a few words, see what Dave was like….

"Okay," she said.

She and Jon spoke little after that, but when the dance ended, he pulled her along behind him toward the table he'd indicated a few minutes earlier.

Dave looked up when they approached, and so did Smal-

ley, who sat on the other side of his father. Smalley's incredible size made it easy for Lucky to recognize him, although
she hadn't seen him in years. He hadn't been present at the
family gathering she'd watched last Sunday.

Two other men had just left the table to play billiards. Jon
yanked out one of the empty chairs and waved Lucky into it.

"Who have we here?" Dave asked when she sat down.

"Lucky Caldwell," Jon said. "She wants to meet you."

Dave's smile tightened the moment he heard her name. At
Jon's added comment about her wanting to meet him, the
warmth fled his eyes. "You must be Red's daughter."

Lucky noted the condescension in his voice and refused to
drop her gaze. "Yes, I am."

"I heard you were back."

"Who from?"

He shrugged. "Can't remember. It's my business to know
what's happening in our little town."

Lucky couldn't see how her return could possibly affect
anything at City Hall and was quickly coming to realize why
Booker Robinson had called this man arrogant.

The mysterious Eugene Thompson suddenly seemed like
the best father candidate Lucky had. She could already tell she
didn't want to be related to Dave Small. "Is my being here a
matter of public concern?" she asked.

Dave took a drink of the clear liquid in his glass, which had
to be tequila. Lucky could smell it from where she sat. "I guess
it is to the Caldwells," he said. "And the Hills."

"You're friends with them?"

"We speak now and then." He leaned a little closer. "And
I have to tell you, I don't understand, any more than they do,
why the hell you'd come back here."

Finally Jon seemed to notice that his father's conversation
with Lucky wasn't all that friendly and stopped grinning like

a fool. "Here, I'll buy you a drink at the bar," he told her, standing up and taking her elbow.

Lucky jerked out of his grasp. "I have every right to come back," she told Dave. "I own property here."

"Not as much as they do. And what you do have should belong to them." He took another drink. The clack of his glass hitting the table served as his exclamation point.

"Morris must've wanted me to have the house or he wouldn't have left it to me," she said.

Dave chuckled. "Yeah, that mama of yours…" He whistled. "She was a smart one, wasn't she? Figured out how to work a situation to her advantage."

"You should know," Lucky said, lowering her voice even further. "You visited her often enough."

When the color drained from Dave's face, Smalley knew he'd missed something significant and leaned forward, over his huge stomach. "What'd you say?" he asked, his dark beady eyes darting curiously between them.

Jon had been standing up, out of earshot. He seemed to care more about getting Lucky away from the table than hearing what he'd missed. Maybe Dave could afford the luxury of being choosy, but after his painful divorce, Jon was obviously too lonely for snobbery and made it quite clear that he didn't want his father to offend Lucky.

"You don't know that," Dave growled to her alone. "I don't *ever* want to hear you say something like that again. I'll deny it to my dying day."

Lucky stood and moved close enough to whisper in his ear. She didn't plan on using her mother's journal as a weapon, had no intention of causing trouble here in Dundee, but she couldn't resist putting Dave Small in his place. "Deny it all you want," she said calmly. "I have proof."

LUCKY WAS SO ANGRY she could feel the blood rushing through her veins. She wanted to stalk out of the bar and head home immediately, pack her belongings and leave this town—forever. But she refused to let anyone chase her away. Especially a hypocrite like Dave Small. And she knew after rambling from one place to another that she wouldn't feel much more satisfied anywhere else.

She could feel Dave's heated glare on the back of her head as she sat at the bar, feigning indifference while she sipped her wine. She glanced over her shoulder a few times to challenge that glare, just so he'd know she wasn't intimidated, and ended up catching Jon's eye a time or two instead. He'd tried to follow her when she left the table, but his father had commanded him, as if he were a dog, to stay. After a brief moment, when Lucky thought Jon might actually defy Dave and earn a bit of her respect, he'd slumped into a seat at his father's elbow.

"Can I get you anything else?" the bartender asked.

Lucky didn't drink much, but she was certainly drinking tonight. She wouldn't allow herself to leave until the Smalls did, and she needed something to occupy her hands. Especially when she realized that Mike Hill was sitting over by the billiard tables. She didn't know if he'd come in before or after she did, but she definitely knew he'd spotted her. Almost every time she looked up, she caught his eye in the mirror behind the bar.

What a night, she thought, wishing she'd stayed home after all. She ordered another bourbon, and when a young cowboy approached and asked her to dance, she decided to pretend she was having a damn good time.

IT WAS MIKE'S JOB to entertain clients when they flew in from out of town. Ever since Josh had gotten married, Mike had more free evenings than his brother did and generally enjoyed taking folks out to eat or over to the Honky Tonk for a few drinks. But he wasn't in the mood for billiards or darts tonight. He wasn't even in the mood for conversation. Not since he'd seen Lucky walk through the door.

He let his focus stray to the dance floor again, where she was swaying to a slow song with a handsome man at least ten years younger than he was—and wished it wasn't bothering him that they seemed to be dancing a bit too close.

"Why so quiet?" Gabe asked, eyeing him suspiciously.

Mike pulled his gaze away from Lucky. Gabe had let the incident in the diner go without comment, but there was still a great deal of tension between them. Mike suspected that he'd only agreed to accompany him tonight because their guests were a father-and-son duo from up in the panhandle who had a lot of land and even more money—perfect fundraising targets.

"I'm a little tired." And feeling old, Mike added silently. Watching Lucky move to the music in the arms of a much younger man reminded him that there were fifteen years between them—a decade and a half. As if that wasn't bad enough, the shoulder he'd injured in a rodeo accident several years back suddenly began to ache.

He needed to get his mind off Lucky and the memories they'd so recently created, memories in which he felt anything but old. "You think they'll contribute to the campaign?" he asked, jerking his head toward his guests, who were taking on Vern Pruitt and Cliff Peterson in a game of pool.

Gabe considered the four men surrounding the billiards table and shrugged. "They said they'd like to meet my father in the morning. I guess we'll find out then."

"Sounds fair." Mike's gaze returned to the dance floor to see Lucky sidling up to her partner for another dance.

Damn, he hated it.

"Mike?"

"What?" Mike masked the frown tempting the corners of his mouth and looked back to find Gabe studying him closely.

"The redhead you're watching is Lucky Caldwell. You know that, don't you?"

Mike wasn't likely to ever mistake Lucky for someone else, not since that first night when he'd pressed her up against the wall. "I know. I've already bumped into her a couple of times."

"Then why are you so fascinated with her?"

"I'm not fascinated with her."

Gabe's eyes sparkled with mischief for the first time in months, but Mike could hardly take it as a victory over that damn wheelchair when his friend's amusement came at his expense. "She's attractive, don't you think?"

Mike could tell it was a loaded question, so he sidestepped it the best he could. "She's young."

"I didn't ask about her age."

"It matters, don't you think?"

"I think what matters more is that you're avoiding the real issue."

"Which is…"

"You can't get involved with her. Your parents, your whole extended family, would disown you."

Mike wondered what Gabe would say if he knew the truth. He'd already been "involved" with her in the most intimate way. And Lucky could have shouted it from the rooftops. But she hadn't. She'd kept it to herself and acted as though it had never happened. He still couldn't figure out what had drawn her to his room in the first place. Why did she wait all those years and then slip into *his* bed? If he hadn't been monitoring his thoughts so carefully, he would've asked her that night they'd decorated the tree.

"I'm nearly forty years old," he pointed out. "I'm not going to let my family dictate what I do."

Gabe seemed to sober. "A man never quits belonging to his family, Mike. Especially out here. Something like this happens to you—" his jaw clenched as he motioned to his chair "—you learn pretty damn fast that everything else is smoke and mirrors. Fame. Money. Success. You realize that life is fleeting and family's what it's all about. It's the only thing that matters."

Mike rubbed his neck, feeling guilty for not keeping his distance from Lucky when he knew that associating with her would hurt the people he cared about most. Even that night they'd decorated the tree had been a mistake, because he felt he knew her so much better, liked her so much more.

When he didn't immediately capitulate, Gabe maneuvered his chair around the leg of the table and lowered his voice. "You get with Lucky, and it'll divide this town in two."

A woman at the next table offered Gabe a hopeful smile—proof to Mike that plenty of pretty women still found Gabe attractive—but his friend ignored her completely and lowered his voice even more, to keep her from overhearing. "Believe me, Mike, as hot as Lucky is, she's not worth it. Look what happened to your grandfather. He fell blindly in love and caused a whole lot of heartache for absolutely everyone in his family, including you. You can bet he regretted that heartache later."

Mike remembered how bitterly his grandfather had wept not long before he passed away.

"If Morris were around, I'm sure he'd back me up on this one," Gabe added.

"Morris loved Lucky."

"I'm sure he did. But she's not for you."

Mike touched the condensation on his glass, telling himself he should just nod and ignore it, but he couldn't. "What if everyone's wrong about her?" he asked.

"In what way?"

"They think she's this…materialistic, self-serving woman out to gain advantage in the world any way she can."

"Sort of like her mother?" Gabe eased back to his normal distance and lifted his beer.

"Exactly like her mother."

"Six years ago Lucky walked off with a sizeable portion of your inheritance. So I wonder where they got that idea."

Mike raised his eyebrows at his friend's sarcasm. "I've survived."

"No thanks to her."

"You're sounding like my family."

"I'm playing devil's advocate. You used to agree with them about Red and her children. I'm wondering why you've suddenly changed your mind."

"I see things a little differently now, that's all."

"Are you telling me Lucky's sweet and innocent?"

Mike jammed a hand through his hair. "Not sweet exactly." He purposely didn't address the "innocent" part. Until he'd accepted her into his bed, she'd been innocent in at least one way—but he definitely wanted to skip that when talking to Gabe. "She's angry and resentful."

"Sounds pleasant."

"Would you feel any differently in her shoes? She's been ostracized and rejected most of her life. Maybe she's grown defensive in order to survive."

"So now you admire her?"

Mike didn't know how to describe his feelings for her. He kept telling himself he didn't have any, at least none that went very deep. He was simply attracted to her. She was different from other women he knew, tough to read, tougher to reach, sometimes belligerent, often remote. Certainly there were less complicated women to want. But—he thought of that night they'd decorated the tree—she needed him, and he wanted to be there for her.

God, what was he thinking? He had to be drunk.

Shoving away from the table, he got up to play some pool before he said something *really* stupid.

CHAPTER FOURTEEN

LUCKY BENT over the bathroom sink so the room would stop spinning, and splashed her heated face. She was feeling a little lightheaded. She wasn't used to drinking and would probably pay in the morning when she woke up with a bad hangover. But at least she wasn't *pretending* to have a good time anymore. The pain and anger of this night were receding; she almost couldn't remember why she'd been so upset in the first place. Who was Dave Small to make her feel cheap and unworthy? She didn't need him; she didn't need anyone. Even the handsome Alex Riley, the cowboy who'd stuck close to her all evening and was waiting at the bar for her to play a game of darts, didn't really mean anything to her.

She liked it that way, she decided. She couldn't get hurt if she didn't care.

Leaning closer to the mirror, she studied the glassy eyes staring back at her. She was fine. Aloof. Anonymous. Indifferent. She could tolerate Dundee; she was just as tough as everyone else in these parts. Tougher, because she'd been through so much. Yet the fleeting memory of Mike standing next to his father at the hardware store still stung, so she quickly banished it.

"See? That was easy," she told her reflection. Then she staggered out—and nearly hit herself with the door.

"Whoops." She laughed at her own clumsiness, but her

smile disappeared when a man yanked her into the dark hall, causing her to smack her head on the pay phone.

"Ow," she complained. "What's—"

"What kind of proof?" Whoever held her pinned between the phone and the wall smelled of alcohol and stale sweat.

Lucky blinked and tried to distinguish the face swimming above her own. She couldn't make out the specific features, but judging by the man's size, it had to be Smalley.

"*What?*" she replied in confusion.

"My father wants to know what you have."

"So he sent his own son to find out the dirty details? Doesn't he care about your opinion of him?"

"I don't give a damn if he slept with your mama. You think that's news to us? Well, it ain't. He's a man, and a man has needs. It's that simple."

"What about your mother's needs?" she asked dryly, beginning to sober.

"It's nothing against my mother. And I'm not gonna let you make it something, either. A man's private business is a man's private business."

"Your father's a public figure, which changes the rules a bit." Lucky tried to jerk away, but he had too strong a grasp on her arm and seemed to be enjoying the way his jagged fingernails bit into her flesh.

Revealing wide-spaced, plaque-covered teeth that made her wonder how his wife ever kissed him, he grinned. "My father has an impeccable reputation, and that's how it's going to stay. It's nothing that he slept with Red. Hell, everyone slept with her, even me and my brother. A whore's a whore."

Remembering the journal entry labeled "Graduation Night," which included Jon and Smalley's names, brought bile to the back of Lucky's throat. She knew she was nothing like her mother, that she and Red had never understood each other, but that fact was never more apparent than at this moment. "Let go of me, you idiot."

Grabbing her by the hair, Smalley banged her head against the pay phone—harder this time, so the dim light above them began to swirl and his voice ebbed in and out. "If you think I'm going to let a whore's daughter ruin my daddy's career, you've got another think comin', sweetheart."

Lucky's knees buckled and she began to sag.

"Just remember—you'd better mind your p's and q's, little Miss Lucky, or your luck's gonna run out."

With that he let her go and she slid down the wall.

BOOT HEELS THUDDING on wooden boards cut through the fog in Lucky's brain, and a swaying sensation nearly made her sick. But that wasn't all that seemed strange. The music of the Honky Tonk was drifting away from her, along with its heat, leaving her cold and shivery and wondering why she felt so weightless.

Opening her eyes, she saw that she was no longer even *in* the Honky Tonk. She was being carried across the porch and through the gravel lot by none other than Mike Hill.

When had he come out of his corner to get her? What had happened?

Wincing at the pain that seemed to be keeping time with his footsteps, she squirmed so he'd let her down.

"Hold still before I drop you," he said, his tone gruff.

Lucky stopped moving, but not because he commanded it. She'd realized almost instantly that she didn't have the strength to stand yet and didn't want to crumple to the ground in front of him. The cold, starlit sky spun around her, and nausea rose and fell in her stomach like great waves.

"What happened?" She let her head fall back against him because it suddenly seemed too heavy for her neck.

"Nothing too earth-shattering," he responded, his voice

rumbling through his chest. "From what I can tell, you got drunk and passed out and have a nasty bump to prove it. When you went to the rest room, you never came back. I nearly stepped on you when I went to see why."

He was talking too fast. "I passed out?"

"Does that surprise you?"

"Considering I've never passed out before in my life, yes."

"That's what happens when you drink too much."

"I *never* drink too much."

"You did tonight."

She thought about that for a moment. "But am I supposed to have a hangover while I'm still drunk?"

"I don't think alcohol agrees with you."

"It agreed with me just fine until—" Suddenly, the memory of Smalley leaning over her, his hand squeezing her upper arm, came back.

"Until what?" he said, his breathing growing slightly labored as they neared his SUV.

"Never mind. Put me down. I'm fine. My car's not far. I can make my own way home from here."

He braced her against his Escalade while digging in his pocket.

"Mike?" she said when he made no move to release her.

"You can't drive." He came up with his keys and popped the locks.

"Then leave me here if I'm so drunk. I'll go inside and get a cup of coffee, sit awhile until I sober up." And try to avoid Smalley and his brother and father....

Mike managed to get the door open, then pushed her into the passenger seat of his SUV.

The interior smelled like aftershave and leather. She was tempted to close her eyes and lie back on the seat. But she remembered all too vividly what had happened the last time she'd let him take care of her—and how carefully he'd kept his distance since then.

Would you want to spend more time with me if I wasn't Red's daughter?...Yes.

Which meant the opposite was also true.

"If you're not careful, you could be *seen* with me," she warned as he fastened her seat belt. "And we wouldn't want that. Other people might figure you sort of like me. You could lose head-honcho status in the We Hate Lucky fan club."

He grimaced at her sarcasm. "You're not a pleasant person when you're drunk."

"That's pretty funny, since it doesn't seem to make any difference whether I'm pleasant or not," she said, but her head hurt too much to laugh—or even to angle her face to observe his response.

He hesitated as if he wanted to say something else. She glanced up expectantly despite the pain, but he simply clenched his jaw and slammed the door.

"What about my car?" she asked when he climbed behind the wheel.

"What about it?"

"I can't leave it here."

"Why not?"

"People will think I'm sleeping around, that...that... Well, they'd never believe I went home with *you*, but they'll think I went home with *someone*."

His eyebrows shot up. "And considering what they already think, that matters to you?"

"Of course it matters."

"Why? In the past you reveled in your bad reputation."

"I only let people think what they want to think," she grumbled. "The fact that there's no real basis for their beliefs makes them look like idiots."

He started the car, backed out and turned onto Main Street. "So you're laughing at us?"

"Laughing?" she said incredulously. "I haven't been laughing at all."

The seriousness of her answer somehow changed the mood in the Escalade and gave Lucky the impression that she might be giving away too much. "I'll finish this conversation when I'm sober."

"Is that why you waited?"

"For what?"

"You held on to your virginity until you were twenty-four just so you could snicker behind everyone's back?"

She'd hung on to her virginity for so long to prove to herself that she wasn't anything like her mother. But she couldn't explain that to Mike. It was a complex issue she wasn't sure she understood herself. She'd just needed to wait.

For the right man, a voice in her head whispered.

She tried to block it out. "Maybe," she said. Propping her chin on her fist, she stared out the window as the businesses flew by, all closed and dark now.

"And is that why you came to my room that night at my place? To show me what an idiot I've been?"

She scowled. "No."

"Then why?"

The alcohol she'd had earlier was starting to do its job again now that she was getting warm. Despite the incident with Smalley, a peaceful serenity stole through her body. She was tired; she wanted to sleep. But the best part of this euphoric state was that she didn't have to think about Garth Holbrook, Dave Small and his "boys," the Caldwells, or even the approach of Christmas.

"Lucky?"

"What?" she murmured, struggling to keep her eyes open.

"Tell me why you came to my room the night of the storm."

She felt her eyes close and once again remembered seeing him kiss Lindsey Carpenter in the barn. That memory was like a favorite dog-eared book—she never tired of it. And now she had her own chapter in that book, which was infinitely more enjoyable than any fantasy could ever be....

"Why'd you come to my room?" he prodded gently, his voice coaxing, curious.

Finally, she turned to him and let a nostalgic smile curve her lips. "Because I'd dreamed of making love with you for years," she said wistfully. "It wouldn't have been the same with anyone else."

Surprise lit his face.

God, had she said that out loud?

"I didn't mean it," she said quickly, alarm chasing away the contentment filling her only moments earlier. "Quit harassing me. I'm drunk. I don't know what I'm saying. I've always hated you, and your family, and everyone in this town. I...I'm leaving soon and that night doesn't matter. I just waited, okay? I don't know why. So don't think otherwise."

A frown settled on his face, but he did nothing to reveal his thoughts, and when he pulled into her drive, she couldn't scramble out of his SUV fast enough.

"Wait a second," he said.

"What?"

"You didn't tell Dave about the journal, did you?"

She didn't answer right away.

"Lucky?"

"No." Not *technically,* she added silently.

"Good. Give me your keys. In the morning I'll have Fernando help me retrieve your car."

She dug in her purse and handed him the keys, then ran for the house.

MIKE WANTED TO FOLLOW Lucky inside. Only Gabe's voice, telling him he'd divide the town if he ever allowed himself to get involved with her, kept him behind the wheel and eventually motivated him to turn around and head home. Gabe was right. His family mattered.

But Lucky was starting to matter, too. At least to him. So much so that he hadn't thought twice about leaving his guests behind for Gabe to bring home. Or about the extra trouble of getting Lucky's car from the Honky Tonk come morning. When he'd found her lying on the dirty floor in that dim hallway, he'd thought she was hurt. He'd seen her talking to Dave Small earlier and wondered if she'd told him about the journal. His heart had begun to jackhammer against his ribs, and his throat had constricted until he could hardly swallow. He'd felt a surge of relief when he realized she was only drunk. But he couldn't leave her to her own devices. He was afraid she'd get behind the wheel and possibly kill herself, or let the handsome cowboy she'd been dancing with take her home.

He felt another trickle of jealousy.

He should never have helped her during the storm; he should never have gone to the motel or bought her a silly Christmas tree. Somehow she'd claimed a piece of his heart, and damned if he knew how to get it back.

I'd dreamed of making love with you for years....

Something quick and powerful had passed between them when she'd made that admission. She'd looked up as if she was shocked she'd let the words escape, and he'd seen a soul-deep hunger in her eyes. Before he could react, the shield of belligerence and indifference Lucky used to keep others at a distance had snapped back into place and she'd begun to vehemently deny what she'd already stated so clearly. But Mike was beginning to understand. The harshness of her words—

her whole belligerent attitude, really—concealed a vulnerability she didn't want him or anyone else to know she possessed.

She wasn't what his family believed. But he knew they'd already made up their minds about her and would never be willing to see her any differently. Hell, they'd probably hate her even if he could prove she was a saint.

With a sigh, he pulled up in front of his house and cut the engine.

He felt a growing suspicion that Lucky was a deep, loyal, generous woman. He was becoming more convinced of that every day. But this time, being right wasn't going to matter.

LUCKY WOKE with a headache, a reluctance to remember last night, and a sickening surprise on her front porch. Someone had stuck a crudely made sign that said, Go Away Bitch, in a dog pile and placed it just outside her front door. She was sure one of the Smalls had left it, but the negative sentiments they expressed seemed to hit her harder than usual. Maybe that was because it was only three days before Christmas, a time supposedly dedicated to loving and giving. And she knew the Smalls weren't the only ones who wished her gone. No one wanted her here, not even Mike.

Grimacing at the stench, she used a shovel to carry the dog pile to the garbage can in back. Then she scrubbed her mat, wondering what she was going to do with the lonely day stretching before her. The town was busy enough. There'd be last-minute Christmas shoppers clogging the drugstore, and little old ladies with blue hair trading holiday recipes at the deli counter at Finley's. But the hustle and bustle and smiles all around—which most often turned to frowns when she caught someone's eye—would only make her feel worse.

She'd planned to spend these days searching for her father, but the way she'd been treated by Garth Holbrook and Dave Small made her glad she hadn't been able to locate Eugene Thompson.

"Thank God for small favors," she muttered and considered flying to Washington for real. When she'd called them, her brothers had muttered the same obligatory invitation they extended every year. She *could* go. But now that they were married, Lucky didn't want to intrude on the peace and tranquility of their Christmas. She didn't know their wives very well, and the emotional baggage she carried made her brothers uncomfortable. Invariably they'd disagree over something. Or she'd want to have a meaningful conversation they couldn't handle.

Still, seeing her nieces and nephews held significant appeal....

Picking up the phone, she dialed Sean's house.

"Who is this?" a small voice instantly demanded.

Lucky laughed. "It's Aunt Lucky. Who's this?"

"Trisha."

Her five-year-old niece. "Hi, Trishy. You sound as though you've been up for a while."

"I always get up early."

"I'll bet. Are you all ready for Christmas?"

"Yep. I sat on Santa's lap at the mall."

"What did you tell him you wanted?"

She listed several items she was hoping he'd deliver, none of which was a Barbie.

"Did you get my present?" Lucky asked, wishing she'd opted for the board games and books she'd almost purchased.

"Daddy made me put it under the tree. He said I can't open it until Christmas, but I told him you wouldn't mind. Can I open it early, Aunt Lucky? Can I, huh? Pleeeese."

"Um, I'll see if I can talk your daddy into it, okay? Is he around?"

Trisha squealed and dropped the phone. Lucky was sure she'd have to hang up and call back and was about to do so when her brother finally answered.

"Lucky?"

"Hi, Sean."

"How are you?"

Her answer, of course, had to be *fine*. He didn't want to hear anything else. "Good. You?"

"Great."

For all she knew, he could have lost his job, and his wife, and be suffering from a terrible depression, but his answer was as predictable and meaningless as hers.

"I'm glad. You off work for Christmas?"

"I've got five days. It's kind of nice, having time with the kids."

"It would be."

"What's happening in Dundee? Are you finished fixing up the Victorian?"

"Not yet. My contractor has another couple of weeks once he starts again in January."

"So have you decided to sell the house?"

Lucky thought of Mike, which wasn't difficult since he was on her mind most of the time anyway. As much as Morris meant to her, as much as part of her longed to keep the house, she knew she couldn't hold out indefinitely. If Mike wanted the house that badly, she'd let him have it. "Yeah, probably."

"Good."

Sean might have added that there was nothing for her in Dundee, but she knew he'd steer carefully away from any comment that could be taken as a lead-in to a subject he'd rather avoid. Namely, anything to do with their mother, their childhood, the welcome or lack of welcome she'd received in their hometown. "Did you get your tree up?" he asked.

Carrying the cordless phone, she walked into the living room to stare at her Christmas tree, with all its mismatched ornaments. Mike had given her that tree, all the ornaments and the expensive, beautiful angel on top. His gift was the best thing about her return. "I did. It's perfect."

"So…" He cleared his throat. "Are you coming out here or… what?"

The obvious reluctance in his voice made Lucky's decision easier than she'd expected. After what she'd experienced here, in Dundee, she couldn't bring herself to crash his Christmas, not if he didn't really want her.

"No, actually I was calling to let you know I'll be joining some friends," she said with as much enthusiasm as she could muster.

"There aren't any soup kitchens you can help with in Dundee."

"Not that kind of friend."

"Really?"

His surprise helped her lie more convincingly. "Really. I met a divorced woman and her roommate at the hardware store a few days ago."

"Sounds perfect."

"I'm excited about it. Will you be spending the day with Kyle and his family, then?"

"That's the plan."

"Well, have a good time and give everyone my love."

"I will. We'll miss you."

In a way, they probably would miss her. She was their baby sister and she'd never doubted that they loved her. She just wished they had more in common.

"I'll miss you, too." She almost hung up, then remembered her niece's plea. "Oh, let the kids open the presents I sent, will you? Since I'm not going to be there, I don't see the point in making them wait."

"Will do. Did you get my card?"

"Not yet."

"It's coming."

"Okay. Merry Christmas," she said and hung up.

At least now she had something to do, she told herself. She had to go shopping and buy enough groceries and supplies that she wouldn't have to go out again, so she could pretend to be gone for the next several days. She didn't think anyone would be paying much attention. The Smalls had already made their point and Mike would be too busy with his family and his own Christmas to notice what was or wasn't happening next door. But she had to be prepared, just in case. She didn't want him, of all people, to know she'd be spending Christmas alone.

CHAPTER FIFTEEN

"DID YOU LET Fernando go early or something?"

Standing at the copy machine, Mike turned to see Josh enter their office from the back. "It only seemed fair. Tonight's Christmas Eve, and the office staff have been off for days."

"You want me to stick around and feed the horses later?"

Mike picked up the pedigree he'd been copying. "I'll do it."

"When are you heading over to Mom and Dad's?"

"Dinner's at five, right?"

"Rebecca wanted to go a little early so she could help out. Since you're taking care of the horses, I guess I'll go with her."

"Go ahead."

He was anticipating several hours of solitude in which he could clear off his desk, but the phone rang as soon as Josh left. Mike grabbed the extension on Polly's desk. "Mike Hill."

"I'm glad I caught you." It was Garth Holbrook; Mike recognized his voice right away. They'd recently had several meetings in conjunction with the senator's campaign and fund-raising efforts.

"How are you, Senator?"

"Good, and you?"

"Busy as always. What can I do for you?"

"I was wondering how well you know your neighbor."

"My *neighbor?*" Mike had assumed Holbrook wanted to talk about the campaign.

"Isn't Lucky Caldwell living in your grandfather's house?"

"She owns the place."

"I remember. She got a portion of your inheritance."

Mike might have stated the situation that strongly before Lucky's return, but something—he supposed a touch of misguided loyalty—made him hesitate to do so now. "I guess you could say that."

"From what I've heard, you've been after that place for years."

Where was he going with this? "That's true...."

"Any chance she might sell out and move away?"

"I don't think she's ready to sell yet. I've submitted plenty of offers and the answer's always been no."

"What if I were to sweeten the pot by a couple hundred thousand, make your offer too good to refuse?"

Mike jerked his head up in surprise. "Why would you do that?"

"I was hoping we could convince Gabe to forget about that remote cabin of his and stay in the old place next to you, for a few years. He'd never let me talk him into moving to town, of course. Ever since the accident, he likes his privacy and the wide open spaces. But you've got plenty of space out there, and I'd feel a whole lot better if he was at least a little closer, and I knew there was someone around to keep an eye on him."

So this call was about Gabe. That made more sense. Gabe was socializing, but only to the extent that his fund-raising efforts required; in Mike's opinion, he was still too distant and remote to be functioning at a healthy level. Evidently Garth agreed. "I'd love to have Gabe next door, but I'm not sure he'd go for it. Have you talked to him?"

"Not yet. I thought I'd see if we can get the house before making any waves. You know how stubborn he can be."

Mike rubbed his chin. "I do."

"So, will you call Lucky? See how much it'll take?"

"I can't call her right now. I think she's out of town." Actually, he knew she was. Once Lucky's car had disappeared from in front of the Victorian, Mike had felt a profound sense of relief. He didn't have to worry about her being alone for Christmas or about his mother or another member of the family bumping into her and saying something unkind. Better yet, he wouldn't be tempted to start the next big scandal, as he'd been tempted almost every night since her return. Lucky's admission of her feelings, and the fact that he knew she'd meant what she said despite her claims to the contrary, only made it harder for him to stay away.

"Where'd she go?" Holbrook asked.

"She mentioned spending Christmas with her brothers in Washington."

"Well, see what you can do once she gets back."

Mike stretched the muscles in his neck as he imagined confronting Lucky with yet another offer. "Is there any hurry, Senator? She might be more amenable to selling when she's finished her renovations."

"I'd rather not wait."

"You're that worried about Gabe?"

There was a long pause. "I'm that worried. And the new arrangement would be better for everyone. From what I hear, Lucky's a real troublemaker."

"To be honest, I don't think she's as much of a troublemaker as others claim," Mike said.

"I spoke to your aunt Cori the other day. She said Lucky really manipulated Morris."

"Most of that time, Lucky was just a child. I'm not sure she was as manipulative as she was needy."

"Everyone else pretty much agrees with your aunt."

"Maybe they do." Mike thought of how difficult Lucky was

to get close to, how she refused to dispute anyone's assumptions about her, how she dared everyone in town to think the worst. "They don't really know her."

"And you do?"

Mike realized he might have sounded a little too sympathetic, but he was tired of all the gossip, and the fact that no one ever looked at the situation through Lucky's eyes. "I know she's proud and fiercely independent." She was also vulnerable despite her desire to appear unaffected. Her hidden pain bothered him, made him want to defend her at every turn. "She's also pretty sensitive, although she doesn't come across that way."

"You like her."

It was a statement, not a question, one Mike wished he could deny. But he refused to join the attack when Lucky already stood against so many. "I live next door, so I've had more contact with her."

Holbrook sighed audibly.

"Is something wrong, Senator?"

"No." Another pause, then, "Just see what you can do when she gets back."

"Okay." After he hung up, Mike sat on the corner of Polly's desk, staring off into space and wondering why he wasn't more eager to act on the senator's call. He'd always wanted the house. He thought Gabe would be better off closer to town. And he wanted Lucky to leave, right? He should jump at Senator Holbrook's offer. Then why did he feel so reluctant to press her?

With a curse, he got up and headed to his office. He'd never been able to care enough about the right women. Now he cared too much about the wrong one—and the irony didn't escape him.

A LIGHT SNOW FELL on Christmas Eve. Lucky stood by the windows at the back of her house as the sun began to set and watched the flakes drift lazily to the ground, as though they existed solely for the sake of their beauty. She'd thought she might be depressed spending this night alone, but she felt unusually peaceful. Maybe she didn't mix well with the people of Dundee, but she had no quarrel with the land. The surrounding mountains rose majestically around her, the ice-covered pond at the bottom of the hill shimmered like a field of crushed diamonds and the leafless trees in the yard resembled nothing more than delicate white lace. Breathtaking...

To her right, she could make out the corner of the large red barn that housed the Hills' best stallions. The paddocks where they penned the mares that arrived during breeding season spread out below the barn, along with the usual plethora of snow-covered vehicles, fences and sheds. Mike's property had been her haven from her mother's shrill voice and constant demands. She could still hear the whinny of his horses, feel the soft brush of their lips against her palm as she fed them apples or carrots. Even the sound of the cowboys talking back and forth had become a fond memory, although she'd only heard them from a distance.

Everything good in her life she'd experienced at a distance. Except the time she'd occasionally spent with Morris—and that night in the motel she'd spent in Mike's arms.

Leaning a shoulder against the windowpane, she closed her eyes and imagined his hands on her once again. They slipped slowly over her wet skin in the saunalike heat of the shower. His lips moved over hers, coaxing her to let go of all reservation. And she had....

She opened her eyes to gaze out at his ranch. Mike had smelled like the scene before her now—of snow and earth and mountain air—and he'd tasted like chocolate mint.

The buzzer on the oven went off and she crossed the kitchen to take out the pumpkin pie she'd baked. She wasn't particularly interested in eating it. She didn't seem to have much of an appetite lately. But she'd spent the day preparing all kinds of food because she didn't have anything else to do, and because she liked the way it made the house smell. The scent of cloves and cinnamon, as well as the crackling fire she'd built the moment she saw Mike's Escalade pass on his way to town, went a long way toward reminding her that this quiet, beautiful night was Christmas Eve.

After setting the pie on a rack to cool, she poured herself a cup of cider, took the lap blanket from the couch and wandered into the living room. She hadn't been able to turn on her tree lights for the past two days for fear Mike would see them and know she was home. But he was gone now.

She plugged the cord into the socket and wrapped herself in the blanket. Then she sat on the area rug she'd bought and stared at the green boughs laden with ornaments. This tree had been Mike's gift. The beauty and serenity of the night was another gift. So were the two cards from her brothers, which waited on the kitchen counter to be opened in the morning.

Briefly she wondered what sort of evening Garth Holbrook might be spending and imagined Dave Small busy with his family. She was probably stupid to have approached either one of them—and yet she still longed to know who her father was.

Lucky considered trading her apple cider for a glass of wine to celebrate the biggest holiday of the year. But her eyelids were growing heavy, and she couldn't make herself move.

"MORE EGGNOG, Mike?"

Mike turned from throwing another log on the fire to see his aunt Cori holding a pitcher of her homemade eggnog. "No, thanks, I'm fine."

"Didn't I spike it enough for you?" she teased.

"It's perfect. I just don't have room for anything more."

Uncle Bunk patted a belly that protruded well over his large rodeo belt buckle. "That was quite a dinner."

"Good thing Christmas comes around only once a year," his wife told him.

Mike smiled as he took his seat on the couch. His two uncles, their wives, his cousins Blake and Mandy, his aunt Cori and his father eventually found seats close by, or dragged chairs out of the kitchen. The rest of his cousins and Aunt Cori's husband were already in the other room, playing the new PlayStation 2 his ten-year-old cousin had brought over to share with the younger crowd. He could hear their excited voices vying for the next turn.

"I hope we wrote down enough movie titles," his mother said as she carried in the glass bowl they used every year when they played charades.

His father, who hated the game but participated under threat of divorce, eyed the bowl with malice as she set it on the coffee table. "Seems like enough to me."

"We could always play Pictionary," she suggested sweetly.

Mike's father hated Pictionary even more than charades, so Barbara's subtle threat succeeded in provoking a little forced enthusiasm. "No, charades is fine."

She laughed. "That's what I thought. It doesn't matter to me. The women will win either way, right, ladies?"

Josh downed half a glass of eggnog. "I think we should mix it up this year," he said, being careful not to jostle his son, who was sleeping in his arms. "I'm tired of losing."

Rebecca squeezed in next to Josh and baby Brian and arched a playful eyebrow at her husband. "Sorry, sweetheart. We're going for a perfect record."

A challenging glint lit Josh's eyes. Josh and Rebecca loved each other desperately, but he'd never seen two more competitive people. "Then it looks to me as if the boys are gonna have to get serious."

"Good luck," Rebecca said scornfully.

"Maybe we should have some pie before we start," Mike's mother suggested.

The entire room groaned in unison. "We're too stuffed right now," Aunt Cori said.

"Okay." Mike's mother sat on the arm of the recliner his father had claimed. "Who goes first?"

They played for more than an hour, stopping only when everyone nearly fell off their chairs laughing at Rebecca's imitation of a samurai.

As the women gloated over their latest win, Mike started for the kitchen to get another glass of wine, but Aunt Cori grabbed his arm before he could take more than two steps. "Hey, Mike, how's your love life these days?"

"Not too good," he said. "I've been too busy to date."

She grinned knowingly. "That's not what I heard. Sparky Douglas asked me just yesterday why you were staying at the Timberline Motel a couple of weeks back, when you've got so much family in town." She nudged him. "I told him there was only one reason I could think of."

Mike coughed to hide his surprise. Very few people had been out and about during the storm, but Sparky was the motel handyman. He'd probably noticed Mike's truck, as well as the fact that Mike hadn't officially registered. "It wasn't anything," he said. "The roads were closed because of the storm, and I happened to know someone passing through town."

"*Someone?*"

"From McCall," he lied.

"Oh, that woman you dated a couple of years ago?"

He nodded, grateful she'd jumped to that conclusion.

"Your mother and I keep hoping you'll get married," she said with a pout.

"Maybe someday." He tried to escape, but she was still holding his arm.

"Sparky said Lucky Caldwell stayed at the motel the same night you did. Did you know that?"

Mike couldn't help shooting a glance at Josh, who shrugged imperceptibly—but if Aunt Cori knew he'd been with Lucky, he would've heard about it long before now. "Actually, I did. I gave her a ride into town. She was stranded out at the Victorian with no heat or water."

"Oh, that's right. Your mother called me that day." She shook her head. "It's too bad Lucky's back. I thought that was behind us."

"I think she's out of town." Mike kept his voice low. He didn't want any other family members to hear Lucky's name and jump into the conversation. He was afraid they might be able to make the connection his aunt had missed. With so few cabins at the motel, he figured it was patently obvious where he'd been and what he'd been doing, but that could've been because he had a guilty conscience. Certainly no one in his family would ever expect him to get involved with Lucky.

"Yeah, maybe she's left town already," Uncle Bunk piped up, overhearing their conversation despite Mike's attempts to keep it quiet. "Seems no one's seen her the past couple of days."

Mike swallowed a groan as his mother joined in.

"Did someone say Lucky's gone?"

The relief and hope in her voice irritated him. "She's just out of town for Christmas," he said.

"What makes you think she's out of town?" Rebecca asked, coming to take her son, who was wide awake and demanding to be fed. Now pretty much everyone was listening.

"She has family in the Washington area."

Rebecca settled baby Brian in her arms and threw a blanket over her shoulder to nurse. "How'd she get to the airport?"

Mike shoved his hands in his pockets in an effort to appear as uninterested as possible. "I guess she drove."

"She couldn't have. Her car's parked behind the Victorian."

Mike blinked at his sister-in-law as he tried to assimilate this information. "Her car's where?"

"Behind the house. We saw it this morning when we went riding, didn't we, Josh?"

Josh frowned, as if he'd rather not say.

"Josh?" Rebecca repeated.

He nodded grudgingly.

His mother shook her head. "I knew it was too good to be true."

Mike tried to look indifferent but felt a scowl descend instead. "She probably had someone give her a ride," he said, and Josh added a "Maybe." But Mike was far from convinced. If someone had taken Lucky to the airport, why would she move her car around back, where there wasn't even a driveway? If it snowed very heavily while she was gone, she'd return to find her Mustang buried.

She *wouldn't* do that. The only reason she'd hide her car was to make people *believe* she'd left. She didn't want anyone to know she'd be alone for Christmas.

ONCE HE KNEW Lucky was sitting in that big Victorian with the tree he'd given her and probably not much else, Mike grew agitated. She always pretended to be so tough, so unconcerned about her own needs. Why couldn't she simply admit she had no plans so he could have—

What? he asked himself. Kept her company? He couldn't do that. He couldn't have anything to do with her.

Jamming a hand through his hair, he did his best to fade

into the background of the celebration he was no longer enjoying. But, after another thirty minutes, he was damn near claustrophobic with all the relatives pressing in on every side.

Mumbling something about not feeling well, which was the only acceptable excuse he could come up with, he apologized for having to leave early and hurried to the door.

His mother intercepted him before he could reach it. "Mike, did I hear your father correctly? He said you're sick. What's wrong?"

Mike struggled to remove any revealing expressions from his face. "I think I'm coming down with something," he muttered.

"But if you go home now, you'll miss opening presents with us."

"I'll come back and open mine in the morning, if you want."

Worry clouded her features, and she put a hand to his forehead. He hated it when she treated him as if he was still a little boy, but he was glad he'd tolerated her ministrations when she delivered the verdict that he did seem a bit warm.

"You don't want to be sick for the rest of the holidays," she said. "Go get some rest."

Now that he had her blessing, he strode outside, trying to convince himself that he'd ignore the uncharacteristic emotions flowing through him and head straight to the ranch. But deep down he knew he wasn't going home.

He was going to Lucky's.

LUCKY WAS AWAKENED by a noise.

She held her breath, waiting to see if the sound would be repeated. A moment later, she heard a soft knock.

Someone was at her door. But who? Who would drop by her house on Christmas Eve at—she squinted to make out the numbers on her watch—nearly ten o'clock?

Whoever it was, she wouldn't answer. She wasn't supposed

to be home, for one thing. And she was afraid Smalley might be back, bent on a little mischief after a few holiday beers.

Crouching low, she crawled over to sit with her back against the wall next to the door, where she couldn't be seen if her visitor decided to circle the house and peek through the windows.

Whoever it is will go away.

Her palms began to sweat as she waited nervously, but her visitor didn't leave. Another knock sounded, this one more insistent than the last, and a voice came through the door. "Lucky, it's me, Mike."

Lucky covered her mouth. She would have preferred Smalley! Why wasn't Mike with his family? Had he come home early and spotted the Christmas tree lights? How had she been stupid enough to fall asleep with them on?

"I know you're in there," he said. "And I'm not leaving until I see you, so you might as well open up."

Obviously it was no use pretending anymore. With a sigh, Lucky stood and unbolted the lock. She hated appearing pathetic, especially to Mike or his family, but there wasn't any way to avoid looking pathetic tonight. How many other people spent Christmas alone? Probably not many, at least not in Dundee, and certainly no one in Mike's big happy family.

Opening the door, she cracked a smile. "Need to borrow an egg or maybe a cup of sugar?"

He didn't respond to her attempt at levity. He was standing on the porch, his thumbs hooked in his pockets. It was difficult to make out his expression in the shadow of his hat and the dark, murky porch—so difficult she considered turning on the light. But she was afraid that would reveal the excitement she felt at seeing him. "Is something wrong?"

"Why did you tell me you were leaving town for the holidays?"

"Because I was. Until I decided at the last minute that maybe it'd be nice to…"

"To what?" he demanded when she couldn't seem to find the words she wanted.

"You know, to spend a quiet Christmas at home."

"Alone."

Lucky lifted her chin defiantly. "Sure, why not?"

Mike stepped closer but resumed the same challenging stance. "You were never going to Washington in the first place, were you?"

Letting her breath seep out between her teeth, she leaned against the lintel. "What do you want from me, Mike?"

He gave her a speculative look but no answer.

"Do you want to hear me say that I don't really have any-where to go? That I'm not close to my brothers the way you're close to your family? Okay, it's true. But it doesn't bother me."

"Bullshit."

"What's that supposed to mean?"

"It means you're as human as the rest of us."

His eyes glittered in the darkness, making her feel as though he could see into her soul. Scrambling to rescue what she could of her pride, she jerked her head toward his truck parked in her driveway. "Okay, so I'm human. Now, you'd better go home before someone sees you here. They might not believe you stopped by just to gloat over my lonely Christmas."

"I'm not here to gloat."

"Why are you here?"

He stared at her for several seconds. Finally he said, "Be-cause I want to be."

Their eyes met, and a powerful yearning swept through Lucky. "I won't be around in a couple of months," she said. She wasn't sure why she felt the need to remind him of that, except she thought it might make things easier.

He stepped closer still, hovering only centimeters away. "Then maybe we should stop wasting time."

Lucky's heart skipped a beat at the promise in his voice. "Mike—"

He ran a finger along her jaw, then lowered his head to press his lips against hers, silencing her with his kiss. She let her eyelids flutter shut at the sweet, gentle contact and felt his hand come up to support the back of her head. "I want to stay the night," he said softly.

Lucky's breath caught in her throat, but she opened her eyes and said what she knew was best for both of them. "You should probably go home."

He must have recognized the lack of conviction in those words because his arms tightened around her. "If I went home, I'd only come back."

She let her lips curve in a seductive smile. "What if I didn't let you in?"

"I'd beg," he whispered, trailing kisses down her neck.

Lucky couldn't help chuckling at the thought of Mike Hill begging at her door. "No, you wouldn't."

"I would, on my knees." More kisses, lightly grazing her skin, sending goose bumps down her spine. "Would you still turn me away?"

"If I knew what was good for me, I would."

His hand curled possessively around her bottom. "We'll worry later about what's good for us."

The little sanity Lucky had left acknowledged the temporary nature of what he proposed, admonished her to pull away and demand he leave. What was the point of falling even more deeply in love with a man she couldn't have?

But it was Christmas, a magical night when anything could happen.

Knocking his hat off, she threaded her fingers through his

short straight hair and her tongue met his in a passionate kiss, a kiss that held nothing back, that said everything she couldn't.

"I'll take that as a yes," he told her, his teeth glinting in a devilish grin. Then he swung her up, cradling her against his chest, kicked the door open wider and carried her into the house.

"What about your truck?" she asked when he paused to close the door behind them.

"I don't know. Ask me again when I can think of something besides you."

CHAPTER SIXTEEN

"WHY AREN'T YOU CLOSER to your brothers?"

Reluctantly, Lucky roused herself from dozing contentedly on Mike's bare chest. The room was cool because she liked it that way at night. Typically, she burrowed beneath her down comforter and a couple of old quilts to create a warm cocoon. But her bed had never been more comfortable or warmer than it was now, with Mike in it. "I admire my brothers, but—" she hesitated, searching for a diplomatic way to state the situation "—they understand each other better than they understand me."

"What's not to understand?" His fingers skimmed her hair lightly.

"Don't *you* find me wildly complex?" She was teasing, hoping to distract him from his serious tone as well as the bent of his questions, but it didn't work.

"You *are* wildly complex. I've never met anyone like you. You'd cut off your nose to spite your face if you thought it might salvage your precious pride—something I'm too practical to understand." He pulled the blankets higher. "But I already know that. What I don't understand is why your brothers aren't taking better care of you."

She rolled her eyes, even though she was still lying on his chest and knew he couldn't see her do it. "Would you quit it? I've been taking care of myself since I was eighteen. Actually, I was taking care of myself long before that."

"Still, they've let you down."

"It's late. Aren't you tired?"

"You don't want to talk about this?"

"No."

"Why?"

"Our families are our families. I don't want to discuss yours, either."

His hands climbed up her back, kneading the muscles that had tensed in the last few minutes, willing her to relax. "I can see not wanting to talk about mine," he said. "But I don't understand why Sean and Kyle left you here alone on Christmas. It makes me angry."

"I told them I'd met a friend, okay? I didn't want to go to Washington." She started to shift away, but his arm tightened around her.

"Don't withdraw. We can do more than make love, can't we?"

"If you want to talk, we can talk about other stuff." She loathed the idea of describing her strained relationship with her brothers because it would lead to the past, which would lead to her mother and the way Red had affected each of their lives. Lucky both loved and hated her mother, and trying to sift through those conflicting emotions was too painful. Especially with Mike, who saw only her mother's bad side, who could never understand the complexities of loving a mother like Red.

"Other stuff?" he repeated.

"Yeah."

"Like the weather? We can talk about that, right? How 'bout the progress of the repairs? Is that superficial enough?"

Pushing away, she sat up. "What's gotten into you?"

"I just need to understand some things."

She glared at him. "What things?"

He regarded her evenly, the seriousness of his expression plainly visible in the silver moonlight falling gently through the window. She'd thought the edge in her voice might make him back off, but he only seemed more determined. "I want to know why you've hung on to this old place, for one. I also want to know what you did during the six years you were gone, what you plan to do with the next six. And I want to know why you've never been with another man and can't trust anyone enough to lose the wariness that insulates you from everyone and everything."

Whoa, this was more than she'd expected. Panic welled up inside her. She was in love with Mike. She knew that, had always known on some level, probably because she'd been in love with him almost as long as she could remember. But he was asking too much. In order to survive the inevitable, when loyalty to his family overcame his interest in her, she needed to keep her most tender self—her thoughts and feelings and painful memories—from him. "Tonight's been fun, but I think it's time for you to go," she said.

He didn't move. "You can't manage it, huh?"

The challenge he tossed out provoked her, but she couldn't answer. Tears began to blur her vision. Why wouldn't he accept what they had right here, right now, and let the rest go? It had been so peaceful in the aftermath of their lovemaking....

"I'd like to hear how you felt about Morris," he said softly. "Why you didn't come to his funeral."

At the mention of Morris's name, a mutinous tear slipped down Lucky's cheek. Cursing her own weakness, she prayed Mike wouldn't see it, but she knew he had when he reached up and wiped it away.

"Come on, Lucky," he coaxed. "Open up."

She struggled to remain defiant and unbending. But her

emotions were getting the best of her. And Mike was pulling her to him, putting his arms around her, kissing her temple, making it that much harder to hold everything inside.

"It's okay," he said as her tears dropped onto his chest. "It's just the two of us."

She listened to his heartbeat. She could take Mike into her bed because making love with him was simply the physical expression of what she'd always felt. Talking about the past, bringing up issues and feelings that hurt to even think about, was much more difficult.

He was waiting, letting the power of his expectation work on her....

Fine, she decided. If he wanted to see the ugly truth, she'd show it to him.

Drawing a deep breath, she started talking. "I remember hearing the bed banging against the wall in my mother's room. I hated that sound. I used to turn the television up so loud it echoed through the whole house."

The hand that had been stroking her stilled. "When your mother was with my grandfather, you mean?"

She chuckled humorlessly. "No. I think Morris was impotent by then. At least my mother screamed that at me once during one of our arguments."

Mike's muscles went rigid. "I knew she wasn't faithful, but you're saying Red slept with other men, right here, in my grandfather's house?"

Lucky nodded, oddly satisfied that her words stung him as badly as they stung her. "One day when I knew my mother was with someone in the bedroom and...and the TV was blaring and I was wishing I was miles away, the phone rang." She cringed, remembering. "It was Morris. 'How's my girl? Finished your homework? Where's your mother?'"

She paused but Mike didn't say anything.

"I lied," she went on. "I told him she was getting her hair done."

"If you really hated what your mother was doing, why didn't you try to stop it? Why didn't you tell him the truth?"

The gruffness of Mike's voice told her how much it bothered him that a man he loved had been made into such a fool. But Mike didn't understand Lucky's position, because he'd never felt so frightened or so helpless.

"I couldn't," she said. "I was sick inside, terrified. If Morris found out, if he was forced to acknowledge what was happening, he'd—" her voice broke but she made herself continue "—he'd leave us."

Several seconds passed. "Were you afraid of being thrown out on the street? Or of going back to your previous life?"

"I was afraid of losing the only person who'd ever truly loved me." That statement laid her soul bare, and she knew it, but there it was. He'd wanted to know why she was the way she was and she'd more or less told him.

"You loved Morris."

She couldn't respond.

"Why didn't you come back when he died?"

"Because I didn't want to see my mother. And I knew my presence would only upset your family, which would bring my mother into the situation again and turn Morris's funeral into a circus."

Silence fell as he continued to knead her back.

"Was it a good service?" she asked.

"It was." He put a finger under her chin and raised her face toward him. "Who were the men your mother slept with? Do I know them?"

"I won't tell you that. It'll only make you hate them."

"Some of them are probably my friends."

"Maybe not friends but certainly acquaintances."

When he cursed, Lucky sat up and dashed an impatient hand across her wet cheeks. "You're the one who wanted to know," she said accusingly and started to get up. "I'll help you find your clothes."

He grabbed her arm. "Lucky."

"What?"

"Come here."

"No."

"Yes. Sleep with me for a little while."

"I don't need that," she said. "Please don't feel you have to stay for me." The last thing she wanted from Mike Hill was his pity.

"I'm not doing it for you." He ran a finger down her arm. "I'm doing it for me."

MIKE BREATHED DEEPLY, taking in the fresh clean scent of Lucky's hair. The sunlight inching across the bedroom floor made him all too aware that he needed to get up and see to the horses. Fernando was off for Christmas. But it was Christmas for him, too, and he didn't want to leave Lucky.

Sliding his hand up her bare stomach to cup her breast, he leaned over to see her eyes flutter open.

"Is it morning already?" she asked, blinking up at him.

"Yes."

"I didn't think you'd still be here."

He hadn't planned on staying the whole night.

"What's the matter?" Lucky murmured, gazing up at him.

He was frowning at some red marks on her neck, probably from the chafing of his whiskers. But he couldn't help admiring the disheveled look of her hair, the endearing sleepiness in her face. Her expression was about as unguarded as he'd ever seen Lucky in daylight. "A certain saying."

"What saying?"

He kissed her neck to make up for the redness. "Between a rock and a hard place."

Her eyes narrowed. "And I'm sure that has nothing to do with me."

"Nothing whatsoever," he lied and rolled onto his back, taking her with him.

"You never moved your truck," she said, resting her chin on her hands and looking down at him.

Chuckling, he toyed with the ends of the long, thick hair that had swept over his body, as soft as silk, when she'd kissed his chest and then his stomach before moving lower…. "You kept me too busy."

She gave him a wicked grin. "Don't blame me if you get caught."

"But it *was* your fault. I didn't have the strength to leave. It's hard for an old guy like me to keep up with a young woman like you."

Her brow furrowed. "*Young* woman?"

"Excuse me. Woman."

"Don't," she said.

"Don't what?"

"*Young* woman? *Old* guy?" she repeated. "Where's that coming from?"

"I'm nearly forty, Lucky."

"Oh! I didn't know." She feigned shock as she sat up and drew the sheet over her. "Maybe you should've said something sooner. Last night probably never would've happened had I known what an old man you are."

He sat up, too. "I'm saying that fifteen years is a lot."

"You're saying it's too much."

Did it matter *what* he was saying? A great deal more stood between them than age. He thought about Senator Holbrook's offer, and rubbed a hand down his face. "It *is* too much."

Her expression turned to one of disgust as she shook her head. "You'd better go before someone sees your truck."

Just like that, Lucky had thrown up the invisible barrier that separated her from everyone else, including him. After last night, he needed to put her on notice that what they'd shared couldn't last. It would be unfair, maybe even cruel, not to do so. But he hadn't expected her to withdraw so quickly and completely.

"Lucky…"

She resisted when he tried to pull her to him. "Give me some credit, Mike," she said. "I know what you're trying to do—I understand the situation."

She was going where he'd been trying to lead her and yet *he* was the one who seemed to be having trouble adjusting. "Last night was…incredible. I didn't want it to confuse you."

Her bare shoulders lifted in a slight shrug. "I'm not confused. Last night was Christmas Eve."

"What does that mean?"

"It was a nice fantasy."

They'd shared some pretty intimate moments, moments of pure reality, but she obviously wasn't willing to acknowledge them right now. Mike almost said so, then realized he'd switched sides. Evidently he was more confused than she was. Instead of explaining all the reasons they'd be crazy to attempt a real relationship, all the people they'd hurt if they continued seeing each other, he wanted to kiss her until she slipped her arms around his neck and brought him down on top of her.

What the hell was wrong with him? He'd always kept a cool head with women, always been capable of letting go easily.

But a cool head was easier when he had a lukewarm heart.

Wait a second. His heart wasn't *really* involved in this, he told himself firmly, and got up to gather his clothes. Lucky was young and beautiful, misunderstood and misjudged. She incited his passion and his protective instincts. That was all. He'd make Senator Holbrook's offer, just not today. Today he'd go home and gain some perspective—somehow. But pounding at the front door surprised him before he could even pull on his pants.

LUCKY FELT the glower slide from her face as the knock downstairs came again. "What should I do?"

Mike started moving more quickly, trying to get dressed. "Who do you think it is?"

Anxiety joined all her other mixed emotions. "I have no idea. The only person who ever comes over is Mr. Sharp. And he's off until after the first of the year."

He zipped his pants but didn't bother to button them because he was in too much of a hurry to find his shirt.

"Maybe if I don't answer, whoever it is will go away," she said, but she knew that wasn't very likely when another knock sounded, more insistent than the last.

"Go ahead and answer it," he said.

"What about your truck?"

"I have several trucks. Say you borrowed it."

"Okay." She could tell Mike didn't believe that the excuse he'd given her would fool anybody. Neither did she, but she couldn't come up with any better excuse for his truck to be parked in her drive. She certainly didn't want anyone to know they were sleeping together. Mike had always been respected and admired in Dundee. She didn't want to leave town knowing she'd changed all that.

Grabbing her robe, she pulled it on and hurried from the room.

"I'm coming," she called as she neared the door.

Whoever it was stopped pounding.

Stepping to the window, she parted the drapes to see the back of a man close to Mike's height, with shoulders just as broad. When he turned, she realized it was his brother, Josh.

"Oh, no," she breathed and cast a worried glance over her shoulder, wondering if she should warn Mike before she answered the door.

"Damn it, Lucky." The voice came from outside. "I know he's in there. Open up."

Josh had probably already confirmed that Mike wasn't at the ranch. With Mike's truck at her place, Lucky didn't see any point in playing games. They'd already been found out.

Making sure her robe covered her well because there wasn't much dignity in being caught in such a situation, she opened the door to a flushed but still handsome Josh Hill.

His jaw hardened as his gaze ran over her disheveled appearance. "Where is he?"

Lucky's spine stiffened at his icy tone, but before she could respond, the stairs creaked. Mike came down, fully dressed, and answered for her. "Here. What do you want?"

Josh's eyes met Mike's and a challenge seemed to pass between the two brothers. "What the hell are you doing?"

Mike scowled darkly. "Mind your own business, little brother."

"This *is* my business. It's Christmas, hardly the time to take this kind of—" he eyed Lucky with no small amount of contempt "—risk, yet your truck's parked out front for anyone to see. What are you trying to do? Make the holidays memorable by tearing our family apart?"

"Get out of here before you say something that really pisses me off," Mike replied. "You have no right to interfere."

"No right?" Josh's hands flexed as though Mike's response angered him beyond words. "You're choosing Red's daughter over your own family, a cheap fling with—"

"Josh!" Mike interrupted, almost explosively. "I'm warning you, watch your mouth."

Lucky felt their powerful wills collide, feared they'd come to blows in her living room, and stepped between them.

Mike moved her out of the way, and Josh seemed to pull his gaze from her only with considerable effort. "You told Mom you were sick last night," he said to Mike.

"You've got something to say about that, too?"

Shoving a hand through his hair, Josh released what sounded like a frustrated sigh. "Only that Mom's on her way out here."

Lucky's breath lodged in her throat, and Mike blanched for the first time. *"What?"*

"She just called and asked me to check on you. She's worried because you're not answering your phone. 'Poor Mike, to be so sick on Christmas Day.' She's bringing you the presents you left behind last night when you walked out on the rest of us—" he shifted his gaze back to Lucky "—almost the moment you learned our new neighbor was here alone."

Mike didn't respond. Lucky wasn't sure he was even paying attention. He seemed to be preoccupied, searching for something.

Josh cocked an eyebrow at him. "If you're hoping to find your hat, it's outside—which says more about last night than I really want to know."

Lucky felt her face burn, but Mike acted as if Josh's words didn't bother him in the least. "I'll grab it on the way out," he said and turned to her. "I've got to go."

"No kidding. Hurry." Stepping back so Mike wouldn't feel he owed her any kind of goodbye kiss, or even a handshake, she gave him a polite nod. "Enjoy the rest of the holidays."

Mike hesitated. When he glanced at her tree, Lucky felt her embarrassment return as he seemed to notice that there wasn't a single present underneath it. But then he strode through the door and was gone, and she prayed he'd make it out of her driveway before his mother arrived.

MIKE REFUSED TO LOOK at Josh as he stalked outside. He found his hat easily enough, fished his keys out of his pocket and had nearly climbed into the Escalade before Josh addressed him.

"Once wasn't enough?" his brother asked as he passed by on the way to his own vehicle, which was parked behind Mike's.

Mike didn't answer, but he knew Josh was talking about that first experience with Lucky in the motel, which he'd admitted to him on the phone.

"What's going on, Mike?" Josh pressed.

Mike tossed his hat in the passenger seat. "Nothing."

"Are you going to be able to stop seeing her?"

Mike scowled irritably. Of course he was going to be able to stop seeing her. He and Holbrook were planning to up the ante on the house until she couldn't say no, right? She'd be packing her bags within the week. Then she'd be gone, and he'd have no choice but to stop seeing her.

Unfortunately, he thought it might take that drastic a measure to get her out of his head and his heart.

"I've got it under control," he said tersely.

"Finding your hat in the snow and your truck in the drive when you could've slipped over here without leaving such obvious signs, had you been thinking *at all,* doesn't make me feel very optimistic about that. If you had to see her, why didn't you use some caution?"

"Let's get out of here," Mike grumbled. He didn't want to explain that he couldn't sneak and pretend. He respected Lucky too much to treat her as though she wasn't worthy to be seen with him.

BARBARA BALANCED Mike's presents in her arms as she climbed out of her Cadillac and walked toward the door. Mike was rarely sick and, when he was, he generally didn't say anything about it. He was like his father; he tolerated discomfort in silence. So this illness, which had been bad enough to take him away from their Christmas Eve celebration, had her worried.

"Mike, it's Mom," she said, letting herself in. She assumed she'd find him in bed, but he came around the corner fully dressed and looking much better than she'd expected. "Oh, you're up."

"Yeah. Merry Christmas." He kissed her cheek, took the presents from her and carried them to the couch. "Where's Dad?"

"He was on the phone with his brother, and I thought I'd give him some time to wish the rest of his family a merry Christmas," she said. "Why didn't you answer when I called you this morning?"

He cleared his throat. "I must've been out with the horses."

"You're feeling better?"

He seemed reluctant to look at her. "I feel fine."

"Well, that's a relief." She waved at the wrapped packages she'd brought. "Open your gifts. I've been anxious to see if you're going to like what your father and I bought you. I love my new sewing machine, by the way. But you shouldn't have spent so much."

"I figured you could use it."

"I can."

He took her box out from under the rest and tore off the paper. When he lifted the lid, he glanced up at her in surprise. "New boots?"

"They seemed perfect for you."

He whistled. "I've never had a pair this nice."

"Try them on."

She knew he preferred simple to ornate and had selected a black leather pair that didn't have snakeskin or anything too fancy. They were simple and masculine, like him.

"They fit," he announced, standing up.

Barbara smiled proudly as she watched him walk across the room. It was tough to believe her oldest was nearly forty. What a great kid he'd always been. He'd gotten into a few scrapes when he was younger, of course. Most kids did. But he'd turned into a fine man.

Gratitude washed over her. She'd been afraid this would be a difficult Christmas with Lucky back in town, but Lucky hadn't affected the holidays much at all. How could Barbara feel bad about anything with two such wonderful sons?

Getting up, she went over and hugged Mike. "I love you, you know that? You and Josh make me so proud."

"Thanks, Mom," he said, but his voice sounded a little choked and when she pulled away she thought she saw a flicker of anguish in his eyes.

"Are you sure you're okay?" she asked.

He frowned and stared down at his boots. "Yeah."

CHAPTER SEVENTEEN

LUCKY SPENT the next few hours cleaning house and worrying about Mike's mother. She'd already vacuumed and dusted yesterday, before she started cooking, so the house wasn't dirty. But mundane chores kept her busy on a day when everyone else was with family and the stores in town were closed.

She opened the cards from her brothers to find a fifty-dollar check from Sean and a Barnes & Noble gift certificate from Kyle, smiled at the pictures they'd sent of the kids and stuck everything in her wallet. Then she waited for Sean and Kyle's call, which came mid-morning. She traded holiday sentiments with each brother, listened to her nieces and nephews talking excitedly about their presents and hung up, tired of housework but with the rest of the day yawning before her and nothing to do.

After an hour of television, she decided to visit Mike's horses. She hadn't been over to the barn since she'd returned to Dundee, and at this particular moment, the stallions she'd always loved seemed to provide a cure for her aching loneliness.

She dragged on her coat and boots and cut up some apples before heading out the door.

Blue, cloudless skies stretched above her but a chill wind almost sent her back for a hat and scarf. She wished Mike had called to let her know how this morning went with his mother, but she quickly redirected her thoughts. The way he'd held her and kissed her so tenderly last night had changed something inside her, something she didn't want to deal with. She needed to protect herself from Mike if she wanted to leave Dundee without a few new scars on her heart.

Taking the long path around the back, because she didn't want to climb the fence like she used to when she was young, she felt warmer by the time she reached the barn.

As she dusted off the snow clinging to her pants, she could hear the horses, could smell the familiar scents of hay and manure. Morris had occasionally taken her riding, but not often enough. He'd always been too busy. Her mother hadn't been interested, and her brothers had preferred not to let their little sister tag along. She missed the bumpy feel of a horse's quick trot—missed Mike's ranch, she realized, and the horses that used to be kept on her own property.

Pausing at the back entrance to the barn, she listened carefully to the noises from within. She wanted solitude and the comfort she'd always received here; she didn't want to run into any of the ranch hands.

When she heard nothing that sounded remotely human, she ducked inside the open door to discover that the barn hadn't changed at all. Fresh straw filled the stalls and the horses munched peacefully, wearing quilted blankets to shield them from the cold. Blankets… She smiled. She supposed horses that cost as much as Mike's deserved to be pampered.

Lucky immediately recognized the tall black stallion standing in the first stall. This horse had been a new acquisition the year she'd left town, the crown jewel of the Hill brothers' breeding enterprise. His name was Midnight, if she remembered right.

"You still around, boy?" she murmured, letting him sniff her hand.

The horse tossed his head and flared his nostrils, suspicious of her unfamiliar presence. When she tried to stroke his nose, he pranced around his stall, swishing his tail.

A slice of apple eventually brought him back to her. "That's it, big boy," she crooned as he took the apple from her open palm. "You're a beauty, aren't you?"

After another apple slice, he actually let her pat his neck. "There you go." She grinned. "See? Don't tell anyone, but I'm not as bad as people think."

"Is your true nature some sort of secret, then?"

Her smile wilted. Because the ranch had seemed so deserted, she'd relaxed a little too much. Turning slowly around, she saw Josh standing at the entrance she'd just used.

"Oh." She shoved her bag of apples into her coat pocket and started edging toward the opposite door, so she wouldn't have to squeeze past him. "I'm sorry. I didn't know you were here. I—" She jerked her head toward Midnight. "He's a beautiful animal. Congratulations."

Pivoting, she set out in earnest, wanting to escape before she had to deal with any more of the contempt Josh had lavished on her that morning, but he stopped her with an unexpected comment.

"I didn't know you liked horses."

Her steps slowed at his conciliatory tone. "I…uh, yes, I do. And of course you have some of the best, don't you?"

"Quality is important when it comes to breeding."

"Exactly."

"Were you hoping to see Mike?"

She rubbed her hands together for warmth. "No, I was just saying hello to some old friends. I used to spend quite a lot of time in your barn." She chuckled. "Fortunately, I was better at going unnoticed then."

"I don't mind you coming over to see the horses."

She hunched against the wind that suddenly blew around the corner. "As long as I stay away from your brother, right?"

"That's complicated, Lucky. My reasons are probably far different than you think."

She doubted it. He didn't believe her good enough for Mike, and most everyone in town would agree with him. "Well, like I said, I didn't come here with Mike in mind. And what happened last night won't happen again. In any case, I'll be leaving soon."

"How soon?"

Obviously she couldn't leave soon enough for him. "When the house is finished."

"What are you going to do with it then?"

"Mike mentioned he'd still like to buy it."

Josh removed his leather gloves and slapped them against his thigh. "So you're going to sell it to him?"

She nodded.

"Why?"

"Pardon me?"

"Why are you finally willing to let him have it?"

She attempted a careless shrug. "I don't know. There's no use letting it sit empty after all the work I'm having done."

"That's not very convincing," he said.

"What's not convincing?"

"Your excuse. You've already let it sit empty for years. That's why it needs the work it does."

"Things change."

"You care about Mike, don't you? That's what's changed."

Lucky ignored his soft-spoken words because life was easier when she held her cards a little closer to her chest. "Did everything go okay with your mother?" she asked instead of answering.

He balled his gloves in one large hand. "Fine."

Relieved, she said, "That's good," and turned to go once more. But he spoke again.

"I can tell what Mike sees in you. You're attractive, young, bright. Not at all what we thought. But..."

She drew a deep breath and braced for the worst. "But?"

He seemed to search for the right words. "You have to realize that a relationship between you and Mike wouldn't work, Lucky. I might be able to live with it, learn to accept it, but my folks and extended family never could. Mike might be able to choose you over them for a while, but he already has problems with commitment, and this is a small, close-knit town. I'm afraid it would eat at him, eat at you both."

"There's no danger of him choosing me." Last night, she'd imagined that Mike felt something for her, had reveled in those few short hours when his caring seemed so real. But she knew she must've been dreaming. She was such a pariah in Dundee that he couldn't even take her out in public, for crying out loud. "I would never ask him to."

Josh's eyebrows shot up. "You care about him that much?"

Lucky scowled. She didn't like giving herself away, but she knew it would be futile to claim she didn't love Mike. Josh had read the signs too easily. "Just take care of him after I'm gone, okay?"

He scuffed one boot in the dirt before glancing up at her again. "I'm sorry. I wasn't trying to hurt you."

She forced as brave a smile as she could muster. "I know."

"You seem distracted, Dad. What's going on?"

Garth Holbrook blinked and focused on his son, who was sitting in his wheelchair near the Christmas tree. "Nothing. I'm just preoccupied with the campaign." He doubted Gabe believed him, but what else could he say? That he was worried sick? Ever since Lucky had dredged up the past, Garth couldn't rest easy about anything.

"Garth, can I get you a glass of wine?" Celeste stood at the entrance to the kitchen. His wife was still pretty if slightly plump. He'd always admired her blue eyes and dark hair, both of which Gabe had inherited. Garth's only wish was that he could reach her on a deeper level than the cordial partnership in which they'd always existed.

He stared down at the torn wrapping paper and open boxes at his feet. What they'd given each other for Christmas this morning said it all, didn't it? She'd given him a tie, some new slacks and a briefcase; he'd bought her an expensive set of pans and a butcher block of knives. All practical items, even though he'd wanted to give her something skimpy and transparent from the lingerie catalogue that came in the mail.

That idea brought a flicker of the sexual desire he worked so hard to ignore, but he quickly squashed it. He knew better than to buy Celeste anything revealing. She promptly threw the lingerie catalogue away without even glancing through it and wore a flannel nightgown to bed. Now that she was long past her childbearing years, he despaired of enticing her to participate in anything she deemed "nasty" or "vulgar."

"Wine would be nice, Celeste, thank you."

She looked at him a little oddly, and he realized he'd addressed her as formally as he would a stranger. He smiled to compensate.

She nodded, apparently satisfied, and went back to the kitchen for his wine. Celeste believed cooking, scrupulous cleaning, waiting on him like a servant, smiling for the cameras and helping with various charities in town constituted being a good political wife. According to her own definition, he couldn't fault her. But there'd always been something missing, something he'd allowed Red to temporarily provide....

Surveying the torn wrapping paper once again, he wondered what Lucky Caldwell's Christmas was like. Mike had indicated that she'd left for the holidays, which meant she was close enough to her brothers that she had somewhere to go.

See? he told himself. She didn't need him. She had no business coming back here and destroying his life.

But he couldn't deny an underlying curiosity. *Could* she belong to him? *Had* Red been lying about birth control? He had to admit it was possible. He hadn't been thinking clearly when he was seeing her. If he could believe that he was somehow special to her, special beyond his gifts and his money, he could believe just about anything.

The phone rang, and he automatically held his breath. He always expected it to be Lucky, pressing him, insinuating herself into his life. But she hadn't contacted him since that day she'd asked him to take the paternity test. And this wasn't her, either. He could hear Celeste wishing her sister a merry Christmas.

"You think we'll be able to hit four hundred thousand dollars?"

The campaign again. Fund-raising was almost all Gabe talked about lately, but at least he was talking about *something*.

Garth tried to concentrate on the conversation. "At the rate you're going? Of course we will. I've never had a better man working for me. I think *you* should run for senate in a few years."

A grimace contorted Gabe's handsome face, and Garth knew his son would disregard the idea as he disregarded all of Garth's suggestions for his future. Gabe didn't feel he had a future worth worrying about. "Even if we reach our target, will four hundred thousand be enough?"

If Lucky breathed a word of what was in her mother's

journal, no amount of money would be enough. But Garth nodded and smiled anyway. "Sure. Butch Boyle's been in office too long already. It's high time we gave him his walking papers." More rhetoric. Garth suppressed a humorless chuckle. He was beginning to speak in clichés even at home. Maybe he'd been a politician for too many years....

"Are you sure nothing's wrong?" Gabe's eyebrows were drawn together in concern.

"Of course."

"You haven't been yourself the last week."

Reenie came marching into the living room, carrying Isabella, her youngest, who had candy cane smeared all over her face. "Grandma's not going to like you getting that candy stuck in her carpet," she scolded.

"Yum!" Isabella responded gleefully, clapping her sticky hands.

"It's a busy time of year," Garth said so Gabe wouldn't glare at Reenie.

Unfortunately, Reenie wasn't quite as preoccupied with Isabella as she'd first appeared. "Maybe Dad wouldn't have to worry quite so much if you'd quit feeling sorry for yourself, Gabe."

An angry muscle jumped in Gabe's cheek, but Reenie was down the hall before he could respond.

Garth knew his daughter was right—Gabe needed to pull himself together, regardless of what he used to be—but he wasn't any happier with Reenie. He'd taken her aside earlier and asked her to back off. Besides, getting Gabe involved in the campaign was creating more progress than Reenie's verbal barrages, even if it was progress by inches.

Shaking his head, Gabe started wheeling himself toward the door, which Garth knew he'd been itching to do almost since he'd arrived. He was on his way back to that damn cabin where he stayed holed up for days and weeks at a stretch. But this time Garth put up a hand to stop him.

"Stay with me today, will you, Gabe?" He'd tried to affect a casual tone, but knew he'd come across too seriously when concern clouded Gabe's blue eyes.

Clearing his throat, Garth tried again. "This Christmas—" *might be our last as a family* "—is important to me."

Gabe's obvious confusion made Garth feel even worse. His crippled son didn't need anything else to worry about. But at least Gabe had stopped moving. After gazing at him for several seconds, he finally nodded. "Sure, I'll stay. Anything you need, Dad."

Anything he needed. What Garth needed was a chance to go back and change the past.

MIKE FROWNED as Josh came into his house and slouched in the chair at the other end of the coffee table. "It's Christmas afternoon. Why aren't you with your family?" he asked, grabbing his beer and glancing away from the football game he'd been trying to get interested in for the past hour.

"I thought maybe you could use some company, what with being sick and all." Josh grinned in an obvious attempt to lighten Mike's mood, but Mike didn't return the smile.

"You don't have to baby-sit me, Josh. I'm not going back to Lucky's."

"I'm not baby-sitting you. I just don't want you hanging out here all alone."

"I live alone." Mike took a long pull on his beer. "How's today any different?"

Josh hesitated until he had Mike's full attention. "Quit acting like it's no big deal," he said, all levity gone. "I know you're having a tough time giving her up."

Mike opened his mouth to tell his brother that he didn't know what the hell he was talking about, but he couldn't get the words out—get them out and make them convincing, anyway. He *was* having a tough time giving Lucky up. And Mike resented the fact that loyalty to his family seemed to dictate he should.

"Think about it, though," Josh went on. "It's better to walk away now, before someone gets hurt. I can't see the relationship going anywhere in the long run, can you?"

Josh had a point there. Mike's relationships never went anywhere in the long run. He didn't seem capable of caring as deeply as other people and had to be extra careful not to hurt the women he dated.

But Lucky didn't seem to fall into the same category as those other women. Somehow, she'd ducked beneath his defenses, made him forget everything and everyone else....

He remembered her warm tears falling on his chest and the overwhelming anger he'd felt at what she'd endured as a child. Since when had he started feeling things so poignantly?

"No, I can't see it going anywhere," he said, suddenly determined to find his old self. He'd been criticized for being too cavalier with women, but "easy come, easy go" had its benefits.

"Yeah, well, she's too young for you, anyway."

Mike shot him warning glance. "Maybe you should stop while you're ahead, little brother."

Chuckling, Josh tossed a coaster at him. "There's the man I grew up with. You had me worried for a sec. I've never seen you sulk over a woman before."

"I'm not sulking." Mike tossed the coaster back at him. "Don't you have somewhere to go?"

"I do now that I know you're going to be okay." Josh stood

and headed for the door. "Are you sure you won't come over in an hour or so and have supper with me and Rebecca?"

"Are you kidding? Rebecca can't cook."

Josh looked wounded. "She tries."

Mike finally mustered a smile for his brother, who was so madly in love with Rebecca that he could eat charred toast at every meal if it made her happy. "She's learning," he said in an attempt to be generous. "I'm just not hungry tonight."

"I'll tell her you're still too sick."

"Good idea," he said, then the door clicked shut and Mike was alone again with his memories of last night.

LUCKY WAS GLAD to see the sun finally set. This Christmas had been the longest of her life. She knew the coming week, which many still considered "the holidays," wouldn't move much faster, but at least the stores would be open. She could distract herself from Mike by going to the diner, getting a haircut, buying a few supplies at the hardware store so she could do some wallpapering. Even facing down Marge at the grocery store seemed preferable to sitting here by herself. The contrast between having Mike's arms around her last night while she slept, and the certain knowledge that he wouldn't be coming back, was too much. She couldn't wait for Mr. Sharp to resume the repairs so she'd have the noise of his hammer or saw in the background.

Fortunately, she was tired tonight. It was barely eight o'clock but—she allowed herself a rueful grin—thanks to Mike and his insatiable *old man's* appetite, she'd slept only a few solid hours when she was with him. If she went to bed, maybe she could block out everything that had happened and feel nothing for a while. She particularly didn't want to think about her conversation with Josh and the stark realization that he was right—the relationship she longed for with Mike would cost Mike more than she ever wanted to see him lose. Especially when he had the loving, supportive, blood-is-thicker-than-water kind of family she'd always dreamed about. How could she expect him to give that up for her? The very foundation on which he'd built his life?

She crawled into bed wearing two pairs of sweats, hoping the added layer of clothing would keep her from missing his warm body. But extra sweats were a poor substitute, and she jumped up five minutes later to change the bedding. She couldn't forget Mike when she could smell him so clearly on the sheets and pillows. She needed to make this *her* room again.

But her memories wouldn't let her. So she took the bed apart and dragged the pieces, mattresses and all, into her mother's room, where she'd be certain to remember who and what she was—and why Mike Hill was completely out of reach.

After she'd managed to put the bed back together, she finally fell asleep. But long before morning she opened her eyes wide to stare at the glowing digits of her alarm clock. 11:00 p.m.

Something had awakened her—but what?

A moment later, she knew. She heard movement on the stairs.

Someone was in the house.

The hair stood up on the back of her neck, but she took a deep breath and told herself to calm down. It had to be Mike. Who else would it be? Who else even lived in the area? "Hello?" she called.

There was no answer, but when she sat up she could see light creeping through the crack beneath the door. She'd turned off all the lights before bed….

"Who is it?" she called again.

"She's in the master."

"I heard her, you idiot."

The gruff voices, voices she didn't immediately recognize, sent needlelike chills down her spine as footsteps pounded along the hall. Her door banged open, hitting the inside wall with a crash before Lucky could scramble out of bed.

She screamed and tried to roll to her right, but the two men bursting into the bedroom reached her before she could escape. Clawing fingers grabbed and gouged, and her hands were forced above her head. Jon Small straddled her waist. Smalley hovered over Jon's shoulder, holding a baseball bat.

"Where is it?" Jon demanded.

Breathing heavily from fear and their brief tussle, Lucky struggled to keep calm. It was the Smalls. She knew them. She didn't think they'd bring her serious harm. But the memory of Smalley banging her head into the pay phone made it difficult to look away from the bat he slapped so menacingly against one hand. She tried to speak, but her throat was so dry she could hardly get the words out. "Wh-what are you doing here?"

"You have something we want."

Jon fairly reeked of alcohol, and the solicitous smile she'd seen him wear on earlier occasions was gone. His expression now closely mimicked the slit-eyed, thuglike menace she saw in Smalley's face.

The Smalls were stupid, but not truly dangerous, she reminded herself. They had jobs, families, respect. Too much to lose. "Get off me," she said, managing to put some conviction in her voice. "You're drunk."

"Give me the proof you told our father you've got, and you won't have anything to worry about," Jon said.

Lucky thought of her mother's journal. She'd come to the conclusion that it wasn't worth the paper it was written on. She couldn't find Eugene Thompson, but she felt fairly certain he wouldn't want to know her any more than Dave Small or Garth Holbrook did. The information in that journal had turned out to be another huge disappointment. But it could still ruin lives—lives like Garth Holbrook's—if it fell into the wrong hands.

"Go to hell." She'd be damned if she'd give anything to Jon and Smalley. She wouldn't be the helpless little girl she'd once been, wouldn't be stripped of the power she'd gained as an adult in charge of her own life.

Surprise registered on Jon's face. He glanced back at Smalley, who cursed and smashed the bat into the bed.

The air stirred near Lucky's ear as the wood landed with a frightening *thwump* only inches away.

"You want to say that again?" Smalley taunted.

The light filtering in from the hall showed Lucky how eager he was to force what he wanted out of her, but she still wouldn't bend. When her mother was alive, she'd been too young to fight the events and circumstances that had left such a mark on her life. She hadn't been able to make a positive difference to anything, hadn't been able to make sure that Morris was treated as he should've been treated. But she was older now. She could resist whatever she had the guts to resist, and she'd had enough. The people in Dundee weren't going to push her one more inch.

"Go to hell," she repeated.

Jon's grip tightened painfully on her wrists. "What now?" he demanded of his brother. "You said she'd cough it up in a heartbeat."

Lucky flinched as Smalley hit the bed again. "Where is it?"

"*What* is it?" Jon asked. "We could probably find it if we knew what we were looking for."

Lucky glared up at them and refused to say a word. Defiance lent her strength, felt oddly liberating despite her fear. They wouldn't win. She wouldn't let them win. Deep down she knew she *couldn't*. The woman she'd become would disappear completely if she did.

"Smalley?" Jon said.

Doubt had crept into Jon's voice, but if Smalley was having seconds thoughts, it wasn't obvious. Deep grooves appeared between his mouth and jowl-like cheeks as he smiled. "Strip her."

Sheer terror seized Lucky. "Wh-what are you going to do?"

Smalley chuckled. "Give us whatever you've got that connects our father to your mother, and you won't have to find out."

"I—I could be your sister," she choked out.

Jon grimaced as though only now realizing the implications, but Smalley laughed. "At least you're prettier than our other one."

Self-preservation demanded she give them the journal and be done with it. She could call the police in the morning and report them. But Senator Holbrook's reputation would be ruined by then. And unless they hurt her badly, she knew the police wouldn't do anything. She meant nothing to this town.

"Lucky?" She suspected Jon felt the tremors going through her because he said her name with hope. She longed to capitulate, but she wouldn't be able to live with herself if she did. She wouldn't sacrifice her self-respect. It was all she had.

"I don't care what you do," she said. "I won't give you anything."

CHAPTER EIGHTEEN

MIKE WAS AWAKENED by the sound of an engine revving up and then down the road. Every time he thought it was gone, it would break the quiet once again.

Finally, he got up. It had to be a bunch of drunken kids drag racing, he decided. If he didn't put a stop to it, someone could get hurt.

Cursing because he'd just fallen asleep after hours of tossing and turning, he pulled on his jeans and an old T-shirt and yanked on his coat. Then he grabbed a rifle and headed outside, only to find the road empty.

He walked down to the end of the drive and looked both ways. Nothing. Of course they would've gone home now that he'd bothered to drag his tired ass out of bed.

He stood there for several minutes, heard nothing and turned back. Before he reached the house, however, the distant sound of a motor hummed on the cold night air.

Mike crossed to his Escalade and sat on the back bumper, resting the butt of the rifle on his thigh as he waited. The truck—he could see it was a truck now, judging by the height of the headlights—was drawing closer. When it was only a few miles away, he moved into the middle of the road and fired a couple of shots into the sky to make sure he got the driver's attention.

At first Mike thought whoever was behind the wheel

wasn't going to stop. He was about to jump out of the way when the truck slowed and Smalley stuck his head out the window. "What do you want, Hill?"

Mike could see someone sitting in the passenger seat and guessed it was Jon. Smalley and Jon spent a lot of time raising hell together. "What are you two doing out here?"

"Just havin' a bit of fun." Smalley glanced at his brother for confirmation, but from what Mike could see through the front windshield Jon wasn't smiling. Jon didn't seem to be having any fun.

"It's getting late. How 'bout you go home or at least have your fun somewhere else?"

"We keepin' you up?"

"I wouldn't be standing out here if I could sleep."

"Okay, sure thing," Smalley said, but before he could drive away, Mike heard someone call his name, softly, shakily and seemingly out of the darkness. Mystified, he put a hand on Smalley's beefy arm, which was dangling out of the cab along with his head, and peered into the bed of the truck. There he found Lucky tied to the side, wearing nothing but a lacy bra and a pair of white panties. Her hair looked like she'd been through a wind tunnel, and she was shivering violently.

"Lucky?" He set his rifle aside and peeled off his coat.

The truck lurched as Smalley put the engine in Park and climbed out. "Hey, leave her be."

Mike's heart thumped wildly as he hopped into the back. What the *hell* was going on?

"This is between Lucky and us," Smalley said. "She knows what she needs to do to get out of there, don't you, Lucky?"

"G-go to hell," she murmured, but she looked beaten. She sat on the cold metal of the truck bed, curled into as much of a ball as she could manage with her hands bound to the side.

Smalley clucked his tongue and shook his head. "See how

stubborn she is? Oh, well. We just got started. She'll be singin' a different tune when she's had enough."

"She's finished *now,*" Mike said, wrapping his coat around her, then working as quickly as possible to untie her.

Smalley scowled. "Hey, slow down a minute, Mike. This here's none of your business."

"It is now."

A grunt reached Mike's ears as Smalley reached over the side to stop him, but Mike gave him such a murderous look that he backed off. "You'll be hearing from me once I have her safe."

"There's no need to act so damn self-righteous," Smalley said. "Everyone knows you don't like her any better'n we do. No one does."

Mike clenched his teeth. Obviously Lucky hadn't heeded his advice and kept her mouth shut about her possible connection to Dave. Mike couldn't think of any other explanation. "What did you figure this would accomplish, Smalley?" he demanded, growing frustrated with the knots. "Where're her clothes?"

"Hell if I know. I'm such a prize, I couldn't keep her from strippin' down." Smalley wheezed as he laughed at his own bad joke.

Mike didn't know he was going to do it—he didn't know until he lurched halfway out of the truck bed and his fist met Smalley's fleshy face. But that moment of impact was immensely satisfying, especially when Smalley stumbled and fell backward, then blinked stupidly up at him from where he lay sprawled in the road.

"You ever touch her again, you'll need crutches," Mike said. "Do you understand?" He slapped the back window to make sure he had Jon's attention, too. "Do *you* understand?"

Jon climbed out and cut through the glare of the headlights

to reach his brother. "Jeez, Mike, what's gotten into you? I think you might've broken Smalley's nose."

Judging by the blood, Mike thought Jon was probably right. He hoped it was broken. A broken nose was less than Smalley deserved. "That isn't all I'm going to break if the two of you so much as look at Lucky again." Finally the knots came free and he swung himself over the side before turning back to get her.

With Jon's help, Smalley clambered to his feet. "I can't believe you did this," he complained. "I can't believe you busted up my face over a…a two-bit—"

"Don't say it," Mike warned, but Smalley wasn't thinking fast enough to stop himself.

"Whore," he finished, and Mike hit him again.

"Mike!" Jon tried to catch his staggering, three-hundred-pound brother and wound up falling to the blacktop with him.

Rage and adrenaline surged through Mike, but he shook the sting out of his fingers and ignored the Small brothers as he spoke gently to Lucky. He needed to get her inside before she ended up with pneumonia. "Come on, Lucky," he said. "Lean out. I'll help you."

She was shaking so badly, she could hardly hold his coat around her, but she managed to do as he asked, and he pulled her into his arms.

"Lucky stole your damn inheritance," Jon said. "She's living in your grandfather's freakin' house—and you make enemies out of *us,* just because we're trying to give her a little motivation to—" His brother made a noise of warning or complaint, Mike couldn't tell which, and Jon seemed to be more cautious about his next words "—to move on down the road?"

Mike shifted Lucky closer to his chest. "From now on, no one hurts Lucky or they answer to me."

Smalley shoved his massive body into a sitting position and

wiped the blood pouring from his nose. "People aren't going to like this, Mike."

Smalley's voice held a distinct threat, which made Mike turn back. "I already know about your father and Red, Smalley. You cause any more trouble, and I won't be the only one."

MIKE LEANED against the kitchen counter, still too angry to sit.

Lucky sipped a cup of coffee at his kitchen table, just as she had the night she'd first arrived in town almost four weeks ago—only this time he was glad, *relieved,* to have her there. What if he'd been sleeping as soundly as usual and hadn't heard Smalley's truck? What if he hadn't gotten up?

At the thought of her being treated in such a cruel, demeaning manner, his jaw tightened and his right hand curled into a fist. Too bad the Smalls had driven off as soon as Jon could get his brother into the truck, because Mike wanted to hit someone again.

"Tell me exactly what happened," he said. He knew she'd been through a harrowing ordeal, but he'd been stewing for more than an hour while she recuperated in the bath, and the thought of what might have occurred if he hadn't stopped it scared the hell out of him. "What were they doing? Threatening you to keep quiet about the past?"

Lucky stared into her cup so long he wondered if she was going to respond. Finally, she lifted her eyes. She was all bundled up, wearing his sweats and slippers and bathrobe—evidence that she was still trying to get her body temperature under control. But her thick, curly hair, the hair he loved to touch, fell down her back in shiny waves, and her skin glowed with a comforting, healthy sheen. She looked fine, which should've helped. Except he kept seeing her tied up, nearly naked and absolutely blue with cold, and the memory provoked him all over again.

"They wanted me to give them my mother's journal," she said.

"You *told* them about the journal?" He realized he was shouting and lowered his voice. "Damn it, Lucky. You had to know Dave wouldn't be happy about that. I warned you he might be dangerous."

"I didn't tell him about the journal, exactly. I merely *alluded* to the fact that I knew he'd been with my mother and that I had proof." She lifted her chin and gave him that "no one pushes me around" look he couldn't help admiring, especially after everything she'd been through.

"When?"

"At the Honky Tonk the night you drove me home. Dave let me know he wasn't too pleased that I'd returned. I let *him* know I didn't care."

"I'm waiting for the part where you told him you had enough information about the past to ruin his reputation and possibly his career."

"I guess that would be when he insulted my mother."

Insulted her mother? *Everyone* insulted her mother. Mike might have chuckled had the situation been less dire.

"Smalley cornered me by the bathroom that night, and you found me in the hall," she went on. "You thought I was drunk."

"You weren't?"

"I was, sort of, but that wasn't why I hit the ground."

"They *hurt* you that night?"

"A little."

"Why didn't you tell me?" He was nearly shouting again. Taking a deep breath, he continued more calmly. "You should've let me put a stop to it right away. You could have frozen to death out there, Lucky. What if I hadn't come out?"

"I'm sure they didn't expect to see you. It's Christmas, it's late, your house is set back. They were just driving up and down a public road."

"They were trying to keep your house tantalizingly close."

"That, too." She toyed with the Sweet'n Low packets his cook always left in the middle of the table. "Anyway, if they thought you'd care about what was happening, they probably would've taken me somewhere else."

"Shows you how stupid they are. I wouldn't let them treat anyone that way. Least of all—" He'd been about to say "least of all *you*," but he didn't feel ready to deal with the fact that it wasn't simply cruelty to others that had him so riled up. In hurting Lucky, the Smalls had somehow trespassed against *him*. He tried to convince himself that it was merely because Lucky was now his neighbor, but he knew it was more than that. He would've been angry no matter who the Smalls had abused, but he wouldn't have been quite this angry.

"Least of all a woman," he finished stiffly and turned to pour himself some coffee before she could read the truth on his face.

"Well, they didn't get what they wanted, that's the main thing." She smiled as though her words held great significance, but Mike was fixated on the fact that she could've stopped them and hadn't.

"Why didn't you give them the damn journal and be done with it?"

The smile disappeared. "I couldn't."

"Why not?"

She sighed. "I don't really want to go into this, Mike."

"Are you kidding me?"

"It doesn't matter anymore." She pushed her coffee aside and stood up. "I'm leaving first thing in the morning."

He could tell by the resolve in her voice that she didn't mean she was heading home. She was leaving town.

He tried to draw a deep breath but couldn't quite overcome the impact of her words. "The Victorian isn't finished yet," he said, even though he was supposed to be making her a huge offer to get her to do exactly what she'd just told him she was going to do. They could find Gabe another place. Mike couldn't imagine anyone, even his best friend, living in Lucky's house.

Lucky's… Since when had he stopped thinking of it as his grandfather's house?

"If you want to continue with the repairs, you can do it after we close escrow," she said.

He swallowed hard. "But I haven't made you an offer yet."

"Make me one."

"I'm not ready." The thought of Lucky driving off with all her belongings in her blue Mustang made him feel hollow inside.

"Then you can mail it to me."

"You're going to let those two bullies chase you out of town?"

He'd hoped he could challenge her, appeal to her fighting spirit. Lord knew not many women possessed a stronger one. But she didn't rise to the bait, which made him fear she was already completely committed.

She shook her head. "It's not just Jon and Smalley. It's your family and this town and—"

"And what?" *As if that's not enough*… He had to keep her talking, get her to reconsider, at least until he could figure out how he felt and what he should do.

She didn't answer right away. Crossing the kitchen, she came to stand before him, so close he thought she might slip her arms around his neck. She didn't touch him, but he longed to touch her—to part the robe and find the warm skin buried beneath those layers of clothes, to reassure himself that she was *really* okay.

If only he didn't feel too numb to move. He'd known she'd be leaving eventually. He'd been *counting* on it so his life could return to normal. But…

"I'm in love with you, Mike," she said softly, her eyes wide and honest, "so in love that I can't even ask you to love me back."

Mike caught his breath. He always did his best to avoid such declarations. "I love you" put him in an uncomfortable position. He generally replied with a polite, "Thank you," then proceeded to distance himself from the person in question—because he'd never felt strongly enough about a woman to become responsible for her future happiness or to risk his own. But he didn't know how he felt right now, except that he didn't want to say thank you *or* goodbye.

"What if I don't want you to go?" he asked.

She gave him a sad smile. "I'd go anyway."

MIKE STOOD AT THE WINDOW of the spare bedroom where Lucky was sleeping, the bedroom she'd used that first night, and stared out at the moon. Damn Smalley. If he and Jon hadn't hurt Lucky tonight, she probably would've let things ride for another month or two. Somehow another month or two sounded much better than saying goodbye to her tomorrow.

She stirred on the bed and he glanced over, wondering if she could sense his presence, and his turmoil. He didn't want her to leave Dundee. He didn't even want her to leave his house. But he couldn't ask her to stay. Not when he'd never been able to commit himself before, not when he couldn't say with some assurance that he was in it for the long haul. His decision affected the happiness of too many people.

He rubbed his eyes. During these last weeks in Dundee, she'd been through enough. It would be kinder to let her move on and eventually meet and fall in love with someone else, someone who wasn't connected to her past and who had a family that would embrace her and love her as she deserved. Better to let her settle in a town with no prejudices or animosity. She was so young; she deserved a younger man.

But her words—*I'm in love with you, Mike*—echoed in his brain over and over again, and tugged at his heart. He wished he could protect her, wished he could tell everyone, including his own family, that if they tried to hurt her in any way, they'd have to deal with him first.

Except he was afraid he'd be the one to hurt her in the end.

She moved again, and he realized she was having trouble sleeping. He told himself he should slip out, before she found him here. But if this was to be their last night together, he didn't want to spend it in his own room.

Crossing to her, he sat on the edge of the bed and smoothed the hair from her face.

A second later, she blinked up at him.

"Hi," he said.

"What is it?" she whispered.

He couldn't say. He didn't want to talk. He only wanted to feel, to touch her, one more time.

Lowering his mouth to hers, he kissed her gently, coaxing her to understand—and he knew she did when her fingers came up and slowly undid the buttons of his shirt.

LUCKY KNEW as she drifted off to sleep an hour later that something significant had happened. She felt it in the way Mike had moved, the way he'd touched her. She guessed he'd recognized the difference, too, simply because he'd been so somber. But when she opened her eyes the following morning, she knew last night hadn't really changed anything. She'd come to Dundee with the childish hope of gaining a father. Instead she'd lost what was left of her heart—and her soul—to Mike Hill.

Rolling over, she reached for him. She wanted to discuss the details of selling him the house, recognized how difficult it would be to speak to him later. But he was gone.

She sat up—and it was then she heard voices coming from elsewhere in the house.

Lucky's stomach tensed as she wondered if it might be Mike's parents.

Getting up, she walked gingerly to the door. After doing her best to fight off Smalley and Jon last night, and being thrown around in the bed of that truck, her sore muscles complained at the slightest movement.

"They're idiots." Mike's voice, filled with impatience, drifted back to her as she quietly opened the door. "Why would they file a police report after what they did to Lucky?"

"Because Dave's furious. You messed Smalley's face up pretty bad, Mike. I saw him when he came in, and I'm telling you he looks like he's been in a damn train wreck."

Lucky couldn't place the second voice. She leaned out of the room to peer down the hall but could see only a portion of Mike's long legs as he sat at the kitchen table. Whoever was with him seemed to be across from him, beyond her view.

"I don't care how bad he looks," Mike said. "They stripped Lucky down in freezing weather and tied her into the back of their truck. When I think about it, I regret that I didn't break a few *more* bones. Jon got off too easy."

"Careful," the other person responded. "Violence isn't going to get us anywhere. Does Lucky have any damage to show for what happened last night?"

"Damage?" Mike echoed.

"Bumps and bruises, that sort of thing?"

"I'm sure she's got a few bumps and bruises from rolling around in the back of their truck. But that's not the point, Orton. She could've caught pneumonia out there. Or worse."

Mike had called his visitor Orton. Lucky tried to place the name and finally realized that this had to be *Officer* Orton. She'd met him once before, when he'd visited her high school class on some antidrug campaign. Did his presence at the ranch mean that Smalley and Jon had gone to the *police?*

"They claim they weren't going to take it far enough for anyone to get hurt, and you don't have proof that they would have."

"You can't kidnap a woman from her house, strip her and tie her into the bed of your truck, just for kicks!"

Orton's voice was so low, Lucky had to listen carefully to catch his next words. "They say they didn't kidnap her. They say she came with them willingly and that it was her idea to tie her up."

"What?"

"Apparently, she's into that bondage stuff. Stranger things have happened."

"That's bullshit!" Mike slammed his fist on the table. A moment later, he wasn't sitting down anymore; he was pacing back and forth.

"Come on, Mike. You know what her mother was like, what her own reputation says about her. Everyone does."

Closing her eyes, Lucky leaned her forehead against the wall. It always came back to Red. But that wasn't the worst of it; by being here and involving Mike, Lucky was dragging him down with her.

"I can't believe Jon and Smalley are really going to claim that." Mike's voice again. "Don't they care about their wives?"

"Jon's not married anymore."

"And Smalley's wife is so cowed he could say or do anything and she'd put up with it," Mike added in obvious disgust.

"Lucky's an attractive woman. Smalley and Jon went out for a little fun, and she jumped on the bandwagon. It's certainly believable."

Mike cursed several times. Lucky opened her eyes to see Orton come into view and reach out a placating hand. "Calm down, you're overreacting."

"I'm not overreacting. Smalley's lying. Lucky would never do that."

"How do you know?"

There was a big pause.

"Mike?"

He whipped around, wearing a determined expression, from what she could see. "Because the only person she's ever slept with is *me*."

Lucky smothered a gasp. Down the hall, this announcement met with an unnatural silence.

Finally, Orton seemed to rally from his shock. "Mike, I don't have to tell you Lucky isn't too popular in these parts. Are you sure you want to feud with the Smalls, just because you're all sleeping with the same woman?"

"We're not sleeping with the same woman. I'm telling you, Lucky didn't go with them willingly."

When he spoke again, Orton didn't sound convinced, but his tone suggested he didn't want to argue. "Well, I know this much. Your families are two of the oldest, most respected in the area. There's never been a problem between you before, and I don't see the point in causing one now."

"I'm not causing this problem, Orton."

"From what your mother's told my wife about Lucky, I think your parents would rather not know you've had any contact with her. Your folks went through a lot of grief over Morris. Let them be done with Red and her kids. Don't dredge up the past."

"I can't change what happened last night."

"You can call Smalley and apologize. Put this thing to rest before it blows up in your face."

"Like hell. Smalley had better be damn sure he stays away from Lucky in future."

"If he presses charges, you could be in trouble," Orton warned. "And he says he's pressing charges. Jon's a witness."

"Let 'em try. Lucky and I will press charges, too."

Lucky nearly groaned out loud. *Lucky and I?* He was linking them together.

"I'm telling you this is going to turn into a mess, Mike. Do you really want to go that far?"

"I'll go as far as I have to. I won't let them twist last night into something it's not."

Lucky bit her lip. She wanted Mike to drop it. She was leaving town and she wasn't ever coming back. It didn't really matter whether the people of Dundee believed she'd had some sort of kinky sexual escapade with the insufferable Smalls, as long as they still thought well of Mike. But now that he'd told Orton about them, it was bound to get back to his family and cause even more trouble.

"You could've called me," Orton said. "You didn't have to punch Smalley."

When Mike responded, he sounded tired but resigned. "Yeah, I did."

CHAPTER NINETEEN

WHEN OFFICER ORTON LEFT, Mike turned to find Lucky standing at the entrance to the kitchen.

"We had a visitor this morning," he said.

"I heard."

He leaned against the counter and shoved his hands in his pockets, wondering how she handled the outrage. He'd been intimately involved in her life for only a short time, and the injustice she faced in Dundee was already driving him mad. To think he used to believe the same thing everyone else did… "So what's your take?"

"I wouldn't sleep with Smalley and his brother if they were the last men on earth."

That much he knew. And he'd be damned if he'd stand back, as Orton obviously wanted him to do, and let Smalley and Jon blame Lucky.

"Smalley's taking a pretty big chance," he said.

"How's that?"

"You said he didn't get what he wanted last night."

"He didn't."

"Then, we could show your mother's journal to everyone in town, which is exactly what he was trying to avoid."

She tightened the belt of the robe she was wearing. "Actually, we can't."

"Why not?"

"There're two other men named in that journal who could also be my father."

More trouble. Mike could feel it coming. He was reluctant to ask, but he did anyway. "Who?"

"A guy by the name of Eugene Thompson."

He *almost* allowed himself a sigh of relief. "Never heard of him."

"I'm pretty sure you'll know the next guy."

The unease was back. "And he is…"

"Do you really want to know?"

Was the truth *that* bad? "Tell me."

"Garth Holbrook."

Mike's jaw dropped. He'd been prepared for a shock, but *Senator Holbrook?* Besides his own father, Holbrook's name was the last one he'd expected to hear. Holbrook was a solid citizen, a good legislator, a real family man. Holbrook was his best friend's *father.* "There must be some mistake."

Lucky shook her head. "No, his affair with my mother lasted about two months. There's no mistake."

"But…" Suddenly, Mike understood the call he'd received from Holbrook the day before Christmas.

Any chance she might sell out and move away?…What if I were to sweeten the pot by a couple hundred thousand?

Evidently, Holbrook was worried about more than Gabe.

"Gabe worships his father," he said.

Lucky seemed to understand that he was talking to himself more than her and didn't respond.

"This will devastate him." It would devastate anyone, Mike thought. Holbrook had cheated on his wife, on his whole family. Gabe and Reenie could have a half sister! They'd feel hurt, angry, betrayed. They'd be humiliated when the whole town found out that their father wasn't as unsullied as everyone had always believed. The scandal could ruin Garth's marriage and his career. The ramifications seemed to go on and on.

No wonder Garth wanted Lucky to move away.

Mike pictured Gabe, already angry and bitter, forcing his chair over the thick pile of the carpet. "We've got to burn that journal," he said. "Right away."

Lucky didn't argue. But when they hurried over to the Victorian, they found the whole place ransacked.

The journal was gone.

LUCKY STOOD with Mike on the small cement pad outside Jon Small's trailer—he'd clearly lost more than his wife in the divorce—waiting for someone to answer the door. It was difficult to believe that only a few hours earlier, she'd been planning to leave town today. If not for the disappearance of her mother's journal, she'd already be on the road. But now that proof of the past had fallen into the wrong hands, she had a terrible feeling that all hell was about to break loose. Leaving now would feel too much like running away, and Lucky was finished running.

Jon finally cracked the door open and peered out at them. "What do you want?"

"To talk to Dave," Mike said.

"He's not here."

"We just spoke to your mother. She said he was."

Jon shook his head in apparent disgust that his mother had been so forthcoming with this information, but if Liz Small felt any resentment toward Mike, she sure hadn't shown it when they were at her house. Before they left, Mike had told her he'd apologize for hitting Smalley, except that Smalley had deserved it, and she'd said she knew Mike wouldn't have done it otherwise.

Too bad Jon and Smalley weren't more like their mother….

Leaving the door ajar, Jon went into the house, presumably to get his father.

"You have some nerve coming here," Dave said as soon as he appeared.

The subtle change in Mike's stance told Lucky he considered Dave a more worthy adversary than Jon or Smalley. She supposed it was the power of Dave's will that caused this reaction. He was used to being in charge and having a say in what happened around him. Plus, Dave was the only one of the Small men who had half a brain.

"We're here for the journal," Mike said.

Dave had obviously been too busy glaring at Lucky to pay much attention to Mike's words, because they seemed to come as a real surprise. "What did you say?"

"Give us the journal."

"I don't know what the hell you're talking about. What journal? Is that what she had on me?"

Confused, Lucky glanced at Mike. She supposed Dave could be playing games with them, but he sounded genuine to her.

"Jon and Smalley didn't go back to my place last night?" she said.

Dave's jaw was set in an angry line. "Jon and Smalley went to the hospital in Boise. Then, in case you haven't heard, they went to the police."

"Not a smart move if you want us to keep our mouths shut," Mike pointed out.

"I figure you're not going to keep your mouths shut anyway. Better to do what I can."

"Let's go," Mike said to Lucky and walked away.

Lucky remained. She could almost see Dave's mind working, trying to figure out a better way to position himself in light of this new information.

"I hope you're not my father," she said, "because if you are, I'd be too ashamed to claim you." She looked him up and down, just to let him know what a pathetic excuse for a man she thought he was, then followed Mike to the truck.

"If *you* don't have the journal and *we* don't have the journal, who does?" he called after her.

Lucky didn't answer.

"What are you going to do? Will you and Mike let this go and keep your mouths shut? Can we count on that, at least?"

Hesitating as she reached the SUV, she turned back. "Drop the charges, Dave."

"If I do, will you keep your mouths shut?"

"Just drop the charges," she said and climbed in.

WHEN LUCKY AND MIKE ARRIVED at Senator Holbrook's house, Mike had to force himself to press the doorbell. He didn't want to confront Garth with what he knew. Worse was the thought of encountering Celeste and having to pretend nothing was wrong. But Lucky said the senator was the only other person she'd told about the journal. Which meant he either had it, or for Gabe's sake, he should know it was now missing.

"Hi, Mike."

Mike swallowed a groan when Celeste answered the door and did his best to return her smile. "Hi, Celeste, how are you?"

"Good." She looked curiously at Lucky. "Who's your friend?"

"This is Lucky Caldwell."

She nodded graciously. "It's a pleasure to meet you, Lucky."

Mike knew Celeste must've recognized Lucky's name and had to be astonished to see them together. But her impeccable manners wouldn't allow her to give any of that away.

"Are you two enjoying the holidays?"

Mike wasn't sure he could claim true enjoyment. This year, the holidays had had their high points, but they'd also had their lows. Too much had happened. But small talk was small talk. "We are, and you?"

"It's been wonderful to have Garth home."

"I'll bet." He hoped she'd continue to be happy about that, but a lot depended on the missing journal. "Is the senator here, then?"

"He is. Please, come in." She ushered them into the marble entryway Mike had seen so many times growing up. It still had the high ceilings and tall mirrors he remembered, but the sculpture on the pedestal in the center had changed. Celeste had always supported local artists. Sculptures, ceramics, paintings of all kinds filled her home. "I'll get him," she said and hurried off.

Mike exchanged a meaningful glance with Lucky. She seemed different all of a sudden, more nervous than she'd been at Dave's. He reached out to squeeze her shoulder in reassurance just as Senator Holbrook came from somewhere in the back of the house.

"Hello, Mike." Garth's tone was cautious, his expression guarded. His eyes cut briefly to Lucky, but he didn't greet her. "What can I do for you?"

Celeste had accompanied him, so Mike chose his words carefully. "I've got some fund-raising concerns I'd like to go over with you, if you've got a minute."

Again his eyes flicked toward Lucky, but he spoke to his wife. "Celeste, would you be so good as to bring our guests some of that delicious spiced cider you make every Christmas?"

"Of course, dear."

"Thank you."

As she left, Senator Holbrook escorted them into his study.

Once he closed the heavy mahogany door, he leaned against it, waiting for Mike to speak.

"Do you have it?" Mike asked.

"I'm afraid I don't know what you're talking about."

The trees outside the only window blocked the sun, making the room darker than the entryway. Mike couldn't read Garth's expression well enough to judge his veracity.

"My mother's journal," Lucky said.

"Someone broke into her house last night and took it," Mike explained.

"I'm sorry to hear that," he said, but he didn't seem distraught in the least, which told Mike everything he needed to know.

"We wanted to alert you, just in case," Mike said and then, because he was so disappointed in Garth, he added, "For Gabe's sake."

Holbrook didn't speak for a second. Finally, he said, "Mike, I—"

The sound of Celeste's heels, clicking across the marble entryway, intruded.

"Never mind." Holbrook moved away from the door. "Thank you for the visit."

Mike nodded and waved Lucky out ahead of him.

Holbrook seemed to be struggling with the role of cordial host and didn't even follow them out. But they immediately encountered Celeste, who was carrying a tray with a pitcher and mugs.

"Oh! You're leaving already?"

Mike gave her his kindest smile. "We just had a quick question."

"Don't you want to stay for a cup of cider?"

"Maybe another time," he said. "You and Garth go ahead. We can show ourselves out."

She seemed torn, but her hands were full and Garth, who

was still in his study, was obviously her priority. "Well, thanks for coming."

Mike nodded, and her gaze fell to Lucky. "You've become a beautiful woman, Lucky."

"Thank you." Lucky seemed to have difficulty meeting her eyes, and Mike could understand. It wasn't easy to accept Celeste's kindness when they were sheltering such a terrible secret. He thought he could understand, a little, how disloyal Lucky had felt toward Morris for holding her tongue as a young girl.

"Enjoy the rest of the holidays," Celeste said, and gave them a parting smile.

MIKE INSISTED on helping Lucky straighten up everything that was at the Victorian. She knew he should probably go home. With Orton's involvement, the missing journal and their visit to the Holbrooks hanging over them, they were only begging for more trouble by spending so much time together. But Mike hadn't mentioned leaving, and Lucky didn't want to be the one to bring it up—not when being with him was the only thing she really wanted.

"Do you think Senator Holbrook was embarrassed that you know?" she asked as she dished up the turkey, stuffing, mashed potatoes and green bean casserole she'd made during the previous two days.

Mike was sitting on the couch in the living room, watching her. "He was feeling something. I'm not sure it was embarrassment."

"He didn't ask you not to tell Gabe."

"He knows I won't tell anyone *because* of Gabe."

"Yeah, I guess you made that clear." She put the first plateful of food into the microwave so she could heat it up.

"Why did you tell Holbrook about the journal in the first place?" Mike asked.

Lucky kept her face averted so he wouldn't know what a disappointment her conversation with Holbrook had been. "I wanted him to take a paternity test."

"He declined?"

"He offered me two hundred thousand dollars to go away."

Mike didn't respond for several seconds. "I'm sorry," he said at last.

"It's okay." She tried to act flippant about it, but Mike was beginning to know her too well. He got up and walked over to her. Circling her waist with his arms, he pulled her back against his chest.

"I know it doesn't change the way that encounter must have felt, Lucky, but he has a lot to lose," he said, kissing her neck in consolation.

"Too much, apparently. Seems like everyone who associates with me has too much to lose, doesn't it?"

She laughed, but she knew he'd drawn the connection to himself when his arms tightened. "It's not fair to either one of us that your mother made such a terrible mess of everything."

Lucky put her hands on his arms, reveling in the solid feel of him behind her, the comfort of his solace. "She wasn't all bad, you know."

She'd spoken the words so softly she wasn't sure he'd heard until he responded. "Tell me some of the good things."

That he was even willing to listen surprised Lucky. She leaned her head on his chest and closed her eyes, searching for happy memories. Somehow the bad ones were so much easier to remember. "She kept me and my brothers together, for one."

His lips moved at her temple. "That's definitely a good thing."

"Occasionally, she'd buy me a small present, some little treat she'd bring home."

"I like that, too."

"She always made a fuss over my birthday. She let me dress up using all her costume jewelry and high heels, and play with her makeup. She didn't care if I ate cake batter instead of baking the cake. And she never made me feel bad that I couldn't stay on a diet—" A lump suddenly swelled in Lucky's throat, making it difficult to continue. But the fact that she *could* continue, that there were more positive things she could say about her mother, made a real impact on her. "She thought I was beautiful. She was proud of me even when I was fat and ugly—"

"Whoa!" He squeezed her reprovingly. "I don't like hearing you say that about yourself. Maybe she saw what I can finally see."

"What's that?" she asked.

He turned her in his arms. "The beauty of your heart."

The lump in her throat grew larger. She attempted a watery smile as he brought her face up with one finger. "Your mother might not have been perfect," he murmured, "but she loved you. And I can forgive her because of that."

He'd said something profound, something that spoke to Lucky on a very deep level. Caressing his whisker-roughened cheek with the palm of one hand, she gazed into his eyes. "Can you really, Mike?"

He nodded.

"If you can forgive her, maybe I can, too."

"It's worth a try."

Lucky ran her fingers through his hair as he kissed her. She felt his body respond, felt her own pulse quicken, but the telephone interrupted them.

Reluctantly, she pulled away, wiping her eyes, and reached for the cordless phone on the counter. "Hello?"

"Lucky, it's Josh. Is Mike there?"

Lucky didn't know whether to lie or not. When they'd returned from Holbrook's earlier, she'd insisted they leave Mike's truck at the ranch and walk over to her place. As far as she knew, there were no telltale signs that they were still together. But they'd been seen in town by both the Smalls and the Holbrooks, and if Mike's truck was at home and he wasn't, where else could he be? Josh would know he wasn't out with the horses. "Just a minute," she said, opting for the truth.

Mike looked at her curiously as she handed him the phone. "It's your brother."

He gave a persecuted sigh before bringing the receiver to his ear. But his expression soon changed. "What?... You're kidding. Are you sure?... When?... Where does he think she is?... Okay, I'm leaving now."

Lucky held her breath, waiting for the bad news. "What is it?" she asked the instant Mike hung up.

"The fact that we've been seeing each other is all over town. Someone at the beauty shop told my mother while she was getting her hair done. She was pretty upset when she left, so Rebecca called to tell my dad she was on her way, but she never arrived."

"Where do you think she is?"

"I have no idea, but everyone's searching, and I'm going to go help, okay?"

"Of course." Lucky grabbed his hat from the counter and put it on his head. "Be careful."

He kissed her, promising he'd call her as soon as he found his mother, and hurried out. She thought she might have a long wait before she knew what was going on.

Fifteen minutes later someone rang the bell.

CHAPTER TWENTY

LUCKY OPENED THE DOOR to see Barbara Hill on her porch.

"Oh…hi," she said, her ulcer voicing a sharp complaint at the sudden tension that gripped her.

Barbara stood ramrod straight, her hands clenching her purse in a death grip. Lifting her chin, she cleared her throat, obviously finding it difficult to speak. "Is it true?" she said.

Lucky knew Barbara was asking about the nature of her relationship with Mike, but she didn't know how to answer. Was it true that Lucky had fallen in love with him? Yes. Years ago. Was it true they'd been seeing each other since she'd returned? Yes. Often and not casually. Was it true that Lucky expected something permanent to come of it? No. She couldn't ask Mike to stand against his family, against all of Dundee. And she knew he'd never leave this place. His business was here. His brother was here. The land was part of him.

"No," she said simply. If they had no future together, the rest didn't matter.

"You're not sleeping with my son?"

Lucky drew a deep breath. She wanted the pain to stop—for everyone. But she couldn't say her relationship with Mike wasn't of a sexual nature when Mike had already admitted to Officer Orton that it was. "We've been together a few times."

Barbara winced and closed her eyes, so obviously and

deeply betrayed that Lucky couldn't help feeling sorry for her. "Does he care about you?"

He did care. Lucky felt quite certain of that. But she knew it would only hurt his mother to hear it. "No." She shook her head. "It was all me. I—I've loved him since I was little. But you don't have to worry. I'm leaving town today, and I won't be coming back."

Her complete surrender left Barbara with nothing to fight about. "Thank you," she said quietly, stiffly. Then she left.

Watching her go, Lucky managed a sad smile. Barbara had believed that her relationship with Mike was one-sided because she'd *wanted* to believe it. Mike had always been such an ideal son, she couldn't *not* believe it. Which was good. If Lucky took the blame, Mike and his family would be able to patch things up and withstand the gossip.

She just had to keep her promise to leave. The sooner the better. Before she had to tell Mike goodbye.

THE NUMBNESS THAT SEEMED to take over the moment Barbara Hill's car disappeared from view made it easier for Lucky. She refused to think while she packed, refused to look at the ranch next door as she loaded her Mustang. She simply left the key to the house above the door so Mr. Sharp could finish up, and drove away. Once the improvements were complete and the rental company had reclaimed their furniture, she could contact Mike about selling. She knew she wouldn't be able to speak to him anytime soon, not without breaking down. She could only hope the ensuing weeks would give her a chance to pull herself together before she had to deal with the past again.

The wind that flooded her car as she drove, with both windows down, nearly froze her despite her hat, scarf and heavy coat. But she didn't close the windows. The cold helped her stay numb, which, at this point, seemed infinitely preferable to *feeling*.

It wasn't easy to pass the businesses as she drove through town and to realize she'd never see them again. Booker Robinson honked and waved as they faced each other at Dundee's only intersection, but she couldn't even wave back. The cold had turned her blood to ice. She felt as if she could hardly move, except to press the gas pedal and put as many miles as possible between her and this town.

Briefly, she wondered where she was going. But that seemed too big a decision to make right now, while her brain was functioning on automatic pilot. She'd go wherever the highway took her and get a motel room when she became too tired to drive.

Finley's came up on her right, the Arctic Flyer on her left. Hair and Now, the library, the Honky Tonk. Lucky wanted to find the anger she'd felt when she'd left Dundee at eighteen; she wanted to hate this place. But she couldn't. The hate and the anger were gone.

Now all she had was a broken heart.

BARBARA HILL SPOTTED Mike's Escalade in her rearview mirror just after she pulled out of Finley's parking lot. She couldn't see his face very clearly, but she could tell he wasn't smiling. She wondered whether he'd spoken to Lucky after she did, whether Lucky had told him about her visit. She hoped not. If Lucky would only make good on her promise to leave right away and not come back, Barbara felt they could ignore the fact that she'd ever returned in the first place.

Barbara didn't like the picture that came into her mind when she thought of her son with Red's daughter, but Mike was single and nearly forty years old. It probably wasn't any big deal that he'd had a fling with a girl like Lucky. If only

Mike had been more discreet, Barbara wouldn't even have had to know. As long as Lucky wasn't a real threat to her son's heart, she preferred *not* to know.

Mike followed her all the way home, where she found Josh's truck already parked out front.

Once she pulled into the drive, she took her time getting out.

"Where have you been?" Mike asked, meeting her as she opened her car door.

She nodded toward the backseat. "Could you grab the groceries?"

"I will as soon as you answer me."

"While I was getting my hair done, Sheila Holley mentioned that you'd gotten into a scrape with the Smalls, so I stopped by the police department to talk to Officer Orton." She left out the part about driving to the Victorian afterward. "You know his wife's a friend of mine. We sing in the church choir together."

Mike studied her as though trying to read her thoughts. "You should've called Dad. We were worried about you."

"Why were you worried? I'm fine. And you'll be glad to know that while I was at the police station, Dave Small called. Smalley's dropping the charges."

He didn't seem particularly relieved, but he retrieved both bags of groceries. "Good. Now I won't have to file charges against *them*. They were in the wrong, not me."

She realized he probably expected her to request his side of the story, but she already knew Lucky played a significant role in it, and she didn't want him to talk about her. She didn't want to hear how he'd defended her. She didn't want him to so much as mention Lucky's name. She was too afraid she might detect something in his voice she'd rather not hear.

Lucky was leaving. Nothing else mattered.

"All's well that ends well, I guess," she said and started up the walkway.

He followed her with the groceries. "All's well that ends well?"

She turned back and actually managed a smile as the tightness in her chest—the panic—slowly receded. Everything was going to be okay. Lucky might be a lot of things, but she'd seemed sincere about leaving. Soon, the world as Barbara knew it would return to normal. "Don't you agree?"

"Mom, I think maybe it's time for us to talk about—"

"I don't want to know any more, Mike." She opened the front door and waved him into the house. "I've heard enough for one day."

He frowned before walking past her. "That's all you've got to say to me?"

"That's it. Now let's eat. I bought some seasoned tri-tip steak that should be fabulous."

"WANT SOME more potatoes, Mike?"

Mike shook his head at his brother's question. Josh had asked him twice if he wanted another helping of potatoes. Rebecca had offered him seconds, too, before she left the table to see if she could get a cranky Brian to nap in the back room. Mike would have pointed this out to Josh, except he knew his brother was only trying to compensate for their father's morose silence. Larry sat brooding over his meal and had barely spoken to Mike all evening.

"What about salad?" Josh said. "You get enough of that, too?"

Mike glanced up. "I'm fine on salad, Josh. *Thanks.*"

Josh sent him a lame grin. "Sure thing."

"What are your plans for New Year's, boys?" Barbara asked. In the face of Larry's surliness, her false cheer seemed more forced than ever.

"I thought I might take Rebecca to Boise for dinner," Josh

said. "It's been a long time since we've been to Asiago's. She loves that place." He gave her a sheepish look. "Any chance you'll be available to baby-sit?"

"Of course." She poured herself a third glass of wine. Mike couldn't help noticing that she was eating little and drinking much, far more than usual. "What about you, Mike?"

"No plans," he said.

"I'll bet Mary Thornton's free. I ran into her at the grocery store and she seemed pretty sad that you don't call her any-more. Maybe the two of you could go to Boise with Josh and Rebecca."

If Mike had needed proof that his mother wasn't quite her-self, this suggestion would have confirmed it. Josh had dated Mary before he'd married Rebecca, so Mary's company wouldn't be very appealing to his sister-in-law, and Barbara knew it.

"Maybe," he muttered. Mike had taken Mary out a few times, too, very casually. He wasn't interested in seeing her again, no matter how obvious she made it that she'd like a relationship with him. But he thought it wiser to sidestep the whole issue.

Barbara finished her wine and began clearing away the plates. Mike pushed back his chair so he could get up and help her, but the moment she disappeared into the kitchen, Larry finally gave him some attention—in the form of a cold stare. "Lucky?" he said through gritted teeth. "*Lucky*, Mike?"

"Don't start, Dad," Mike said. "You don't really know her."

"I don't *want* to know her. And I can't believe you'd bother making nice to her, either."

Josh spoke. "Maybe we should wait a few days to talk about this."

Larry ignored him. "After everything your mother's done for you, how could you knowingly hurt her? And start the whole town talking about it, besides?"

"I wasn't trying to hurt anyone, and I certainly wasn't trying to start a scandal."

"Excuse me if I find that a little difficult to swallow. You slept with her, didn't you? What were you thinking? Do you have any idea how many men she's probably been with?"

Mike felt a muscle twitch in his cheek and couldn't help the hard edge that entered his voice. "I know exactly how many men she's been with, Dad. She's been with one. *Me.*"

"You don't really believe that."

"She's not what you think," Josh said.

Larry glared at Josh as malevolently as he'd been glaring at Mike. "Whose side are you on?"

Josh's eyebrows shot up. He'd never been asked to choose between his parents and his brother before, and Mike didn't want him to have to choose now. "Stay out of it, Josh."

"I think we should *all* let it go," Josh said. "No one's perfect. And Lucky told me herself she's leaving town in a month or two. There's nothing to worry about."

"You don't see anything wrong with what Mike's done?" Larry said.

Josh scowled. "He cares about her, Dad."

Larry shook his head in disgust. "You two stand together on absolutely everything. But this is one time you both should've stood with us." With that he tossed his napkin onto the table and stalked out of the room.

As Mike watched him go, he was tempted to follow him and finish the argument. But he knew it wouldn't make any difference. He hadn't planned on getting involved with Lucky. He hadn't planned on caring about her. But Josh was right— he did. And he was sure his father wouldn't approve.

"What's wrong?" Barbara asked as she returned for more plates. "Where's your father?"

One look at the empathy in Josh's face, and Mike figured

it was time to go. "I guess he's not comfortable with the company I'm keeping," he said and headed for the door.

MIKE SPOTTED Gabe's truck outside the Honky Tonk on his way home and decided to stop. He needed a beer and some time to think. After what he'd learned about Gabe's father, he also felt he should connect with his best friend, make sure Gabe was still okay—as okay as Gabe ever was since the accident.

"How's it goin'?" Mike asked, approaching the table where his friend sat, nursing a beer.

Gabe gave him a rueful smile. "From the rumors spreading all over town, I'm probably a hell of a lot better than you are."

"You heard about me and Lucky, then."

"Everyone's heard about you and Lucky. You told *Orton,* for God's sake. He might wear a uniform, but he's the biggest gossip in town."

"I had to tell him." Mike waved to the bartender, indicated he'd have a beer, too, then sat across from Gabe.

"Why?"

"Because Jon and Smalley were saying crazy things about her."

"So you rode to the rescue."

"I told the truth."

"Too bad you didn't take my advice and stay away from her."

"Your advice came a little too late," Mike said, but he suspected it wouldn't have made a difference, no matter when Gabe had warned him off. Mike had known from the beginning that he should stay away from Lucky. He just hadn't been able to do it.

"What do your folks have to say about the situation?" Gabe asked.

"What do you think?"

"I'm sure they're not happy."

"My mom's in denial. My dad's mad as hell."

"What about Josh?"

"Josh is playing the middle man."

"And Lucky?"

Mike scrubbed a hand over his face. He'd told her he'd call as soon as he found his mother, but he couldn't do it from his parents' house. The situation had been too volatile, too tense. Excusing himself to give her a call would've been like tossing a match into a puddle of gasoline.

He could call her now, he supposed, but he didn't want to feel the craving he felt every time he heard her voice. He couldn't go from his father's accusing words—*After everything your mother's done for you, how could you knowingly hurt her?*—straight into Lucky's arms.

"None of this is fair to Lucky," he said.

Gabe took another drink of his beer. "My mom actually likes her."

Mike chuckled. "Your mom likes everybody."

"She said you and Lucky came by earlier. What was that all about?"

"I met someone from Pocatello who might be willing to make a campaign contribution," Mike said, spinning the lie as quickly as possible, then hiding his face in his beer.

"You think he might be a heavy hitter?"

Someone played "Long Black Train" on the jukebox, and Mike felt as though he'd gotten on a long black train to somewhere. He just didn't know where. "Sounds like it. I guess we'll see," he said. "What are you doing in town so late, anyway?"

Gabe toyed with the matches in the ashtray, turning them over and over between fingers callused from maneuvering his wheelchair. "Trying to decide whether or not to go home."

"Why wouldn't you?" Mike asked. "You love that lonesome cabin."

"I don't know." Gabe sighed. "Something's going on with my dad. It's driving me crazy. He hasn't been himself for a couple of weeks now."

Mike tried not to fidget uncomfortably. "What does he say when you ask him?"

"He says he's fine. But then he adds little comments he doesn't typically make."

"Like…"

"Like how proud he's always been of me." Gabe stared into his beer, shaking his head. "He loved watching me play football, man. He was there at every game."

"He's *still* proud of you, Gabe."

"Right." Gabe rolled his eyes, but before Mike could say any more, he continued. "Earlier, out of the blue, my dad said that Reenie and I are the best things in his life. He said he wanted me to know, no matter what might happen, that he—" Gabe paused, drawing a line in the condensation on his glass "—that he'll always love me."

Conner Armstrong, who'd developed the Running Y Resort a few miles out of town and turned it into a tremendous success, came in, along with his wife, Delaney, and some of the cowboys who worked for them. Mike and Gabe waved to acknowledge their entrance. Conner had been a big help with the campaign so far, and Mike had always liked Delaney.

Conner and the others stopped long enough to say hello and chat for a minute or two. When they moved away, Mike went back to his conversation with Gabe. "Garth *has* been a good father, hasn't he?"

"The best." Gabe's eyebrows lowered. "So why the sudden insecurity?"

"I can't say," Mike said, cringing a little at how literally he meant that.

"I'd think maybe he and my mom are having marital trouble or something, but Mom's more devoted to him than ever."

"How does he seem to feel about her?" Mike couldn't resist asking. There had to be problems or Garth wouldn't have broken his marriage vows.

Gabe shrugged. "He treats her well. I've never heard him say a negative thing about her. And he certainly demanded that Reenie and I give her the proper respect while we were growing up."

"Whatever it is, it'll blow over," Mike said. Garth had probably already destroyed Red's journal. The Smalls hadn't even known the journal existed. Mike and Lucky were the only other people to know Garth's terrible secret, and they were never going to say anything. Garth was probably just rattled by what could have happened. Once he calmed down, everything would be fine.

"I hope so," Gabe said.

"Have you thought about what I said at the diner?" Mike asked.

"God, you're not going to bring that up again, are you?"

Mike finished his beer. "It might not make me very popular with you, but sometimes a friend's got to do what a friend's got to do."

Gabe studied him for several long seconds and finally nodded. "I guess that's what makes you the kind of friend you are," he said with a grudging smile.

MIKE WASN'T SURE what to think as he drove home an hour later. He and Gabe had spent considerable time talking about ways to start a viable business selling handmade furniture, and Gabe's growing enthusiasm encouraged Mike. Gabe might actually follow through with some of their ideas. But Mike couldn't figure out what to do about his own situation. Maybe he shouldn't see Lucky for a day or two, take the physical aspect out of their relationship and try to get to the bottom of how strongly he felt about her.

At least he was leaning that way—until he drove past the Victorian and didn't see her car peeking out from behind the old fountain. Then he couldn't help turning in at the drive.

Where could she be? He hadn't seen her at the Honky Tonk, and except for Billy Joe's pickup, which was often seen around town in the wee hours of the morning, Jerry's Diner had been deserted when he passed by. The gas station was about the only other business open so late, and he didn't think she'd drive into town just to fill up.

Anxiety caused his muscles to tense as he parked and got out. After what had happened with the Smalls, he found himself imagining the worst. He should've called her.

The Smalls wouldn't hurt her again; he was almost positive of that. He'd made it perfectly clear that they'd pay a high price if they did, and he'd meant every word. But revenge would be little consolation if she'd been hurt.

He jogged up the steps, rang the doorbell three times in quick succession and banged on the door. "Lucky? It's me."

The house remained dark. He couldn't hear any response, no movement from within.

"Lucky?" He reached above the door for the key he'd located when he delivered her Christmas tree and was relieved to find it still there. Letting himself in, he glanced around.

The dark, quiet house had grown cool, as if Lucky had turned off the heat. That only increased his foreboding.

He charged upstairs. The furniture was there, but Lucky's clothes, makeup and shoes—all her personal things—were gone, along with her luggage.

"Son of a bitch," he muttered and hurried back downstairs. Surely she'd left him a note, telling him where she was going and when she'd be back. Depending on how long it'd been since she drove off, she could be just about anywhere by now.

His heart pounded frantically as he headed to the kitchen. He searched the counter, the floor, even the fridge. No note. Nothing. The kitchen and family rooms were as empty as the rest of the house.

Mike couldn't believe it. He'd been counting on her leaving; he'd thought it would solve everything. But it solved nothing. It hit him like a blow to the chest, nearly knocking the breath from him.

He had to find her. But until she sent him her address so he could forward her monthly check from the trust, he wouldn't even know where to look.

Walking slowly into the living room, he stared at the Christmas tree they'd decorated together. The ornaments were still there, he noted dully. But the angel on top was missing.

CHAPTER TWENTY-ONE

GARTH SAT in his study while Celeste slept, the clock ticking loudly on the wall as he stared down at Red's journal. He'd tried to make himself destroy it at least a hundred times over the past two weeks. He was terrified their housekeeper or Celeste would come across it while cleaning. But he hadn't been able to burn the damn thing as he'd originally intended. It felt too seedy, too dishonest, to have stolen it in the first place. If he hadn't found the door to the Victorian standing wide open when he'd gone to speak with Lucky, to plead his case, he never would've considered doing this, despite the book's terrible ramifications.

But the door *had* been standing open. Seeing it as the answer he'd been praying for, he'd taken advantage of the opportunity—and now he could contain the past. What he did with the journal was his decision and no one else's. It was better to perpetuate a lie than to let the truth hurt so many, wasn't it?

He pictured Lucky as she'd looked standing in this very room and sighed. He'd heard a lot of disparaging remarks about her since she'd returned. He'd used them to justify his own feelings and behavior. But he didn't usually measure a person according to gossip. And the fact that Mike Hill was so supportive of her said something. Garth respected Mike, considered him almost a son.

Mike… Garth shook his head. How was it possible that

Gabe's best friend had become embroiled in one of the biggest scandals to rock Dundee in years? When the *real* scandal, the scandal that should've erupted but hadn't, was right here in this book.

Slowly, Garth thumbed through the pages again, scanning for his name, the dates of his visits, the gifts he'd bestowed on Red. The sight of it turned his stomach. How could he have been so weak? Red's notes about his favorite foods, wine and movies made it all so impersonal—as if she were sleeping with such a multitude of men she had trouble keeping everyone straight. It certainly didn't do his ego any good and completely destroyed her mystique. But what could he say? He'd been a damn fool, and he'd had to live with that for years.

Snapping the book closed, he shoved it back in his drawer. Because he didn't destroy it, he had to wonder if part of him was hoping Celeste *would* find it. Then he wouldn't have anything left to hide. Then maybe he could wipe the slate clean.

A soft knock intruded on his thoughts. Locking the drawer in which he'd just deposited the journal, he dropped the key in his paperclip holder.

"Come in." He pulled a stack of papers in front of him to make it look as though he'd been going over correspondence.

Celeste opened the door and slipped inside, wearing her flannel nightgown. "You're working late again."

He mustered a smile. "Yes, well, there's always more to do, it seems."

"But the legislature isn't even in session. Can't you relax a little? It worries me when you work so hard."

"I'm fine, Celeste."

"You never come to bed with me anymore."

He felt fairly certain she used to consider that a blessing. He knew for a fact that there'd been many times when she'd feigned sleep so he wouldn't expect to make love. After all these years, he supposed her reluctance to welcome any kind of sexual advance had worn him down. He rarely approached her anymore.

"It's easier to use the guest room. That way I don't disturb you."

"Are you seeing someone else?" she asked suddenly.

Garth felt his mouth drop open. "Excuse me?"

"Are you in love with someone else, Garth? Is that what's going on?"

He blinked, reined in his surprise, and found his voice. "No. No, I'm not."

"Reenie seems to think it's a possibility."

"Reenie's wrong."

"I'm glad." Celeste smiled in obvious relief. "You're a good man, Garth."

A *good* man? A good man didn't lie. A good man took responsibility for his actions. He'd preached that concept to his children over and over again while they were growing up.

"Good night." Celeste stepped toward the door.

Turning his face to the ceiling, he fought the panic surging through him. He had the journal; he didn't need to do this, a voice in his head cried. But in reality he knew he had no choice. Either he risked losing everything he loved, or he lost his self-respect. And who could love a man who loathed himself?

"There *is* something you should know, Celeste."

He saw a hint of fear in her expression as she turned, smoothed her nightgown and squared her shoulders. "What's that?"

"I did have an affair. Once. A long time ago."

The ensuing pause stretched his nerves taut.

"*How* long ago?" she finally asked, her voice now choked with the fear he'd seen in her face.

"Two and a half decades."

Her chest lifted as though she'd just drawn a deep breath. "That is a long time ago."

It wasn't long enough. No amount of time seemed capable of dulling his remorse.

"Did she mean anything to you?"

He thought of Red's notations—*Favorite dessert: Pecan Pie*—and almost laughed out loud. "No. I got confused and made a terrible mistake, for which—" he struggled to control his voice "—for which I'm very sorry. I've been sorry ever since. I should've told you long before now."

She crossed the room and put her arms around him, drawing his head against the soft folds of her stomach. She smelled so familiar, so sweet and comfortable, he couldn't help closing his eyes and simply breathing her in. His marriage wasn't perfect. It never had been. But he and Celeste had been together for forty years, and she was a good woman. He'd done the right thing in staying with her. He knew that now.

"It's okay, Garth," she said. "We're not always everything we want to be."

Garth got the impression she was acknowledging her own weaknesses in that statement as well as his, and loved her all the more for it. She knew. She knew he'd been disappointed in certain areas of their marriage and she accepted responsibility for it.

What a big person—someone he could definitely admire.

He almost told her about Lucky…but caught himself. He didn't want her to have to deal with something that might not be a problem. Before he said any more, he had to find out if Lucky *was* his daughter. Soon.

"Thank you, Celeste," he murmured.

"I love you, Garth."

He felt the first peace he'd known since Lucky's call, and

the physical aspect of his and Celeste's relationship suddenly meant far less to him than the comfort and support she'd always offered. "I love you, too."

MIKE PACED his brother's office. "It's been two weeks."

Josh dropped his pen, propped his hands behind his head and stretched out his legs. "You want to fill me in on what you're talking about?"

"You know what I'm talking about. I haven't heard from her. Has she contacted you?"

"She?"

"Lucky." Moving to the edge of Josh's desk, Mike thrust his hands in his pockets and kept a close eye on his brother's face. "If she has, you'd tell me, right? You wouldn't hold out on me in some misguided attempt to appease Mom and Dad—"

Josh rocked forward. "Hey, slow down, big brother. I wouldn't hold out on you. I told you I'd let you know if Lucky called. She hasn't."

Mike went back to pacing. He hadn't had a good night's sleep since she left, not that he'd been sleeping all that well before. She'd wreaked havoc on his orderly, peaceful life. But now that she was gone, he couldn't get her out of his mind. He kept thinking he'd hear from her, have the chance to convince her to come back, deal with the house, take a more measured and thoughtful approach to the future. But she hadn't contacted him or anyone else he knew of, and worry was quickly overtaking all other emotions.

"She has to be out of money by now," he said. "Her monthly check is waiting in my office. I can't mail it because I don't have an address to send it to."

"She's probably fine. She arranged for an equity loan against the house, remember? She could be living on that."

"Fred Sharp told me she left him a check in an envelope taped to the wall. He's already been paid in full."

"Maybe she borrowed more than she paid him."

"According to Byron Reese down at the bank, she didn't—at least not much more."

"Byron Reese gave out that information?"

Mike scowled. "Come on, this is Dundee. Privacy in lending isn't an issue when everyone already knows everyone else's business. How's she getting by?"

"I don't know," Josh said with a shrug. "You've been frantic ever since she took off and you're only getting worse, but I can't help you. She didn't leave a forwarding address."

Mike had tried searching Boise. It was the only place he knew to look, the closest "big" city in Idaho. In the first two days after she left, he'd called every hotel or motel in the area, but had come up empty. He'd even driven down there and prowled the streets and local hangouts. He'd known it was a hopeless endeavor, but it was better than sitting around Dundee doing *nothing*.

"What should I tell her if she does call?" Josh asked.

"Put her on hold and get me. Or jot down a number where I can reach her."

"What if she just wants an offer on the house?"

"Don't give her one. If she wants to sell that house, she's going to have to deal with me."

"She could always list it with Fred Winston and sell it to someone else."

Mike didn't like the fact that she could do any number of things besides come back. But he was betting she'd eventually contact him about the house. Despite what he'd originally believed, she cared as much about the Victorian as he did. And she cared about *him*.

"She'll call," he said, trying to keep his hopes up.

WAS THIS PHOENIX? If so, it wasn't the better part of the city.

Lucky stared through a dirty motel window at the crumbling blacktop parking lot that was empty except for a few banged-up cars, including an old Oldsmobile that had a flat tire. Judging by the mobile-home park that served as a retirement community across the street, the flatness of the surrounding land, and the desert plants and pale rock below her window, it sure as hell wasn't Oregon. She'd already been to Oregon. And Utah. And California. She couldn't remember where else. The states were beginning to blur. Road signs didn't matter much when you didn't know where you were headed in the first place. She just kept driving and drinking coffee and blasting the stereo to drown out her thoughts, then driving some more, finally checking into little hole-in-the-wall motels. She could scarcely recall the past three weeks, except for the pain she felt every time she woke up and realized she'd never see Mike again.

The heater in the corner kicked on with a noisy rattle. Closing the drapes against the cloudy day, she fell back onto her bed and gazed up at the cottage-cheese ceiling. She tried to occupy her mind by asking herself how anyone had ever found the white, sparkling substance above her attractive enough to spray on almost every ceiling built in the seventies. But visions of Mike touching her, kissing her, crept in. As usual. Whenever she shut her eyes, she saw his face, felt his warm skin against her own—

Time to go. Shoving herself off the bed before the crushing pain could incapacitate her, she started stuffing her belongings into the backpack she'd brought in from the car. She couldn't stay here anymore, couldn't even stop long enough to volunteer for a few days. She had to keep moving, keep driving…forget.

Maybe New Mexico would feel more like home.

Somehow she doubted it.

"WHERE'S MIKE?" Barbara asked, pinning Josh with a searching look the moment he, his wife and baby Brian came into the house.

Josh glanced awkwardly at Rebecca before responding. "He told me to tell you he can't make it for dinner today."

Over the past few weeks, when Mike hadn't shown up for their usual Sunday dinner, Barbara had put a brave face on her disappointment. Today she couldn't seem to manage the effort. "Again? He hasn't been here for weeks."

"He's pretty busy," Josh said. "Breeding season's nearly upon us and—"

"Breeding season has never interfered before."

Normally Barbara took Brian the moment she laid eyes on him. She worshipped her grandson. But she was too upset and preoccupied right now. When the baby started to fuss, Josh handed him to Rebecca instead. "If you want to know the truth, Mom, I'm a little worried about Mike."

"Why?"

"He's miserable."

"Miserable? He's always been happy in the past."

"Well, he's miserable now." Josh put the diaper bag on the floor, next to the wall. "I think he's in love with Lucky."

Barbara clutched her chest. She'd expected Josh to say *something* about Lucky. He'd been trying to talk to her about Red's daughter ever since Lucky had left town. He'd said Mike wasn't the same, that Mike *cared* about her, but Barbara couldn't believe he cared too much. Mike would get over Lucky in a matter of weeks. He respected women, treated them well, but he never fell too hard.

"Love's a strong word, Josh," she said.

"I know, but there it is," he replied. "I doubt Mike even realizes what's wrong with him, but he can't think of anything or anyone else. I'm sure that's part of the reason he's not here today. He's hoping she'll call and he doesn't want to miss her if she does."

"That's silly," Barbara said. "He's not here because he's still angry at your father about that little spat they had a few weeks ago. Larry?"

Hearing his name, her husband muted the football game he was watching on television half a room away. "What?"

"You called Mike, right? Told him you're not holding a grudge?"

"Of course."

"Mike just hasn't forgiven him yet," Barbara said.

Rebecca's expression plainly revealed that she agreed with Josh. "I'm not so sure that's it."

Barbara remembered Lucky standing at the door. *Does he care about you?... No...it was all me...*

Strange words from someone who wanted to hurt her...

Barbara's conversation with Lucky nagged at her late at night, as did the lovesick expression she'd seen in Lucky's eyes. But Barbara couldn't think about that. Lucky was gone. For good. Mike had never fallen in love before; he wasn't in love now. Certainly not with Red's daughter. He'd eventually meet and marry someone else. And if Lucky loved him as much as she said she did—well, that was unfortunate. As a good Christian woman, Barbara wished Lucky no harm. She just wanted Red, and everything to do with her, out of her life.

Tightening her apron, she finally managed a brittle smile. "He'll forget her," she insisted. "Come on, let's eat before the food gets cold."

CHAPTER TWENTY-TWO

THE PHONE RANG.

Pulling himself out of a light sleep, Mike lunged toward it. Lucky. This late, it had to be her. She was finally calling....

"Hello?" he said eagerly.

"Mike?"

It was his mother. Slumping back onto his pillows, he cleared his throat to buy enough time to keep the disappointment from leaking into his voice. "Hi, Mom. Something wrong?"

"No, I was just up late, puttering around the house, and thought I'd give you a call. I didn't wake you, did I?"

He squinted at his glowing alarm clock. She couldn't have called earlier? It was nearly eleven-thirty on a Sunday night. "Not really," he said, because he knew the past few weeks hadn't been any easier on her than they had on him. "I only dozed off a few minutes ago. What's up?"

"We missed you at dinner earlier."

So that was it—she was upset about dinner. He hadn't skipped out to make any kind of statement. He simply couldn't sit through another dinner and pretend, as she obviously wanted to, that nothing had changed. "I had a lot of work to do, stuff that's been piling up," he said vaguely.

"Are you still angry with your father?"

Mike wasn't sure he had a right to be angry. Considering

what he'd thought of Lucky in the past, he couldn't blame
Larry for his reaction. Of course his father felt betrayed. Mike
would have felt the same in Larry's shoes. "No. Dad called
and we talked about it." He rolled away from the glowing digits of his clock. "How's he feeling now?"

"He's putting the past behind him."

"Good."

"I think we should all do that."

"It's probably best," Mike agreed.

"So you're okay?"

"I'm great. Just busy. Breeding season's around the corner and—"

"Business picks up," she finished. "I know."

A strained silence fell between them. "Well, I'd better let
you get to bed," Mike said.

"Josh seems to think you're in love with Lucky," she
blurted out. "Is that even a possibility, Mike?"

Mike opened his mouth to deny it. But he couldn't. He knew
it was true. "My feelings don't matter," he said. "She's gone."

"She hasn't called, then."

"Not once."

"If she were to contact you, what would you say to her?"

He hesitated. He knew his mother wouldn't want to hear
the truth, but he'd already tried to dodge her. This time he
couldn't keep from voicing the two words that sprang immediately to his lips—probably because he'd said them to Lucky
so often in his mind. "Come home."

"What?"

Mike made no reply.

"You're not saying she could become my *daughter*-in-law
someday…."

He might have reacted to the panic in his mother's voice.
But the idea of marrying Lucky hit him like a club over the

head. He'd been so busy trying to fight his attraction to her, trying to minimize what he felt for her, that he'd never allowed himself to imagine anything permanent. Now he pictured her smiling up at him as he slipped his ring on her finger, and felt a tremendous surge of pride and desire.

"Well?" his mother pressed.

"I don't know," he said. "We're wrong for each other in every way." He blinked up at the ceiling. "Except..."

"Except?" she echoed weakly.

Mike remembered Lucky's "I don't need you" look, the one she used to reject people before they could reject her, and couldn't help smiling to himself. "Except the one that matters most."

MIKE USED A PEN to trace the number he'd jotted down a few minutes earlier. According to Rob Strickland from the telephone company, Lucky had made only two calls to the state of Washington while staying at the Victorian, both to the same number. Which meant it belonged to one of her brothers. Lucky had mentioned that she and Sean and Kyle weren't particularly close, but it'd been more than three weeks since she'd left. Surely they'd know how to contact her by now.

"Hello?"

It had been so many years since Mike had spoken to Kyle or Sean that he couldn't place the voice. "Sean?"

"Kenny."

Feeling the tension of approaching someone he'd always considered an enemy, Mike got up from his desk and crossed the room to gaze out his back window at the barn below. He'd thought a lot about making this call. Lucky had left and wasn't looking back. If he wanted a clean break, to go on as he was before she'd returned, he could do that now.

But he didn't want to go on as he'd been; he *couldn't*. He

wanted Lucky, and he knew he'd contact anyone and everyone who might be able to help him find her. "This is Mike Hill."

The sudden silence seemed deafening, but then, he'd expected a chilly response.

"What can I do for you, Mike?" Kyle's voice sounded clipped. Mike had purchased the land Morris had left to both Kyle and Sean almost as soon as they'd inherited it, but that wasn't the full extent of their past dealings. There'd been many times when the animosity between Mike and Josh, and Sean and Kyle, had almost come to blows, usually at the Honky Tonk, when Sean had consumed too much alcohol. Fortunately, Kyle had always pulled his brother outside and driven him home.

But that was years ago, Mike reminded himself, better forgotten. "I'm looking for Lucky," he said.

"Lucky?"

"Your *sister?*"

"Isn't she staying next door?" Kyle's confusion seemed authentic, heightening Mike's concern. Could something have happened to her?

"She left here almost a month ago. You haven't heard from her?"

"No. Is there some sort of problem?"

Mike hadn't been able to keep his hands off her, which had definitely turned out to be a bit of a problem. But he didn't feel inclined to share that with Kyle. "Not that I know of. I just…" What could he say? *Your little sister's too young for me, but I can't live without her?* It was true…. "She mentioned that she might be ready to sell the house. I was hoping to get in touch."

"With another offer."

"Yes."

"How much?"

"Just have her call me when you hear from her, okay?"

Kyle obviously didn't like the answer he'd received. "Maybe I will and maybe I won't," he said and hung up.

Mike frowned as he walked back to his desk and placed the phone in its cradle. Obviously, Lucky's family didn't like him any more than his family liked her.

LUCKY'S HEART POUNDED so hard she could scarcely hear above it. The in-home pregnancy test she'd purchased at a nearby grocery store boasted that it could be used as early as the first day after a missed period. But she didn't have to worry about testing too soon. Although she'd never really bothered to keep close track of her menstrual cycle, she'd always been regular. She was pretty sure she should've started her period three weeks ago.

According to the pamphlet that came with the test, the display on the little plastic indicator would read "Pregnant" one minute after testing and "Not pregnant" inside of three. She knew she'd have her answer soon—but sixty seconds had never lasted so long. Mouth dry, eyes riveted on the little oval where, barring an "error" code, the words would appear, she told herself to pray for a negative result. She hadn't expected this kind of complication. She didn't have a home or any real direction in her life, and she certainly didn't want to raise a child in the homeless shelters where she often volunteered. She had no support from family or friends. No business having a child.

And yet the thought of carrying Mike's baby made her feel a strange, yearning sensation. If she was pregnant, she'd definitely keep the child. She'd love and cherish a baby with all her heart.

She glanced at her watch. Fifty seconds and counting... Fifty-five... Sixty...

Nothing. She wasn't pregnant. The condoms they'd used had done their job. Another two minutes would confirm it.

Relief *and* disappointment swirled inside her while she waited. Sixty more seconds... Seventy...

The digital letters appeared, faintly at first, slowly growing blacker and more distinct. Lucky expected to see two words: *Not pregnant.* But it didn't look like two words to her. She blinked disbelievingly, then held the indicator closer to the light. Sure enough, there it was, clear as day. Only one word: *Pregnant.*

"MIKE, IT'S Senator Holbrook."

Mike swiveled slightly away from Josh, who was sitting across from him at the conference table going over some layouts for their new brochure. "Hello, Senator," he said. "What can I do for you?"

"Is it true that Lucky's left town?"

"Yes."

"Could you give me her telephone number, please?"

Mike felt his eyebrows shoot up. "I'm afraid I don't have it."

"Do you know anyone who does?"

"No."

"What about her family, her brothers?"

"I've already called them. No luck."

"So you don't know where she's gone."

"No." Mike had hired a private investigator to track her down, to ease his worry, if nothing else. But he couldn't admit that in front of Josh. Mike hadn't heard from his mother or father since he'd admitted how he felt about Lucky while talking to Barbara on the phone over a week ago. They hadn't even invited him to Sunday dinner.

Holbrook seemed unsure of how to proceed.

"Is there something you'd like me to tell her if I happen to hear from her?" Mike asked, wondering why the senator was trying to reach Lucky.

There was a long pause. "Please tell her I'm ready to take the test," he said and hung up.

Mike stared at the handset. The test? The *paternity* test? But what about Gabe and Reenie and—

"What'd Holbrook want?" Josh asked.

Quickly pulling himself together, Mike hung up and made a halfhearted attempt to come up with a lie. But nothing, except the truth, presented itself quickly enough.

"What?" Josh pressed.

"He wants the same thing I want," Mike admitted.

"And that is…"

"To find Lucky."

LOS ANGELES WAS as good a place as any to start a new life, Lucky decided as she wandered through the small blue house for sale. The mild weather appealed to her. So did the sandy beaches only a block away. She liked sitting and watching the waves tumble over themselves as they crashed against the shore. She even liked what most other people complained about—the miles upon miles of concrete and teeming masses. Probably because nothing in L.A. reminded her of a small town tucked into the mountains north of Boise, where she'd briefly spent time with the handsome cowboy who still owned her heart.

"What do you think?" The real estate agent stood at the door, frowning impatiently at her watch. "As I said, these properties don't become available very often. If you want it, we'll have to move fast."

Lucky turned away from the window, and the voices and laughter drifting in from outside. The living room was situated above a small garage. This little house, with its fresh paint and hardwood floors, was more than forty years old and had only two small bedrooms and one bath. But the view, in addition to the quaint, clean neighborhood, made it special. Lucky knew she should probably rent an apartment before buying any real estate, get a feel for the city, make sure she was going to like it here. Except, if she could move on easily, she was afraid she would. This time she intended to put down roots. For her baby. Her son or daughter might grow up without a father, as she had, but Lucky was determined to give her child more than her own mother had been emotionally capable of giving her—stability, direction, a strong self-image.

That was going to start with a permanent home.

"I'll take it," she said. "But my offer will have to be contingent upon selling the house I own in Idaho."

"What?" The sour expression that crossed the Realtor's face revealed how unwelcome she found *this* news, but Lucky couldn't do anything without selling the Victorian first. The beach house was going to cost everything she could conceivably get from the sale of the property she'd inherited. Small in L.A. certainly didn't mean cheap. Without her monthly check from the trust Lucky couldn't even make a rental deposit. She had barely a hundred bucks left in her bank account. She'd been holding out as long as possible, trying to put a buffer between her and Mike before she had to deal with him again.

But time had just run out.

"You didn't tell me you had to sell your own house first," Priscilla Hathaway said.

"It won't be a problem," Lucky assured her. "I have an eager buyer who definitely has the money. It shouldn't take more than a couple of weeks to close escrow."

Her face instantly brightened. "Oh, well… Let's go ahead and write up the paperwork, then."

Lucky took a deep breath and nodded. This was the right

thing to do. She'd get a job, work, somehow become the kind of mother she'd never had.

But she didn't have the nerve to call Mike. She couldn't bear to hear his voice. So she called Josh instead.

CHAPTER TWENTY-THREE

"MIKE, I FINALLY heard from her."

Mike jumped as Josh flung open the door to his office and let it crash against the inside wall. But what his brother was saying made an even greater impact. Mike knew Josh was talking about Lucky even though he hadn't said her name.

"When?"

"Just now."

Mike stood and glanced anxiously down at the buttons on his phone. Two of them were lit. "Which line?"

The question seemed to cast a pall over Josh's excitement. "Um…she's not on the phone anymore."

"Why not?" Mike asked. "I told you I wanted to talk to her. Did you get her number? Somewhere I can get hold of her?"

"I have a fax number." Josh shrugged helplessly. "That was all she'd give me."

"A *fax* number?"

"She asked for an offer on the house. I told her I had to talk to you about it. She said to fax it to her when we were ready and hung up."

"That's it?" Mike tried not to feel stung that she hadn't called *him,* that she wouldn't even speak to him.

"Just about, other than the fact that she asked me to act quickly."

Mike sank back in his seat. "Why the rush?" he asked,

his initial excitement turning into a variety of other emotions.

"She didn't explain. I think she needs the money."

Of course she did. She should've called long before now. "Did you tell her Senator Holbrook is trying to reach her?"

"No. She was all business, quick and to the point, and I was too busy trying to get her to slow down so you'd be able to talk to her." He hesitated. "What does Holbrook want with her, anyway? You never did tell me."

"I can't say."

Mike thought Josh might push him, but he didn't. "Well?"

"Well, what?"

"Are we going to fax her an offer?"

Lucky… What did *she* want? he wondered. Was she happier without him? Was that the message she was trying to send?

He hoped not.

"Yeah, we'll fax her an offer," Mike said at last.

"How much?"

Considering what was at stake, he had to go for broke. "Whatever it takes."

LUCKY SAT primly in the Beach Front Realty office, awaiting Josh's fax. She'd asked him to respond right away and felt quite confident that he would. The Hill brothers had waited too long to get their hands on Morris's house to be unresponsive now.

Priscilla, the Realtor she'd been working with, caught her eye while talking animatedly on the phone and smiled. Lucky knew it was simply a professional courtesy, an automatic reflex, which was too bad. She felt she could use a real friend at this moment. Her palms were sweating, and she was finding it difficult to breathe. She was letting go at last, taking a stand for her future, moving on with her life. She was saying goodbye to Dundee and Mike Hill—forever.

Hoping to calm the butterflies in her stomach, she willed away the sense of loss and regret "goodbye" engendered, along with the terrible questions that had haunted her since she'd found out about the baby. Should she tell Mike? If so, when? How?

She pictured his friends and family, the town. Everyone admired him. Surely, if he knew about the baby, he'd feel even more split between her and the rest of his life.

She wouldn't tell him now, she decided. Maybe not ever. He had everything he needed, everything he wanted. She had only this.

As the fax machine in the corner began to spew out paper, apprehension tightened every nerve. When Josh had asked her how much she'd like for the Victorian, she'd given him the minimum amount she absolutely had to have in order to buy the beach house. She wasn't after Mike's money. She wanted as little of it as possible. But she owed it to her baby to make sure they had a good start, and that meant she needed a decent roof over their heads. Besides, she'd set the price low enough that she felt fairly confident she could get that amount from someone else. She just didn't have time to go through the motions of marketing a piece of real estate.

Lucky watched the fax machine until the light turned off and the humming stopped. She was tempted to get up and retrieve the fax herself. But this was a busy real estate office, and several faxes had come in over the past thirty minutes. There was no guarantee this one was hers.

She waited instead for Priscilla to get off the phone and do the honors, but with every second her anxiety grew. Although Mike and his family had wanted the house for years, she suddenly feared that they wouldn't come through in her hour of need.

Finally, Priscilla finished her conversation and hung up.

"I think my fax arrived," Lucky said.

"Something's here." Priscilla crossed the room and shuffled through whatever it was that had come in. But a deep frown creased her forehead as she walked slowly back to Lucky.

"What's wrong?"

"I'm not sure what this is...."

Lucky's heart fell. It wasn't what she needed, then. Maybe Josh and Mike hadn't agreed on how much they'd be willing to pay. Maybe—

"Hmm...I guess it's an offer, after all," Priscilla said, straightening the papers. "Just not the kind I was expecting."

"Who's it for?"

"You." She passed her the fax, then propped her hands on her hips.

Lucky stared down at the cover sheet. It was from High Hill Ranch, all right. Only it wasn't from Josh. It was from Mike. She spotted his name on the "sender" line and couldn't help running a finger over the ink. The message read: *Attached please find my best offer.*

His best offer? What did that mean? That he wasn't open to negotiation?

Lucky removed the top sheet and studied the first page. Now she understood why Priscilla had had difficulty figuring out what she was looking at. It took Lucky a moment, too, but eventually she realized she was holding a picture of a ring. A diamond ring.

Why would Mike be sending her a picture of this?

She turned to the next page—and then she knew. It said: *I don't want the house. I want you. Marry me.*

Lucky couldn't believe it. She glanced up in astonishment to see the hardened, career-woman Priscilla-the-Realtor grinning like a thirteen-year-old schoolgirl. "I'm single, so I'm not a specialist in this area, but from the size of that diamond, I'm guessing it's not a bad offer."

Lucky couldn't seem to find her voice. Mike wanted her to *marry* him? To be Mrs. Mike Hill? To live with him and sleep with him and…

Their baby! She felt her chest constrict. They could raise their child together.

But what about his family? The town? The big fuss he liked to make about his age? Could they love each other enough to compensate for all that?

"There's one more page." Priscilla helped Lucky bring it to the top. This one looked curiously like a contract. A fancy heading read: *Offer.* Below that was one line of text: *Everything I have. Everything I am.* A signature block, where Mike had signed his name and even scrawled the date, made it all seem very official.

Now she knew why he'd said it was his best offer. There wasn't anything more he could give.

The Realtor was positively beaming now. "God, if you don't accept this, I think I will."

He was willing to stand against everyone he knew—for *her?* Tears filled Lucky's eyes, but she tried to laugh through them.

"As your agent, it's my job to respond." Priscilla cocked a playful eyebrow at her. "What should we fax back to him?"

MIKE STOOD next to his fax machine, waiting, his heart racing with anticipation. Would she accept? She'd once told him she loved him, but with Lucky, he wasn't sure love was enough. She'd been through a lot in Dundee. Maybe she'd had all she could tolerate and wasn't willing to come back. Maybe loving him was too simple a motivation to get her to settle down in one place….

"I don't think I've ever seen you so nervous," Josh said.

Mike didn't respond. Since the day Josh was born, he'd shared almost everything with his brother. He supposed it was fitting that he'd included Josh in this moment, too, since it was one of the most terrifying of his life. But he was more than a little worried about how he might handle his disappointment if she said no. He'd never committed himself before, never been in this position.

"I know she loves you," Josh said as if trying to convince them both. "I could tell that day I was talking to her in the barn. She didn't even bother to deny it. She—"

Mike interrupted to shut him up. He was stressed enough without Josh's anxiety adding to his own. "If you're really so sure she's going to say yes, quit wearing a hole in the damn carpet."

"Actually, I don't think I'm worried about her saying no. Yes might be worse."

Mike stabbed a hand through his hair. "Mom and Dad?"

"And Uncle Bunk and Aunt Cori and all the others." Josh shrugged and pivoted for another pass. "Oh, well, maybe I'll get to be the family favorite for a while."

"You're the baby of the family. You've always *been* the favorite."

"Well, I guess it doesn't hurt to solidify my position." Josh checked his watch.

"How long's it been?" Mike asked.

"Fifteen minutes."

"Seems like longer."

"I know. The wait's killing me. You'd think I was the one who'd just proposed."

Mike started to chuckle but fell silent the second the fax machine whirred to life. "Here it is," he breathed.

Josh came to stand next to him. They both watched the papers slide smoothly into the receptacle, then Mike retrieved what Lucky had sent.

The cover sheet indicated it came from some real estate

company in Los Angeles. But her location was no surprise to them now. They'd already called information to check the area code on the fax number and knew she was in southern California. Mike just wasn't sure she'd be willing to return to his little corner of the world. L.A. was a far cry from Dundee.

Shooting a quick "here goes" glance at Josh, he flipped to the second page. It looked like some kind of magazine clipping of a—he held it closer—a...*baby?*

"What's that?" Josh asked, his eyebrows gathering in confusion.

"A baby, I think," Mike said.

"But what does it mean?"

Mike had no clue. There wasn't any writing on the page. He moved on to find that the last sheet had only one line of text. *Does your offer still stand?*

Mike met his brother's eyes.

"I'm lost," Josh said. "What's going on?"

Mike couldn't imagine. He—

Suddenly the realization of what Lucky was trying to tell him began to sink in. The fax fluttered to the floor as shock stole his strength. A baby... A...*baby. His* baby!

"Whoa," he said and grabbed the nearest table for support.

Josh's eyes cut back to the picture Mike had just dropped. Then his mouth formed an O. "She's *not* saying..."

"I think she is." Mike bent over, drawing several deep breaths to ward off the dizziness. He'd almost lost Lucky *and* his baby. If she hadn't contacted Josh about the house—

Anger swirled through him, and he shot back upright.

"Are you okay?" Josh asked.

"How could she leave without telling me?" Mike cried. "How could she leave without even saying goodbye?" He took up pacing in Josh's place. "Do you suppose she was ever *going* to tell me? She called *you,* for Pete's sake. What about *me?*"

A sheepish expression claimed Josh's face, but Mike was so busy ranting and pacing that it took him a moment to recognize that his brother knew more than he was saying. "What?" he said insistently. "Did *you* know? Did you threaten her to leave or something?"

Josh looked offended. "I wouldn't do that. But…" He stretched his neck, acting as though he wasn't sure whether or not to proceed.

"Tell me everything," Mike said darkly. "Now."

Josh grabbed the picture of the baby and gazed down at it. "Okay. Remember the day we couldn't find Mom?"

"Yes…"

"And I was already at the house when she got home and you were with her?"

"Yes…"

"I'd quit looking because…"

"Because…"

Josh frowned. "At that point I already knew she was okay."

"How?"

"I saw her pulling out of Lucky's driveway and flagged her down at the end of the road."

"Did she say if she'd spoken to Lucky?"

"She wouldn't tell me, which was indication enough. She mentioned that she was going to Finley's to get some stuff for dinner, so I went home to tell Dad."

Mike dropped his head in his hands and massaged his temples. He'd wondered at the suddenness of Lucky's departure. Now he knew. Unfortunately, it didn't bode well for future relations with his family.

But he hoped his mother would come around some day. Once she had the chance to know Lucky, he couldn't see Barbara—or anyone else in the family—continuing to dislike her. Besides, he and Lucky would have an ace in the hole.

They were going to have a baby, maybe two or three over the next ten years, and the mother he knew would never be able to reject her own grandchildren.

"Send Lucky another fax," he said.

"What do you want me to say?" Josh asked.

"Tell her I want to consummate this deal right away."

Josh grinned. "That's it?"

"No." Mike imagined holding a soft, squirming bundle in one arm and Lucky in the other and couldn't help returning his brother's smile. Life was going to change—a lot. But he was ready. Evidently the big 4-0 was his year. "Tell her I love her."

EPILOGUE

HEARING THE DOORBELL at ten o'clock on a Wednesday morning surprised Lucky. The initial two weeks after the birth had been a flurry of excitement and activity, what with all the visits and gifts from her brothers and Mike's friends and family, and Mike himself being home so much. But the past few days had slowed to a leisurely crawl. Although Mike appeared for lunch every day—sometimes an extended lunch because he seemed to have difficulty leaving—he worked mornings and most afternoons, which afforded her a few quiet hours with their new daughter.

The bell rang again before she could reach the front door. She parted the lace drapes she'd just bought for the Victorian to see Senator Holbrook standing on the porch. He'd called her occasionally over the past few months, to ask how she was doing. He'd even offered to go ahead with the paternity test. But there'd been so many positive changes in her life, Lucky had decided against it. Privately, she wanted to know, but she understood how worried Mike was about Gabe's reaction. She didn't want to cause a problem for Gabe or Reenie or anyone else. She and Mike were happy together. Her health was good; the ulcer she'd fought for more than a year before returning to Dundee was finally gone She already had more than she'd ever dreamed.

"Good morning," she said, smiling as she opened the door.

The senator's eyes swept curiously over her. "I hope I haven't come at a bad time."

"No. As a matter of fact, I could use the company. Sabrina's been sleeping all morning."

She invited him in, and he sat on the antique couch she and Mike had bought at an auction in Boise.

"You've done a lot with the house," he said, gazing around. "It's beautiful."

Lucky experienced a moment of pride as she sat across from him. When she and Mike had decided to live in the Victorian, they'd seen it as a symbol of peace—the coming together of his family and hers. And it had been a good choice. She finally felt as though she *belonged* here. "Thank you. I'm not as good as Celeste at filling my house with fabulous paintings and other works of art, but I'm trying."

"I'm sure she'd help you, if you'd ever be interested in shopping with her."

"I'd like that," Lucky said.

"Maybe we can make it a day when all three of us could go to lunch."

Lucky hesitated. She wasn't sure quite how to respond. The *three* of them? "Senator—"

"Please, call me Garth."

"Garth, I understand why you responded the way you did in the past. Please don't feel as if you have to make it up to me."

His eyes strayed to Sabrina's infant seat sitting by the door, which reminded Lucky of the day she'd bumped into him on one of her first forays into town after the birth of her daughter. He'd stopped her so he could see the baby, and had seemed oddly touched by the whole encounter. Lucky supposed she could be wrong in thinking that it held special significance for him, but something about the senator's demeanor today seemed to confirm it.

"I think Mike's done the right thing," he said, surprising her by changing the subject.

"In what way?"

"He's made it a point to let the whole town know how much he loves you, how much he respects you, and it hasn't left any room for the past to intrude on the future."

Lucky smiled at Garth's comment. Mike's actions and attitude had gone far toward neutralizing the old rumors and resentments. If someone turned away or whispered in her presence, Mike would only put his arm around her and stand taller. Even his family, his *mother,* had started making overtures of kindness, especially since the baby was born. "Sometimes I can't believe I'm married to him," she admitted. "I've loved him since I was sixteen."

"I was as blind as everyone else at first, but I'm beginning to see that he's the one who got the catch of the century."

The unexpected compliment made her feel a comforting warmth. "Thank you."

Garth opened his mouth to say something else, but Sabrina's cries interrupted him. Excusing herself, Lucky went into the kitchen to scoop her daughter out of her baby swing. When she returned, Garth couldn't seem to look at anything except Sabrina.

"Would you like to hold her?" Lucky asked.

He nodded and she put the baby in his arms.

"She's beautiful."

Lucky grinned. "Mike worships her."

Garth didn't respond right away. He kept staring at Sabrina, who seemed equally mesmerized by him.

Finally, he raised his eyes. "Lucky, I want to take the paternity test."

Lucky blinked. "What?"

"I want to be part of your life, part of *her* life."

"But what about Gabe? And Reenie?" Lucky asked.

"I've already told Celeste. With her support, I think Gabe and Reenie can handle the news. She keeps telling me that I'm underestimating them, that if I want to get to know you, I should do so. And I think she's right. She even said they might benefit from having someone like you as a sister."

Lucky had never expected to hear such words from Garth Holbrook. "I've never been so flattered," she said. "But there's still your bid for Congress, right? The election is only a couple of weeks away. A scandal could cost you your career."

"That's possible, but…" He gently kissed Sabrina's head. "Some things are more important to me than a seat in Congress."

Lucky reached out to rest a hand on his arm. "I hope you *are* my father," she said and meant it.

* * * * *

Come back for another visit in May!
Gabe Holbrook, who's become a stranger to the people of Dundee ever since his accident, is slowly resuming his life. A new life. Does that include finding a new love? And what if Lucky really is his sister? How will he feel about that?

Find out in Stranger in Town *(May 2005).*

Mother and Child Reunion

A ministeries from
2003 RITA® finalist

Jean Brashear

Coming Home

Cleo Channing's dreams were simple: the stable home and big, loving family she never had as a child. Malcolm Channing walked into her life and swept her off her feet and before long, she thought she had it all—three beautiful children in a charming house she would fill to the rafters with love.

Their firstborn was a troubled girl, though, and the strain on their family grew until finally, there was nothing left to do but for them to all go their separate ways.

Now their daughter has returned, and as the days pass, awareness grows in Cleo and Malcolm that their love never truly died.

Except, the treacherous issues that drove them apart in the first place remain....

Heartwarming stories with a sense of humor, genuine charm and emotion and lots of family!

On sale starting January 2005
Available wherever Harlequin books are sold.

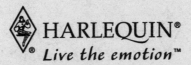

Forgotten Son by Linda Warren
Superromance #1250
On sale January 2005

Texas Ranger Elijah Coltrane is the forgotten son—the one his father never acknowledged. Eli's half brothers have been trying to get close to him for years, but Eli has stubbornly resisted. That is, until he meets Caroline Whitten, the woman who changes his mind about what it means to be part of a family.

By the author of *A Baby by Christmas* (Superromance #1167).

The Chosen Child by Brenda Mott
Superromance #1257
On sale February 2005

Nikki's sister survived the horrible accident caused by a hit-and-run driver, but the baby she was carrying for Nikki and her husband wasn't so lucky. The baby had been a last hope for the childless couple. Devastated, Nikki and Cody struggle to get past their tragedy. If only Cody could give up his all-consuming vendetta to find the drunk responsible—and make him pay.

Available wherever Harlequin books are sold.

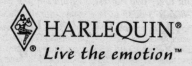

HARLEQUIN®
Live the emotion™

If you enjoyed what you just read,
then we've got an offer you can't resist!

Take 2 bestselling
love stories FREE!
Plus get a FREE surprise gift!

Clip this page and mail it to Harlequin Reader Service®

IN U.S.A.	IN CANADA
3010 Walden Ave.	P.O. Box 609
P.O. Box 1867	Fort Erie, Ontario
Buffalo, N.Y. 14240-1867	L2A 5X3

YES! Please send me 2 free Harlequin Superromance® novels and my free surprise gift. After receiving them, if I don't wish to receive anymore, I can return the shipping statement marked cancel. If I don't cancel, I will receive 6 brand-new novels every month, before they're available in stores. In the U.S.A., bill me at the bargain price of $4.69 plus 25¢ shipping and handling per book and applicable sales tax, if any*. In Canada, bill me at the bargain price of $5.24 plus 25¢ shipping and handling per book and applicable taxes**. That's the complete price, and a savings of at least 10% off the cover prices—what a great deal! I understand that accepting the 2 free books and gift places me under no obligation ever to buy any books. I can always return a shipment and cancel at any time. Even if I never buy another book from Harlequin, the 2 free books and gift are mine to keep forever.

135 HDN DZ7W
336 HDN DZ7X

Name	(PLEASE PRINT)	
Address	Apt.#	
City	State/Prov.	Zip/Postal Code

Not valid to current Harlequin Superromance® subscribers.

Want to try two free books from another series?
Call 1-800-873-8635 or visit www.morefreebooks.com.

* Terms and prices subject to change without notice. Sales tax applicable in N.Y.
** Canadian residents will be charged applicable provincial taxes and GST.
All orders subject to approval. Offer limited to one per household.
® are registered trademarks owned and used by the trademark owner and or its licensee.

SUP04R   ©2004 Harlequin Enterprises Limited

eHARLEQUIN.com

The Ultimate Destination for Women's Fiction

For FREE online reading, visit
www.eHarlequin.com now and enjoy:

Online Reads
Read **Daily** and **Weekly** chapters from
our Internet-exclusive stories by your
favorite authors.

Interactive Novels
Cast your vote to help decide how these
stories unfold...then stay tuned!

Quick Reads
For shorter romantic reads, try our
collection of Poems, Toasts, & More!

Online Read Library
Miss one of our online reads?
Come here to catch up!

Reading Groups
Discuss, share and rave with other
community members!

For great reading online,
visit www.eHarlequin.com today!

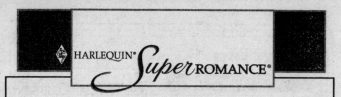

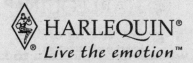

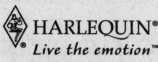